"Did you miss me?"

"I missed you." His arms came around her and she didn't move away, couldn't move away, but no more could she have stepped into his embrace.

"Do you know how often I've wished we could change the past?" Kyle's voice was low, his breath warm against her hair.

"I don't think there's a person living who hasn't wanted the very same thing at least once." She tried to smile but she wanted to cry out against the great tide of longing that washed over her. When she opened her mouth to tell him they couldn't change anything that had gone before, his mouth lowered to cover hers.

Alanna felt her knees start to buckle. Lowering her gently, Kyle followed her down onto the sand. "I've dreamed of you so many nights." His voice was rough with longing. "So many long, lonely nights."

ABOUT THE AUTHOR

Marisa Carroll is the pseudonym for a writing team of sisters, Carol Wagner and Marian Scharf. The siblings share interests as well as backgrounds—Carol is a nurse, while Marian is an X-ray technician—and describe themselves as being "awfully ordinary" yet "hopelessly romantic." They also write together under the pseudonym Melissa Carroll. They live in the small Ohio town where they were raised, with their respective husbands and children.

Books by Marisa Carroll

HARLEQUIN AMERICAN ROMANCE
127–NATURAL ATTRACTION
160–JENNA'S CHOICE

Don't miss any of our special offers. Write to us at the following address for information on our newest releases.

Harlequin Reader Service
901 Fuhrmann Blvd., P.O. Box 1397, Buffalo, NY 14240
Canadian address: P.O. Box 603,
Fort Erie, Ont. L2A 5X3

Tomorrow's Vintage
Marisa Carroll

Harlequin Books

TORONTO • NEW YORK • LONDON
AMSTERDAM • PARIS • SYDNEY • HAMBURG
STOCKHOLM • ATHENS • TOKYO • MILAN

To Mom and Dad for all your help
through all the years.

Published March 1987

First printing January 1987

ISBN 0-373-16190-5

Prologue

Perhaps it was the shade of high blue sky overhead that was the cause of it? Kyle Stafford deliberated. It was exactly the color of the wide fanlighted door of that little inn, tucked away in the hills of Maryland, where he'd taken Alanna when they first made love.

Or it might as easily be the weather affecting his concentration. He narrowed his eyes, more hazel than brown, with gold flecks thick around the irises, to glance out over the light blue-green waters of Lake Erie. That was it. It was the weather, so much like a hot muggy spring day in Washington, that kept tugging his mind back to the time he'd spent with her.

Or, more truthfully, was it simply her proximity?

Despite his present preoccupation with his memories, the tall rugged-looking man, crowded among the holiday-spirited passengers on the Port Clinton to Put-in-Bay ferry, didn't consider himself given to bouts of nostalgia. But he couldn't get Alanna Jeffries out of his thoughts or erase her from his memories. He hadn't been able to, his own innate honesty made him admit, for the better part of two years.

Her likeness was lodged very firmly in his heart.

Kyle was dressed as casually as the rest of the passengers, but more conservatively, in lightweight flannel slacks and an

open-necked sport shirt in shades of gray that complemented his darkly tanned skin and gold-brown eyes. He
wore no jacket or hat in the midsummer afternoon, and
heavy layers of silver hair lifted off his forehead in the
freshening breeze. He was almost completely gray now.

Distinguished was the word his older sister Irene used, but
Kyle wasn't sure he liked the transformation from raven
dark to gray, which his only sibling found so interesting.
What man a good five months from his thirty-eighth birthday would be comfortable with hair almost as white as a
grandfather twice his age?

Had Alanna also changed?

Kyle continued to stare out beyond the rail of the crowded
boat, oblivious to the noise and activity around him, as he
tried to discover answers to his musing in the opaque
churning reflections on the lake's surface. But the images in
the water remained as cloudy and unenlightening as the
meaningless whorls of light in a gypsy's crystal ball.

He leaned his forearms on the metal rail, propping one
suede-shod foot on the bumper pipe a few inches above the
steel deck. He appeared to be studying the fishing and pleasure craft bobbing all around the heavy, low-riding car ferry,
but his mind refused to register the festive sight.

If you were rash enough to ask, Kyle Stafford would reply that he wasn't a man prone to self-analysis or useless
inward reflection. He preferred to take life one day at a time,
reducing it to neat equations, easily labeled components or
profit-and-loss statements. This compartmentalizing of his
life, of his emotions, worried Irene, bringing out the moth-
ering instincts in her that were no longer required by her two
nearly grown sons; but it didn't worry Kyle. He'd learned
not to look beyond tomorrow a long time ago—except for
those few fleeting days when Alanna had almost been his—
because you might find the future. And always the past.

What the hell was he doing here?

It wasn't fair to either of them. He should leave the running of Island Vineyards in Alanna's capable hands, precisely where it had been since her father's stroke. Her winery was turning a good profit. It was one of the Stafford Foundation's biggest success stories. The perfect example of what his work was all about, the concept his grandfather had first envisioned thirty-five years ago: keeping small, unique, usually family-owned businesses profitable and out of the hands of big impersonal conglomerates.

Three years ago Alanna Jeffries's father had contacted the foundation, just before he was taken ill, to ask for help in sidestepping a hostile merger attempt by a multinational distiller. The foundation had agreed to represent him, and Island Vineyards had become Kyle's corporate responsibility—until the day Alanna left him in Maryland. Then he'd turned the account over to Irene.

But his sister didn't know what demons she was awakening from restless slumber when she asked him to take her place on the trip to Ohio. How could she? He'd never spoken to her about what passed between him and Alanna that spring. Now Alanna's formal request for additional funding to restore and refurbish her family's century-old winery had created the need for a foundation representative to be on the scene. And his beloved and astute sister's recent water-skiing accident had left her with a shattered ankle, a lousy temper and scant patience for the few lame excuses he could find to avoid making the trip in her stead. Irene's misfortune had put the responsibility for Island Vineyards' dealings with the Stafford Foundation right back in his lap.

And the simple truth was that he needed and wanted to see Alanna again.

She'd touched something deep within him during the short time they'd been together. She'd sparked something young and bright within him that hadn't been atrophied over the years. Something restless and eager that refused to be lacquered over, subdued and tamed with successive, ruthlessly applied layers of caution and reserve.

Her image, also, insisted on staying with him always, just below the surface of his awareness, much like a shining crystal cat's-eye marble in a small boy's pocket. It wouldn't go away no matter how hard he'd tried at various times to eradicate it. So in a way, he supposed, he was trying to exorcise those private demons without the proffered help of Irene's latest shrink.

He needed to see Alanna, to be close enough to touch her, embrace her, inhale the light, airy fragrance of her skin and glorious sun-bronzed hair, absorb the light and energy she radiated like a small, bright sun. He'd give everything he owned to see Alanna come running to him, full of vibrancy and life, spirited and prickly, young and exuberant as she'd been when they almost fell in love.

Those days had been the happiest in his life, before they knew each other's secrets, the damnable coincidences of their past, the realities that had separated them almost as quickly as they'd been joined.

Chapter One

"It must be the *Goose*," Alanna Jeffries observed to her fidgety companion as she shut off the roughly idling engine of her 1952 GMC pickup. The engine sputtered to a hacking, gasping halt. It needed a good overhaul, she decided peripherally, wondering where she'd find the time for that chore. "Nothing else gets the tourists gawking like that but the *Tin Goose*."

Alanna leaned back against the leather seat as she surveyed the brightly dressed summer visitors crossing helter-skelter in front of the truck, pausing in their stroll around Put-in-Bay's busy main square to crane their necks at uncomfortable angles. Without exception their sunburned noses pointed to the heavens.

"It's the *Goose* all right, Mom," her son yelled, leaning precariously out of the truck window. The decibel level of his voice, even from his position outside the truck, brought a pained wince to Alanna's clear-skinned piquant features. But thankfully, since he was caught up in his own excitement, her inner anxiety went unnoticed. To most of the three hundred fifty or so year-round residents of Lake Erie's South Bass Island, the sight of a pre-World War II Ford Tri-Motor aircraft in a blue July sky wasn't an anachronism. It was a common event, hardly an occasion for rejoicing. Unless, of course, you were an all-American male of eight summers.

"Not so loud, please," Alanna cautioned, covering her ears with ringless long-fingered hands. David Harris Jeffries had lately come to the conclusion, it seemed, that since his mother was fast approaching the advanced age of twenty-nine her hearing was obviously impaired.

Or was his volume merely indicative of his unbounded enthusiasm for everything mechanical, colorful and interesting in his small island world? Alanna suspected as much and let the scolding drop, her attention once again focused on the approaching ferry riding low in the water. She shivered as a small frisson of anticipation, mixed with unease, skittered over her ivory skin, raising tiny goose bumps that she absently smoothed away with the palm of her hand. Kyle Stafford was on that boat.

"D'ya think Jack could see me from up there?" Davy asked in a more conversational tone. "I waved real hard," he added, pulling his cropped dark-red head back into the truck cab.

"He might have, but I doubt it," Alanna replied as seriously as her laughing gray eyes would allow. She hastily swallowed an indulgent smile. The *Goose's* pilot, and owner of Island Airlines—the shortest scheduled airline in the world—was a special hero to David. Her son craved male companionship; he needed role models even more than most boys his age, and Alanna encouraged the friendship. "You'll have to ask Jack the next time we see him—on the ground."

"I bet if I yelled loud enough he'd still hear me now." Devilment sparked in David's eyes.

Consternation and love followed each other in swift succession across Alanna's face as her son bounced out onto the pavement. His interest had already diverted to other matters with the speed of light, or an eight-year-old's ability to switch thought and destination in mid-synapse, a phenomenon Alanna believed to be very nearly as quick.

"There's Billy, Mom," David hollered over his shoulder. "I'll be right back. I have to talk to him. It's urgent." He raced off among the trees of DeRivera Park to meet his towheaded buddy, scarred knees pumping rhythmically below cutoff school jeans. The two boys were best friends and comprised the entire third-grade class of the island's school.

Alanna leaned her forearms along the steering wheel and rested her chin on her layered hands. A small satisfied smile quirked the corners of her lips. She never tired of watching her son go about the fascinating business of being a child. And if his antics kept her mind from the man fast approaching on the ferry, so much the better.

David. Her son. Her life. What a dynamo he was: tall, strong, with her red-brown hair and her gray eyes. Although David's were a lighter shade of gray, nearly silver and less likely to darken with storm signals at the drop of a hat, possibly because his eyes were shot with blue lights, not black as Alanna's were. It certainly couldn't be, as her mother suggested every now and then, that Alanna's temper was far less even than her son's

Alanna let a smile curl the corner of her mouth. She tilted her head, soft curls brushing her cheek as she followed her child's pelting progress across the busy park. David had her father's and her late brother's strong, square features and long lanky build, while she favored her mother's family. The Harris clan was shorter and finer boned than the Jeffries. Well-padded bones in her case, Alanna admitted ruefully. She didn't carry an ounce over the recommended weight for her five-feet, five-inches, but her body was lushly feminine with rounded, enticing hips, a small curving waist and high firm breasts that proclaimed her every inch a woman.

And her face. Alanna sighed, glancing at her reflection in the rearview mirror, pulling her lips down into a mocking grin. Beneath her layered, shoulder-length curls her face had an impish quality, a gamine prettiness that was at odds with her rather serious view of herself as a mother and a vintner.

At least, thankfully, she no longer had quite the look of an ingenue. That was a relief. Alanna studied herself a moment longer, more critically than was her usual wont. What would Kyle Stafford think of her new maturity? Would he even notice the changes in her? Possibly not. All he would remember was her last hysterical outburst; the way she'd run away, never returned his calls, never talked to him again.

Why was he coming here today?

Rationally, she knew it was because his sister, Irene, had broken her ankle and couldn't make the trip. He also knew how important the proposed renovations were to Island Vineyards' continued success, and that she needed a "go ahead" from a foundation officer.

And was it possible he still cared?

No! This was business, nothing more. Alanna was getting the hang of this maturity thing and her new outlook on life dictated that it be so. There was no room for reminiscences, or regrets. The future was what was important, not the past.

Alanna took one last look in the mirror. She was pleased with the sense of purpose shining out of her clear gray eyes, the firmness of her full cinnamon-tinted lips that hadn't always been there. Certainly hadn't been there when she knew Kyle. Now a few tiny lines appeared around her eyes when she smiled. And there had always been a temper line between her slightly curved brows. She definitely looked, in her admittedly biased opinion, far more womanly than she had two years ago.

David was back, hopping up on the running board, breaking in on her self-assessment. Alanna faced him with more relief than she liked to reveal. Her recollections had been threatening to get the best of her.

"Mom, I need a quarter," he panted. "Billy has one and we want to play a game of Space Wars. Please?" His voice had taken on a wheedling tone. He danced from one sneak-ered foot to the other in an agony of impatience. The coax-ing, cajoling grin to which Alanna had no natural resistance creased his urchin face.

"I suppose that can be arranged. But you haven't taken out the trash yet, and there won't be any more where this one came from until that chore is done. Understood?" Alanna fished in the pockets of her soft, faded denims for the coin.

"Yes, ma'am," David responded with a frown. "I won't forget."

"Okay, it's a deal. Here you go. And hurry back. The ferry's already loading up at Middle Bass."

It was a journey of only a few minutes between the two larger of the three inhabited Bass Islands, part of the archi-pelago of eleven or so small pancake-flat landfalls rising out of the shallowest of the Great Lakes. They all seemed, when viewed from the air, to cluster around the base of the three-hundred fifty-two foot granite column that celebrated Commodore Oliver Hazard Perry's victory over the British in these waters off the Ohio mainland in 1813. For Alanna the fertile, wave-swept islands had always been, simply, home.

She watched David and his alien-zapping cohort disap-pear into the eighty-year-old white clapboard building that housed the video arcade. It amazed Alanna that they could enjoy themselves in the dark, stuffy building on such a glo-rious day. Yet it wasn't easy for her to deny David anything he wanted. Alanna worked very hard at treating him as firmly as she felt she should. Her son was such a bright child, intelligent, inquisitive, full of an insatiable curiosity about everything. She supposed she had Elliot's genes to thank for that. Her family was hardworking, blessed with good business acumen and a great deal of common sense, but David was very gifted indeed. It must have come from his Ph.D. father.

Alanna shut down her musings with an ease born of long practice. What was done was done. David was hers alone. She'd worked hard to gain her present serenity and peace of mind. Thanks to the backing of the Stafford Foundation money, there was no reason for David to ever have to contact his father, none at all. Perhaps it was the trepidation she felt at meeting Kyle again that had started this unbidden, unsought chain of remembrance?

She wondered if he had changed?

"Mom...Mom...Mother!" David's voice was strident. His hand yanked on her sleeve, bringing Alanna to swift attention as he bounced up and down on the running board of the truck. "You look like the Alien Overlord just zapped you with his megalaser," her son said in disgust.

"That's about how I feel. Sorry. You're back in a hurry." Alanna leaned out the window to wrap David in her arms for one of the quick hard embraces he tolerated in public and still openly solicited in private, for which she was grateful. He hugged her back, jumping down off the running board almost at once to glance furtively over his shoulder to see if anyone he knew had spied him acting like a baby, letting his mom hug him in broad daylight.

"The ferry's in and you didn't even notice." He turned around to scan the crowd disembarking from the boat. "Everybody's almost off already. What does this guy we're waiting for look like?" David queried, narrowing his eyes against the bright flashes of sunlight darting through the tree branches.

Alanna pushed at a strand of escaping russet hair. She should have worn it up, she fumed inwardly stepping out of the truck. She should have made herself look more like a hardworking executive—more professional, as she imagined Kyle's sister Irene to be, like the women he must deal with every day. How could she bring off that image of maturity and sophistication she'd been congratulating herself on in faded denims and an open-necked teal-blue cotton shirt? Should she redo the second button at her throat? Was the cleavage too suggestive? Would Kyle think she wanted to remind him how beautiful he thought her breasts?

Alanna smoothed her palm over the offending blue jeans. Perhaps she should have changed into something more appropriate? She still had the tailored gold shirtwaist with its myriad of tiny pleats and tucks and plethora of fabric-covered buttons that she'd been wearing at the Washington reception the afternoon Kyle Stafford had entered her life.

"Mom, pay attention!" David's little-boy soprano had gone up several tones in pitch.

"I'm sorry, Davy, my mind wandered." Alanna laughed suddenly, gaily and without reservation, causing more than a few heads to turn in her direction with answering smiles of their own. She could not have chosen anything more inappropriate for her present nautical setting than the expensive, understated gold dress hanging in her closet. There was nothing like an impetuous eight-year-old to keep your feet on the ground and banish the ache of the past.

"I asked you a question." David was clearly still a little miffed.

"What was it?" Alanna wiped the lingering smile off her face and considered David seriously.

He preened under the attention and repeated his question. "I said, what does this guy look like?"

"He's tall, has dark hair with some gray in it and eyes that change color depending on the light ... or what he's wearing ... or something." Memory threatened to take control. Kyle's eyes had fascinated her so. They did seem to change color, like the mood ring she'd had as a child, to different shades of forest greens and golds and browns, each corresponding to his inner feelings although many times little emotion could be read in his face.

Alanna summoned all her considerable willpower to fight the drag of the past. Her gaze ranged anxiously over the people surging forward onto the roadway now that the ferry had lowered the hydraulically controlled gangplank. It was a useless exercise. She had only to close her eyes and summon his image, even with her son only inches away, even with a hundred people laughing and calling all around her, and the sights and sounds of a busy waterfront competing for her attention. She could almost reach out and touch him, taste him, smell the clean spicy scent of his soap and the faint lingering odor of pipe tobacco on his clothes. She could feel his arms around her, strong, and yet gentle too, his body pressing her into a soft conforming mattress, his lips teasing hers to open while his knee coaxed apart her thighs....

His body would be lean and strong of frame, all bone and muscle and lithe controlled movements. He was tall with mahogany tanned skin and thick dark hair graying at the temples. He had a square jaw and high angular cheekbones framing an oval face that drew her attention upward to his remarkable hazel eyes. His laugh was rare, seldom more than a quick smile that lightened the depths of his eyes, setting them dancing for a few breathtaking seconds before he became serious again. All this she recalled and so much more....

"How old is he?" David insisted, cutting straight to the heart of the matter. Alanna concentrated her entire attention on her son. He tilted his head back and squinted up at her for all the world like her brother used to do—exactly like the older David. Although, sometimes Alanna wondered if she found so many similarities between them because she'd known so little of her son's father.

"Mr. Stafford isn't so old." She never said anything like "about your father's age" so she searched her brain for a suitably aged male. "A little older than Jem Harlan, I suppose." Jem was Billy's father.

"Then it can't be that old guy over by the fence watching us, can it?" Alanna's gaze flew in the direction indicated by Davy's cocked head. At least he wasn't pointing, she observed with a grateful maternal corner of her brain. Maybe he'd absorbed some of her lessons on etiquette despite his resistance.

"Kyle?" The name slipped out before she could restrain her tongue.

"Is that the guy?" David was staring openly now.

"Yes." Alanna found her hand at her throat and forced herself to stay where she was. She dropped her hand and wiped the dismay from her face.

"I'll help him with his bags." David was off, sneakered feet flying onto the concrete pier before she could call him back.

It was Kyle. And he had changed. He looked older, weary, an unaccustomed hesitancy in his bearing. He didn't look forward to this meeting any more than she did, Alanna realized. She squared her shoulders. She hadn't expected anything else. Certainly not after the way she'd behaved when they parted.

Oh, but Kyle, how sad you seem.

His hair was completely gray now. He looked even more
distinguished than he had two years ago when he had moved
out of the crowd of people in Senator Thurston's overdec-
orated and overheated Georgetown town house and changed
Alanna's world forever. Yes, he was more distinguished, but
also more distant and reserved. There were lines between his
nose and chin that hadn't been there in Washington, deep
permanent grooves that would never smooth away. Was that
her fault too?

Alanna watched wide-eyed and apprehensive as Davy
skidded to a halt in front of him; watched as Kyle bent at-
tentively and extended his hand in formal greeting to the
small boy, man-to-man. Her throat tightened as David returned the handshake importantly before reaching for the
canvas-strapped tote that Kyle indicated. The child stag-
gered under its weight but moved steadily forward toward
his mother.

Alanna's son. Kyle glanced down at the T-shirted swirl of
redheaded energy beside him. They were as alike as two peas
in a pod. He'd been watching mother and child for some
time before she spotted him. Alanna hadn't changed a bit
from the picture he carried in his heart. She was still healthy
and happy, wonderfully sane and loving. He'd seen that
immediately in her son's bright, trusting face. Alanna was
doing a good job of raising him alone.

She was still so dear to him. Kyle had never admitted that
even to himself before this minute. Why was he chasing a
lost dream? So many things stood between them, obstacles
solid and substantial. He was tired. He didn't want to contemplate the battle of winning back her trust and laying
siege to her heart. Perhaps he didn't have the right. Just by
being who he was and what he was, he had caused her anguish in the past.

Nothing had changed.

"Alanna, it's good to see you again." She was staring at his hair. Kyle resisted an urge to run his hand through the thick steel-gray swath. The changes in him had shocked her, that was certain. He held out his hand, watched her pull herself together, not quite sure what he should say next. He tried to gauge from her actions the way she wanted him to react to their being together again.

"I hope you had a smooth trip over," Alanna replied stiltedly. She took his hand with reluctance. She was almost afraid to touch him and the admission made her more nervous still. "The lake gets pretty choppy when the wind's from the southwest." *Lord, wasn't there something she could say that didn't sound so mundane?* She hated being so constrained, to being reduced to talking banalities. A muscle twitched along the granite line of Kyle's jaw. The hazel and gold of his eyes dulled noticeably. She'd meant to let him know that bygones were bygones, but her emotions had betrayed her again. Flashes of that last terrible scene between them kept rushing across the screen of her mind's eye. All the hurt and the disillusionment must have left traces of their passing in her voice and manner.

Alanna broke the contact of their fingers. She rubbed her hand along her pant leg without thinking. Her palm burned with sparks of sensory fire that shot out through her body in threads of tactile pain. How could it be, now that Kyle stood before her, that two years seemed like nothing more than two days? That the issues that had separated them were so fresh, so immediate, at least to her?

"The boat was so loaded down it would have taken a gale force wind to make her wallow." Kyle grinned, speaking with deliberate lightness. Alanna managed a smile of her own but it was a travesty of her usual bright reaction.

"You should be relieved, Lake Erie is known for its bad temper. And it's much worse coming out from Port Clinton on weekends—cars, campers, bicycles, you name it. It's a circus." She motioned him forward. David was growing restless under the weight of the tote, but machismo forbade him resting it on the ground. "The truck is right this way."

Kyle wasn't paying her the slightest attention. Alanna turned back to see him, neck craned upward in the familiar awkward tourist pose.

"Is that what I think it is?" One hand shaded his eyes as he stared skyward. "I'll be damned if it isn't." He glanced back down to catch Alanna's attention. His quick, rare smile twisted up the corners of his mouth and lightened the depths of his changeable hazel eyes. "Is it really—"

"A Ford Tri-Motor. She's just about the last one of her kind flying anywhere in the world." She copied his stance and waved toward the red-white-and-blue plane as it circled the Perry monument.

"I'll be damned," Kyle repeated reverently.

"Quite a sight, I agree." Alanna felt a little of the tension drain out of her arms and legs, allowing her to move forward with a graceful purposeful stride, not the jerky marionette steps she'd been taking. "She's been part of our islands since the thirties. You're not seeing a ghost plane; although it's hard to get insurance for her these days so we don't see her overhead as often as we'd like."

"The only one I ever saw was in a museum," Kyle revealed, shaking his head. The beginning of another faint smile twitched at the corner of his mouth. "How do I go about getting a ride in her?"

"That's the *Tin Goose* and I know the pilot personally," David broke in, braggadocio evident in his posture as well as his voice. "I'll fix it up, no trouble."

Kyle dropped to the balls of his feet bringing his eyes level with David's. "No kidding." There was no adult condescension in his words, only genuine interest.

"You bet." David preened and stood a little taller.

"David." Alanna made her tone severe. "Mr. Stafford is here on business with the winery." She felt obliged to qualify her son's invitation. She didn't want David's feelings hurt by this man. She couldn't face that now. Men who weren't used to being around children could be cruel without meaning to. Kyle wasn't used to children. He had never been used to children.

"I'd really like to fly in the *Goose* if you can fix it up," he answered David with grave formality. They regarded each other in a measuring silence. Kyle glanced fleetingly in Alanna's direction, his expression plain to read. He'd interpreted her thoughts; it hurt her to see the pain she'd caused him needlessly. Kyle would never be deliberately unkind to her child. She knew that, in her soul, but she'd let her actions in the present be dictated by the pain of the past once again. It was only a small occurrence but it frightened Alanna, made her more determined than ever to keep a po lite distance between herself and this man. Male-female relationships were hard for her to manage. For too long after David was born she'd been in thrall to the trauma of that long-ago time. She didn't want to slip back into the same insecure, destructive patterns ever again.

"Piece of cake," David crowed, satisfied with what he evidently read in Kyle's expression. "Me and Jack are just like that." He held up two grubby fingers and twisted them around each other. He grinned from ear to ear revealing a gap where a bright new tooth was coming in. "He'll take us up whenever you want to go." His chest swelled with pride as he shifted his burden to the opposite shoulder. "And you can come camping with Billy and me if you want sometime," he added generously.

"David." Alanna was compelled to interrupt again. All at once she felt as if she'd been totally excluded from the conversation. "Mr. Stafford hasn't got time to go camping with you."

"I just might find the time," Kyle answered. He stood, turning to face Alanna, towering over her by a good six inches. "Unless your mother objects." One still-dark brow rose a fraction of an inch.

"No, no, plan anything you like." Alanna threw up her hands in denial of any effort to thwart their outing. Strain undermined her nonchalance. Her hands trembled and she brought them quickly back to her sides. It would be so easy to drift back under Kyle's spell. His rapport with David was genuine, even she could see that, as unwilling as she might be to accept the fact. Kyle's enthusiastic reaction to sighting the *Goose*, his interest in the islands as a whole, was sapping her will to resist his old attraction for her. David should have been her shield against Kyle's charismatic drain on her senses, but Kyle had won him over effortlessly within ten minutes of his arrival.

David, her bastard son. Alanna used the hateful oldfashioned term purposefully to bring her wayward emotions back under control. And Kyle's daughter—a child he had fathered out of wedlock. Two innocent and beautiful children, the bright and loving consequences of past mistakes, the symbols of a gulf dark and terrible, and far too wide to bridge.

Chapter Two

They piled Kyle's luggage into the back of the truck that already held a roll of copper tubing, a stepladder Alanna had picked up at the hardware store and David's bicycle. After only one false start the engine coughed to reluctant life, and they bounced off down the road.

David chattered nonstop, lively and unconcerned by the wary adult silence, as he wiggled around on the hot seat between his mother and Kyle. A tour of the marina to examine close up the biggest of the East Coast yachts anchored there and a climb to the top of the Perry column were added to the agenda. "It's three hundred and fifty-two feet straight up," David proclaimed knowledgeably, pointing out the window as they passed by on the county road skirting the monument. "But don't worry. They just fixed it all up," he assured. "You should have seen the—" He broke off his travelog to dart his mother a beseeching glance.

"Scaffolding," Alanna supplied, her eyes on the road to avoid looking at Kyle as well as to avoid running down pedestrians, bicyclists and stray tourists in electric golf carts.

"Yeah, scaffolding. It looked just like the Statue of Liberty did when they were redoing her."

"It's a long climb." Kyle looked dubious. The breeze from the open window stirred the heavy layers of his gray hair. Alanna caught the movement from the corner of her eyes and all at once, superimposed on the everyday scene before her, was a vision of him smiling and bareheaded as they ate ice cream from a vendor's cart outside the Air and Space Museum on a spring day. His hair had been dark then, though just as thick, and a little longer than it was now, with only a frosting of gray at the temples.

"There's an elevator," David explained with enthusiasm, happily unaware of his mother's stress. "It's awesome up there. You can see Canada and everything. Then we'll go over to the Arcade," he inserted hastily, glancing at Alanna to gauge her reaction. She didn't even catch the words, preoccupied with banishing the memories that Kyle's younger, happier image before her mind's eye had produced.

"I think you're trying to get even for our whirlwind tour of Washington by abandoning me to David's tender mercies," Kyle said half-teasingly a few minutes later as they pulled to a stop behind the winery. Alanna's carpenter Gothic home was out of sight a hundred yards farther on, below the low limestone bluff on which the winery was located. Kyle waited a moment for her response. When none was forthcoming he opened the door and climbed out of the truck with David on his heels.

"It would seem that way." Alanna's delayed reply was toneless as she alighted from the vehicle. A faint hint of embarrassed color flooded her cheeks then ebbed away. Her door slammed forcefully. So she hadn't been able to forget those lovely spring days any more than he had. But she didn't recall them with the same pleasure, that was all too obvious. Kyle could have kicked himself for forcing her thoughts back to the past. He'd have to watch what he said carefully if there was any hope of rebuilding their relationship.

"My son has a habit of sweeping everything and everybody along in his wake. Please don't feel obligated to spend time with him."

Alanna was warning him against coming too close to the boy. Kyle flinched inwardly at the verbal blow but allowed no hint of the discomfort to show on his face. Her words were bitten off, precisely enunciated so that he couldn't misunderstand her reluctance. Alanna lowered the tailgate on the truck and pulled David's bicycle down onto the ground without allowing Kyle to even offer his help.

Nothing had changed.

If he hadn't given way that long-ago morning to that one mad impulse to tell her about his daughter, could they have found a way to work things out? Alanna would have revealed David's existence to him in her own good time, and he would have had a warning, a reprieve, time, to prepare her for what he had to say.

"Kyle." He blinked against the strong sunlight and focused on Alanna's face. There was a flush high on the delicate curve of her cheekbones. She'd apparently repeated his name several times.

"I'm sorry." Kyle sounded as if he meant much more than a simple apology for keeping her waiting in the sun. Alanna was ashamed all at once of her abruptness but she couldn't seem to help it. The old hurting was still there, and even more upsetting was the realization that just below that layer of anxiety was an attraction as profoundly compelling as it had been in the beginning. Kyle frowned and Alanna came to her senses. He didn't want to be here any more than she wanted him to come.

"David will show you to your room." She wheeled the cycle into her son's waiting grasp. "Get one of the boys to help unload the truck, honey." She made herself smile as the child looked curiously up at her, over to Kyle, and back again.

"Okay, Mom. I'll go get Rich. He's the strongest. Bye, Kyle." David began to roll the bicycle up the incline.

"It's the green room upstairs remember, Davy." Alanna raised her voice to remind the small boy toiling up the hill.

"Are you coming, Kyle?" David shouted over his shoulder.

"Soon, go on ahead, I'll find my own way," Kyle answered with a wave of his hand. The gesture was strong and vital and very male.

Alanna drew a quick ragged breath. She was determined not to fall prey to Kyle's tug on her senses. It was, after all, only a residue of the past, but he was far too close to ignore it at the moment. And it was so good to see him again, to talk to him, to be near enough to touch, to kiss, to...to care again.

"I'm sorry to be such a poor hostess but I have a tour to lead at seven," Alanna blurted out, looking at her watch. "The regular guide leaves then and Bette, my friend, will be all alone in the gift shop. She's pregnant and I don't want her to get overtired in this heat." She held out her hand in a pretty gesture, half regret, half dismissal. "Ordinarily my mother could take over," she hurried to explain, hating sounding so ungracious. It shouldn't be this hard to make small talk. When the tiny flame of animation kindling in Kyle's gold-rimmed eyes died away Alanna rushed on with her explanation. "My dad flies to the mainland for therapy tomorrow..."

"Alanna." Kyle's voice was sharp with old regrets. "Quit treating me like some visiting potentate." Kyle stopped speaking, his mouth a straight taut line, his own memories betraying him. Abruptly he turned to pull his tote and suit bag out of the back of the truck.

"Are you referring to my...royal suitor by any chance?" Alanna responded pertly before she could curb her unruly tongue. "Sheik Abdullah ben Ahmed was a force to be reckoned with. He was more than ready to sweep me off my feet and into his harem. You're very nearly as determined to get your own way as he was."

"I am?" Kyle swung the lightweight suit bag over his shoulder, responding to the faint jesting note in her words. His shadow fell across her feet. Alanna looked down at the ground to delay meeting his eyes. "You looked frightened out of your wits that day."

"I wouldn't have used quite those words but he certainly had me flustered," Alanna replied with a considering shake of her head that caused the light to catch and hold in the auburn strands. She risked glancing recklessly up into his hazel eyes. "In that respect you're both very much alike." Alanna never saw the trap until she'd stumbled into it.

"In that we both...fluster you?" Kyle asked leadingly.

Alanna colored faintly but kept most of her composure intact. "No. It's because you're both very...shall we say...determined men."

"Very tactfully put, Ms. Jeffries. From the gleam in your eye I'd say you'd been considering using another term...obstinate or stubborn, perhaps?" One dark brow rose a fraction of an inch, again nearly meeting a wave of silver gray hair on his forehead.

"Perhaps." Alanna couldn't resist the heady danger of this verbal sparring.

"You're spoiling my image, Alanna." Kyle's laugh was self-mocking and sounded rusty, as if he didn't use it enough. "I want to go down in history as the corporate rescuer of vintners in distress." There was a hint of that devastating smile lurking in his eyes and at the corners of his mouth. "I thought I was very gallant that afternoon at the senator's reception, rushing to your side from across a crowded room, risking life and limb on those very treacherous, highly waxed parquet floors."

"In imminent danger of being trampled by a horde of hungry, tipsy diplomats and Congressional aides storming the buffet tables. I remember." Alanna repeated the two words more softly, her gray eyes dark with feeling. "I remember."

But she didn't want to. She'd tried so hard to forget the pleasure of his company, the evocative verbal fencing they'd both delighted in.

"Here I thought I had saved you from the clutches of an amorous desert chieftain with all the aplomb and flair of James Bond, at least." Kyle made his words deliberately light, sensing an opening, a chink in her armor of polite indifference. He didn't want to let her get away so quickly, but he was leery of allowing their conversation to drift too far into the past.

"You did save me. Like a knight on a white charger. And I showed my appreciation by buying you dinner." Alanna giggled, her laughter like the chime of tiny temple bells. "At McDonald's."

"And never one to be ungrateful I repaid the compliment by selling His Royal Highness your Sparkling Catawba juice." Kyle laid his hand on the fender of the green truck very near hers. Sunlight glistened on his bronzed skin. His nails were cut square and straight. The hair on the back of his knuckles was dark and curling. His wrist was strong and corded with tendons and a dark blue pattern of veins that Alanna could barely keep herself from reaching out to trace with the tip of her finger.

"He's still ordering it by the planeload, bless him. He said his guests can't tell it from champagne. And his wives *adore* it. Not a bad endorsement for a nonalcoholic drink, don't you agree?" Sparkling Catawba juice, made from the native American grape that had been the backbone of the Ohio wine industry for over a century, carbonated like ordinary soda pop, had been around for years and years. But when the current mania for more healthful, nonalcoholic drinks had escalated a few years previously, Alanna and her family had redesigned and repackaged the old standby and introduced it into markets in the East. It caught on immediately with health-conscious young adults and the more conservative members of the new administration. But convincing the absolute ruler of a desert kingdom to buy it to serve at all state functions had been a real marketing coup. "Thank you." Alanna's gratitude was heartfelt.

"I was only doing my job," Kyle said, still in the same light teasing manner.

"Your job. Yes, of course." Alanna came back to a sense of time and place with a painful mental jolt. She stiffened and backed away a step, putting distance between them emotionally as well as physically. "It was only bad luck that brought me to the Shiek's attention that afternoon anyway. I was only at the reception to give the senator my father's regrets in person. They're old friends. They have been since the senator was first elected to Congress from our district twenty some years ago."

"It wasn't luck that brought you to the prince's attention." Kyle moved closer as if drawn by an inclination too strong to deny. His movements were jerky, unlike the fluid grace he usually commanded. His voice was a dark rasp of sound, low and enticing, spilling over Alanna like smoke. "It was your freshness, your beauty amidst that overdressed, exotic crowd. You looked so warm and lovely in that dress. It was gold, wasn't it? With tiny buttons all down the front, so many of them." He reached out as if he couldn't help himself, to skim the neckline of her shirt.

His caress burned like fire against her skin. "Kyle...
don't, please." Alanna's throat tightened and her words
came out in a croak.

Kyle stopped speaking; his hand dropped away. He
blinked as if coming back from the edges of a beckoning
dream. He took one look at Alanna's defensive stance, the
stiffness in her arms and back, the tiny unconscious movement she made to keep space between them and stepped
back, but some private cutting devil made him go on. "Is his
Royal Highness still trying to entice you into his harem?"

"No! He never asked me again to be one of his wives. It
was all a mistake I'm sure. He must have thought... I was
someone else," Alanna stuttered and her words dwindled to
a halt. She could still feel the panic that had beat low in her
stomach when the figure straight out of *Lawrence of Ara-
bia* had backed her, literally and figuratively, into a corner
behind two towering potted palms and began a very practiced and skillful seduction within three feet of the senator
himself.

"I disagree. He wanted you." Kyle's voice was flat, hard,
brooking no argument. He bent to pick up his tote from the
dusty gravel parking lot. He'd gone to the senator's reception that afternoon purposefully, to meet his new client as
well as to see and be seen, an activity foreign to his privacy-
loving nature but an absolute necessity when doing business in the nation's capital. Alanna had been pointed out to
him just moments before the lusty diplomat had backed her
into the secluded corner. Even then her innocence and vulnerability had attracted him. He'd seen her distress and offered her an excuse to break away from the shiek's
unwelcome attention.

"He wouldn't have wanted me after he learned I already
had a child." Alanna's voice was high, strained, as she
glanced down at her watch. At the time Kyle had indeed

seemed like a gallant knight on a white steed. She didn't like to remember her unease in the awkward situation. She had never been very good at fending off a pass. Especially in a place where she was so out of her natural element, nervous, anxious about dealing with the foundation in her father's stead—and so very vulnerable emotionally.

She changed the subject hurriedly. "I'm running late." She raised her eyes to his face, felt her gaze caught and held for a long moment before she wrenched her attention away from the bleakness reflected there to check her watch a second time, emphasizing her busy schedule yet again. "Just follow David over the hill. Your room's all ready. It's the green one, second on the left at the top of the stairs. The bathroom's right down the hall. You can get a sandwich at the tasting room kitchen. I'm sorry, I don't cook much anymore...no time..." She clutched the roll of copper tubing to her chest as if it were some kind of shield. Already she regretted her curtness but it was too late to bring the words back.

"A sandwich is fine with me. It's been a long day. Will I see you again this evening?" He couldn't seem to keep himself from asking the question.

"I think not...I have to close up, and there are several points in the grant proposal that need a last going over before you see it." Alanna let her words fade away into silence.

"Breakfast then." He made it just less than a question. Kyle shifted the weight of his suit bag on his shoulder. The wire coat hangers bit into the flesh of his fingers as he flexed them absently. His eyes were shadowed by the pattern cast by the leaves and branches of the huge old maples above their heads.

"I'm not sure." Alanna relented when she heard how harsh and ungracious her words sounded. "We'll see." She gave a little shrug of her shoulders that molded the soft cotton blouse to the shape of her breasts.

"I'll look forward to it." Kyle brought his glance up from the tempting curves outlined so beguilingly.

"I'm usually up early so don't be surprised if we don't make connections..."

Kyle watched the nervousness and anger follow each other swiftly across Alanna's expressive features and knew he was the cause of her distress. "I understand." He wanted to say a great deal more, but he didn't. He probably never would tell her all the things he had bottled up inside. It wouldn't change anything. With a short, curt nod he turned away to follow David's slight energetic figure up the hill.

"Yoo-hoo, Alanna. I'm up here." Alanna stood a moment to let her eyes adjust to the light airy interior of the gift shop after the gloom of the back hall leading from her office. Both rooms were situated toward the rear of the winery, the gift shop connecting with the terrace that led off the old dining hall, which Alanna hoped to be able to renovate and reopen to the public next season.

"Over here." A tall dark-haired woman, big-boned and decidedly pregnant, straightened up from her precarious perch on the third riser of an old-fashioned wooden stepladder. "Here, take this box, will you?" She handed Alanna an unwieldy cardboard container.

"Betts, you shouldn't be up there," Alanna scolded, accepting the box, relieved to find it wasn't very heavy after all. "I told you to get one of the boys to help with the lifting and climbing."

"Couldn't find anyone. Relax, Alanna, this is my third, remember? I know what I can do and what I can't do," Bette Harlan answered with a wave of her hand. "I want this display of T-shirts to be ready for the next batch of tourists to be turned out of the tasting room. We've only got about ten minutes.'' She brushed a strand of chocolate-brown hair out of her eyes and grimaced.

''Rough day?'' Alanna studied her friend with concern. Well advanced in her third pregnancy, Bette refused to give up her job in the winery gift shop until the end of the season, no matter how often Alanna hinted that they could manage without her if necessary.

''No, just busy. Lots of tourist dollars flowing into the Island Vineyards' coffers.''

''Just what I want to hear.'' Alanna laughed, glad for the reprieve from her tightly strung emotions. She began pulling brightly colored T-shirts out of the box, checking the sizes and the quality of the design that reproduced the Island Vineyards' logo in various complementing colors. ''This batch looks just fine.''

''Of course it does,'' Bette said complacently. ''I really let the printer have it after that last anemic batch he tried to pawn off on us. These are perfect. I think I'll up the price another dollar.''

''Bette...'' Alanna couldn't help laughing at the avaricious glint in her friend's blue eyes.

''All right, all right, but fifty cents at least. They are much nicer than the others,'' Bette insisted.

''Okay,'' Alanna capitulated, folding several large-sized shirts onto a glass shelf near the arched windows looking out over the terrace at the edge of the lawn. The lake was restless today, small whitecaps curling at the edges of the swells and breaking into white foam out of sight at the foot of the bluff.

''I knew you'd see it my way,'' Bette murmured half under her breath. She picked up a felt-tipped pen to change the price on a cardboard sign below the shirts with a flourish.

The two women had been best friends all their lives. Bette was four inches taller than Alanna, and admitted to being thirty pounds heavier even when she wasn't seven-and-a-half months pregnant. She was effervescent and fun loving, the life of every party. In their teens she'd fallen in and out of love with the summer boys with amazing regularity while Alanna, smaller, quiet and more serious had added needed ballast and caution to Bette's vibrant personality. And in her turn Bette had brought laughter and mischief into Alanna's more serious days. Only a year's difference separated their ages, but Alanna felt a hundred years older more often than not.

"Did you see Father Tim while you were in town?" Bette asked, folding the ladder to return it to the curtained alcove that served as the chronically strained storage area of the shop.

"I did see his Tri-Pacer go over about two hours ago," Alanna conceded, finishing with the shirts and beginning to straighten a display of fine crystal taster's glasses also etched with the winery logo.

"Priests shouldn't take up flying in their old age. It isn't seemly." Bette wriggled her head in disapproval, totally dismissing the irrefutable fact that flying was the only way the sixty-year-old Catholic priest could tend to his duties on the inhabited islands of the chain. "I say a prayer for that man every time he goes up in that crate. It's nearly as ancient as the *Goose*," she added, blessing herself absently before twitching her flowered smock over her denim skirt. She ended her sentence by pasting a friendly smile on her face as the first of the tour group drifted into the rough-cut cedar-paneled room.

"Another hitch in Leslie's wedding plans?" Alanna questioned sotto voce, moving over to join Bette behind the high wooden counter near the back.

"Always. I told that baby sister of mine not to get married on an island. I don't know where we'll put everybody who wants to stay overnight. You know how limited the accommodations are out here. The logistics of this affair are incredible!"

"You ought to know," Alanna couldn't help pointing out as she checked over a running tally of the day's receipts. "You insisted on doing the same thing. And as I remember we bunked a lot of people down on cots and sleeping bags right here in the winery."

"That's right. I don't suppose we could impose on you again old friend . . ."

"Impose away. You're renting the dining hall for the reception, aren't you?"

"You're right, we are. Good, that's settled. I'll have Leslie make some calls to all the aunts and cousins. If they want a regular bed they'll have to make reservations at a motel in Port Clinton." A light on the phone console beside the cash register began to flash. Bette picked up the receiver. "It's for you. They want you back in the bottling room."

"Tell them I'll be right down. It's the new line down again I'll bet." Alanna frowned and rubbed the tense muscles at the back of her neck. "Seventy-five thousand dollars worth of equipment and we can't seem to keep it running for more than an hour at a time."

"She'll be there in five minutes," Bette informed the unseen caller and hung up the phone. "It never rains but it pours." Bette was fond of platitudes.

"I'll tell Father Tim you want to talk to him if he stops by to play chess with Dad later on."

"I'd appreciate it. Did you get your mysterious Wall Street tycoon settled in up at the house?" Bette's tone was deceptively offhand.

Alanna halted her advance toward the door. She should have known Betts wouldn't let her get away so easily. She didn't even have to ask how the other woman knew Kyle Stafford had been on the four-thirty boat, although she hadn't told a soul. It was telepathy of some kind, or voodoo, or a sixth sense that certain islanders had seemed to acquire down through the years that accounted for the precognition.

"He was on this boat, wasn't he?" Bette looked over their handiwork of the last few minutes with a critical eye, adjusting one or two shirts with a master's touch before swiveling to face Alanna with a cocky grin.

"As a matter of fact Mr. Stafford is here. He phoned from the mainland just before you came on duty and asked me to meet him." Alanna swallowed a further confession. She wasn't about to divulge that merely hearing Kyle's voice after two years had set off neural alarms deep within her. Subsequent events had proved their warning to have been correct.

"I can't wait to meet him." Bette settled herself on a stool, one foot swinging free, one eye keeping watch over the two well-dressed, blue-haired matrons near a display of unframed but skillfully matted yachting prints. Her attention however was directed fully at Alanna.

"Betts, I..." Alanna didn't want to hurt her friend but she was reluctant to talk about Kyle to anyone at the moment. She wasn't sure why seeing him again had so drastically affected her equilibrium, but it had. Their affair that spring had been so brief, so based on fantasy and illusion, its end so traumatic, that Alanna was totally confused by her present reaction. The pain was still there, raw and unhealed, but so, too, were the memories, equally strong, of the pleasure they'd given each other.

"I don't mean right this minute, silly. He is staying at the house?" Bette eyed the smaller woman sharply, all traces of levity gone from her broad, placid face.

"He needs access to the winery operation." Alanna shrugged and willed herself not to blush. There was no need to feel as if she was on the verge of committing some kind of sin by inviting a man to be her houseguest. But she supposed Bette was only expressing her concern because other people would have plenty to say on the subject. Small communities were always prone to gossip about unattached women.

"I for one can't wait to set eyes on this corporate marvel—the mystery millionaire who saved Island Vineyards from the big bad distilling conglomerate; the man who's funding the renovations to this pile of stones; keeping the wolf from my door, my children in shoes and frozen pizzas, bless him." Bette raised the back of her hand to her brow and sighed theatrically.

"Hey, girl, remember I'm still the one who signs your paycheck," Alanna laughed but decided that no matter how rushed she was it was time to set the record straight on at least some points. "Kyle Stafford is not a millionaire." Alanna paused thoughtfully. "At least I don't think he is. Of course his family is very wealthy. And he's not a Wall Street tycoon. The Stafford Foundation is based in Virginia; Arlington, actually. You know that's why I went to DC after Dad had his stroke." A trip that had indeed kept the vineyards free of the distillery's takeover attempts, but one that had resulted in so much anguish for Alanna.

"It sounds better my way." Bette pretended to pout as she fiddled with the tape reel on the cash register. "You can't deny he did save the winery. What do they call those guys who come in and prevent a smaller company from being taken over by a big one?" Bette screwed up her face in a comically grave and concentrated expression. "Something romantic...I've got it." She snapped her fingers. "A 'white knight,' you know, doing battle with corporate raiders like Burgher Distilling."

"Knock it off Betts. You make it sound like an episode of *Dynasty* and it wasn't like that at all." Alanna didn't want to think what might have happened to her vineyards, to her son's future, if the conglomerate had acquired her family's business as it had so many other Ohio wineries. Island Vineyards hadn't been in any condition to fight the unfriendly merger. And Kyle Stafford had seemed like a white knight to her in those troubled days.

Bette watched her friend slip back into the past with sympathetic blue eyes that countered a great deal of her airheaded facade. They were soft with love and attachment for Alanna. "Hey, come back. It didn't happen. Island Vineyards still belongs to the Jeffries. A hundred years of winemaking tradition, just like it's always been. And just like it will always be."

"Now that the state has added us to the Historical Register we can keep this 'old pile of stones' from falling down on our heads." Alanna patted the exposed stone wall by the doorway. Her smile was faint, her eyes bright with suppressed emotion. "We'll always be right here where we belong."

"Amen." Bette wasn't about to ask Alanna point blank if Kyle Stafford the businessman was the cause of her preoccupation. Or if it was Kyle Stafford, the man, who was at the root of Alanna's discomfort. Certainly something about that week she'd spent in Washington two years ago had affected her friend greatly. She hadn't spoken of it then, wouldn't speak of it now, Bette knew, but whatever had occurred had driven Alanna deeper into the shell of caution and mistrust she'd erected around herself after David's birth. "Shall I take Davy home with me for the evening? Billy'd love to have him."

"No." David was Alanna's buffer, her protection against a too-hurried renewal of relations with Kyle. "You need the time alone with Jem."

"With two kids in the house? No way. Anyway, he won't be in from his charter until midnight. The walleye are still biting like gangbusters out on Niagara reef. He's booked solid for the next ten days. Besides, with this figure I doubt he's even interested in being alone with me." She scowled facetiously down at her ballooning stomach, arching her spine in the age-old stance of pregnant women the world over. "Lord, I'm tired of looking like the Goodyear blimp."

"You and Jem should have thought of that when it would have done some good," Alanna retorted with a holier-than-thou smirk. She wished she could have been as proudly smug and complacent about her one and only pregnancy.

"Get out, Boss, you're taking up space better occupied by paying customers," Bette threatened good naturedly. "And while you're at it, hit our big-city visitor up for another loan to enlarge this place. We could use the room. In for a penny... well, you know. With Landmark status and the excursion boats coming in from Toledo we have the excuse we need to get on with the renovations. I think your ideas for a restaurant are first-rate. It'll be a big boost to the whole island's economy. Get every cent you can out of the old coot."

"He's not an old coot." Alanna couldn't help correcting.

"All the better," Bette crowed. "I thought you looked too starry-eyed to be indulging in thoughts of a senior citizen." She nodded sagely, ushering a pair of prosperous-looking yachtsmen, husbands of the blue-haired matrons, toward the display that held the privately printed and extravagantly expensive history of the winery that a historical society member had written and illustrated with dozens of old photographs. "Use a little of that Jeffries charm on him. I'm tired of you living like a nun. You're not even Catholic." With that parting shot she turned her full attention to her customers.

Alanna moved through the doorway but not before she saw the well-to-do sailors pick up two of the books and head for the cash register. For Bette everything was simple, either black or white with no murky complicated shadings of gray in between. Women and men were made to love and support each other. Alanna couldn't help that she'd made so disastrous a choice in caring for David's father, but neither should she do penance for an early mistake all her life. She should try love again. The right man would come along.

How Alanna envied Bette that assurance. Her friend was happy, confident, uncomplicated, loving and still madly in love with her childhood sweetheart. Her husband Jem was an elementary science teacher and summer charter captain whose devotion had outlasted all the crushes Bette had had on the rich summer boys. Her life wasn't without its problems, it was true, but it was also busy and richly fulfilling.

Bette was cherished, secure in her relationships, proud of her growing family. She had everything Alanna had always wanted and been denied a long time before. Blessings she had once thought she might find with Kyle, at least for a brief and shining time....

Chapter Three

It was an exercise in futility trying to keep her mind off the past when there were no physical tasks to occupy her thoughts. Alanna stared at the glass of Riesling wine sitting on her desk. It was the product of a very small trial plot of the varietal grape and still unfinished; tart and a little woody, but promising. She swirled the pale yellow liquid, sniffed, tasted, sighed and gave up the attempt to concentrate on her work. Her office was shadowed; the sun was sliding over the western basin of the lake even as she watched. As twilight deepened, the only light in the room came from a gooseneck lamp on her desk. The remains of a sandwich, mostly untouched, lay beside the colorful file folders holding the grant requests destined for Kyle's appraisal. She pushed them aside, closing her eyes, resting her head on the high back of the cracked leather swivel chair. Behind closed lids the negative image of the room grew brighter, taking on the dappled texture of sunlight shining through lace curtains. The Ross Hotel for women; how they'd laughed at the prim straightlaced hostelry that Senator Thurston had suggested for her during her Washington stay.

"I didn't think places like this actually existed," Kyle had proclaimed several hours after they left the senator's reception. He craned his neck for a better view of the tall weathered brick exterior of Alanna's hotel.

"I didn't think so either," she admitted, giggling as he held open the etched glass double doors of the small narrow lobby. It was incredible how much you could learn to like a person while sharing a Big Mac and fries. That Kyle Stafford would appear out of the blue and remove her from the clutches of a real desert sheik's overzealous advances, spirit her away in a Mercedes and then calmly announce that she could buy him dinner—at McDonald's of all places—seemed too fantastic to have actually occurred. But it had, and what was more, she'd enjoyed the evening very much. That was by far more surprising. Alanna could count on the fingers of one hand the hours she'd spent alone in a man's company since her son was born.

Now to have this man standing in the lobby of her hotel, making plans to meet again the next morning was a lovely continuation of the fantasy. It was like something out of a dream, a very nice dream and she meant to make it last as long as possible.

"It reminds me of something out of one of those old Hollywood musicals about Broadway." Kyle cocked his dark head and stared down at her. "You know, where Ann Southern played the heroine's best friend and they were all stage struck actresses waiting to make it big when the aging star got laryngitis and couldn't go on. I expect to see Ginger Rogers come tripping out of the elevator to go dancing up the street with Fred Astaire any moment now."

"Me too." Alanna smiled, understanding exactly what he meant, slipping further into whimsy herself.

"Is there a curfew?" Kyle murmured bending closer. A woodsy clean after-shave mingled with the smell of wool and pipe tobacco and something less easy to describe and by far more heady, a scent elementally male. Alanna took a quick instinctive step backward, alerted once more to the dangers of allowing her feelings to override her common sense.

"No." She looked up into his eyes and was surprised to find them sparkling with humor and a gentle teasing. "And no bed checks either that I'm aware of." Alanna gave a deliberately saucy toss of her head, then marveled at her own willingness to join in Kyle's banter. But it was because the guise of unreality held; because she was twenty-six years old and away from her family and her son for the first time in years; because she'd been drinking champagne from a crystal goblet and been asked to marry or at least to enter the harem of a prince not three hours ago—and because she'd been rescued by a knight in, if not shining armor, at least a very well-tailored black dinner jacket, that she could handle this sensual repartee. "Actually it's very quaint, don't you think? Most of the ladies who live here are retired federal employees." She shrugged expressively. "Anyway, I'll only be here three more nights."

"Then it's back to your island..." He seemed about to say something else but changed the subject abruptly. "I think I'm overstaying my welcome."

"Oh, no..." Alanna spoke before she had time to follow the direction of his eyes. The sign was prominently displayed alongside the elevator: Men Not Allowed Beyond the Lobby. This edict was given added weight by the presence of the desk clerk, a heavyset woman regarding Kyle with a basilisk stare from behind a glassed-in counter. Her iron-gray hair, drawn into a bun on top of her head, was wound so tightly that not a single strand escaped. Her several chins quivered importantly as she eyed the clock pointedly before returning her scrutiny to Kyle's rugged features.

"It's *very* respectable." Alanna faltered, trying hard not to laugh. "I don't think there are a lot of assignations carried out within these hallowed halls." She gave the desk clerk a smile. The older woman nodded stiffly.

"More's the pity," Kyle said so softly Alanna wasn't sure she'd heard correctly.

"I beg your pardon?" She accepted her room key from the dour clerk with a second tentative smile.

"I said: Good night, Ms. Jeffries." Kyle smiled disarmingly at the desk clerk who glowered in return.

"Oh." She had misunderstood apparently. He wasn't really reluctant to leave her company. "Good night, Kyle." How inadequate those conventional words sounded. She didn't want him to go—not yet. "Will I see you tomorrow?" She hurried into speech before she could think better of it. "I mean to finalize the business arrangements with the foundation, of course." She sucked her lower lip between her teeth and studied the tips of her dull gold shoes for several seconds before recalling her dignity and raising her smoky-gray eyes to Kyle's face.

"Yes, tomorrow." His voice was low and raspy. Alanna felt a shiver of sensation race across her nerve endings. It was a very sexy voice. "Is this your first trip to Washington, Alanna?" Kyle watched her closely, thick dark lashes fringing his fascinating hazel eyes, lashes so thick they cast shadows on his high cheekbones.

She nodded. "I haven't seen very much, only on the bus ride in from the airport..." She cleared her throat, trying to filter out her excitement at being in the nation's capital. "I thought I'd catch the tourist shuttle, see some of the city. I've always wanted to go the the Smithsonian...but only after we've concluded our business, naturally." She finished in a rush, making her tone as brisk and nonchalant as she could manage when her breath seemed to be coming in quick shallow gasps. Lord, she must sound like a high school senior on her graduation trip. "I don't want to inconvenience you any more than I already have."

"Tonight hasn't been an inconvenience. It's been more like an adventure. I've enjoyed every moment, Alanna." He reached out to take her cold hands in his. Jabs of pain from scars around her heart that were only partially healed throbbed a warning. He sounded sincere. She searched Kyle's face carefully for any sign that he was not. She couldn't find any falseness there and gave a tiny sigh of relief.

"I've enjoyed it, too." What an understatement that was. It had been a wonderful evening. "Thank you." Her voice was very soft and low.

"But you are determined to do the whole tourist bit?" Kyle's eyebrow quirked upward in a gesture she already recognized. "I can't talk you out of it?"

"Why, no." Alanna laughed, striving for sangfroid, but all she could think of was that a wonderful warmth from his strong brown hands was radiating up her arms and through her bones and muscles to her cold, aching heart before spreading lower, slowly, like warm syrup to the very center of her body. "I want to do the whole tourist bit."

"Okay." Kyle's tone was exaggeratedly martyred, deliberately light as though he'd sensed her silent fears, although she hoped desperately that he hadn't. "I'll pick you up at nine for breakfast, and we'll make a day of it."

"But you said we have business to discuss." Again the excited child slipped from behind her facade of worldliness.

"We can discuss it anywhere. That's one of the perks of being the founder's grandson. I don't have to conduct interviews behind a desk. Is nine too early?"

"Nine will be fine," Alanna replied dazedly.

"Then I'll say good-night, Ms. Jeffries." Kyle still smiled down at her but the teasing glint in his eyes was gone, replaced by a lambent flame that nearly took Alanna's breath away. "May I ask for a good-night kiss, merely in the interest of cordial business relations?" The flame was gone, his eyes were clear, unclouded, as though he sensed her reading of his intentions. Alanna blinked and focused on his entire face. Still no hint of insincerity. Could she trust him? Alanna smiled. This wasn't the time to analyze every nuance of speech and body language to death. What was a good-night kiss after all? She'd been kissed before.

"In the interest of cordial business relations, I think that can be arranged." She was dizzy with the elation of playing this age-old but very unfamiliar game between the sexes. If she didn't let it go too far, lose her head, what harm could it do? "I'll be thinking you're a corporate raider if you keep doing things like this."

"Things like what?" Kyle's face was very near her own. Alanna stood her ground, refusing to lower her gaze although she was shaking in her shoes. "Stealing a kiss."

"I never steal what might be mine for the asking." There was an edge of steel to his words. "I am asking, Alanna, nothing more." His hands were still on her shoulders. The rush of her own blood through her veins made her breath catch and she swallowed against the sensation.

"I'd like a good-night kiss very much." She couldn't think of anything else to say.

His lips swooped down to cover her mouth and Alanna braced herself for the impact. It never came. Kyle's lips played lightly over the silky surface of her cheek, moved to the corner of her lips, rested a moment in the honeyed crevice, as though tasting her skin, and lifted. Alanna's eyes had closed at the first touch, now they flew open.

Kyle was grinning but his hands were shaking. She could feel the fine tremors just before he released her. "That's the kind of kiss that goes with our surroundings, don't you agree? Just like in one of those old musicals. I'm not too sure I didn't see Gene Kelly use it on some starlet one night on the late show, if the truth be told. Chaste and respectable like this hotel, soft and sweet and innocent like you, Alanna Jeffries." He lifted her chin with his fingers. "Good night, Alanna."

"Good night, Kyle." *Soft and sweet but hardly innocent,* Alanna thought, too bemused to deny the claim. Kyle ushered her to the elevator and watched as the doors rolled shut. She had to be imagining things but he looked almost as confused as she was.

Alanna was up early the next morning, her stomach full of flitting butterflies, her thoughts full of Kyle Stafford and snatches of hopes and dreams long put aside. She was half afraid he wouldn't come, half hoping that he would. She didn't like being ambivalent. It took the situation out of her control, made her feel even more vulnerable than usual, prey to all sorts of girlish whimsies and flights of fantasy.

Alanna studied herself in the mirror as she piled her hair haphazardly on top of her head. It added essential inches to her height and hopefully several years to her... impish... there was no other word for it... features. But wayward curls persisted in hanging softly against her temples and the nape of her neck, defeating any hope she might have cherished that the arrangement added to her sophistication.

With a grimace Alanna gave up trying to subdue them. She was going to be late. She hated keeping people waiting, probably because she herself abhorred waiting. She took the stairs two at a time to avoid the arthritic elevator and sailed into the lobby with thirty seconds to spare.

Kyle was there before her, his back to the stairs, studying the view of ethnic restaurants and shop fronts on Constitution Avenue from one of the plate glass windows. Alanna took the opportunity to observe him for several seconds. There was something about him, some aura, some field of quiet energy that defied explanation. She hadn't imagined it at their first meeting yesterday. His bearing, his manner, all spoke of wealth, position and success, but tempered by an inner solitude that set him apart. Sadness perhaps? Was that the empathy that had called to her, allowed her to put aside her usual reticence in dealing with men and enjoy his company so thoroughly?

She was finding this man's attraction just as devastating, exciting and exhilarating as she'd found that of David's father all those years ago. The comparison gave her pause.

Remember. Remember!

And she might have, if Kyle hadn't chosen to turn away from the window at that moment and smile at her.

"Good morning, Alanna. Did you sleep well?"

"Good morning, Kyle," Alanna whispered, not wanting to wake the tiny old lady in a canary-yellow pantsuit dozing in a nearby chair. "I did sleep well, thank you," she lied. She'd spent at least two hours tossing and turning and replaying the day's events in her mind. He looked rested, as if he'd slept soundly from the moment his head hit the pillow, and Alanna found she was slightly and uncharacteristically annoyed.

"I'm all ready to go," she informed him, holding out both hands to pirouette before him. "Do I pass muster?"

"I like that color on you. What do you call it? Peach?" He finished tamping down the aromatic tobacco in his pipe as Alanna watched the unfamiliar male ritual with interest.

"Apricot", Alanna replied, pleased he liked the simple cotton shirtwaist she'd chosen. "I like the way you look, too," she responded boldly. His pale blue shirt was crisp and well tailored, open at the throat to show deeply tanned skin slightly furred with dark curling hair. His body was long and lean, as that of a runner or a sprinter, finely honed and steel hard. There was more silver threaded through his thick dark hair than she'd noticed last night, but it only served to emphasize his good looks, not detract from them.

"I have croissants and a thermos of coffee in the car," Kyle said, holding open the door. "I promised you breakfast, but if you want to see as much of the city as you can today we'll have to keep on the move." He sounded like a military commander planning a campaign. Alanna knew intuitively that she was getting a glimpse of how he kept his employees on their toes.

So much for any faint daydreams she'd harbored of long leisurely meals in small elegant restaurants with hovering, attentive maître d's and white linen tablecloths while she discoursed, knowledgeably and intelligently, on her future plans for Island Vineyards, dazzling him with her savoir faire and scintillating wit.

They did talk a great deal it was true, but about everything under the sun, not just wines and wineries. Kyle was easy to talk to and laugh with, although his laughter was rare. Even more astonishing was the fact that it was easy to be silent with him. He attracted her a great deal. He struck sparks from her sexuality that Alanna'd thought long immured from any male charm. It was a little frightening but also very, very nice.

Still he managed to learn a great deal about her, Alanna realized later when she analyzed that day. She told him about her brother's death in the last days of the Viet Nam war. How she'd gone in his stead to study at the University of California at Davis, at first from a sense of family loyalty and duty and later from a real and growing love of winemaking. "It's in the blood," she said with a touch of reserve, not wanting to dwell on those days for very long.

Kyle sensed her unease and changed the subject. He couldn't know that her grief at the death of her laughing, high-spirited brother was only partly to blame. She'd returned from her second year at Davis pregnant and alone. Her parents had been horrified and angry at what had happened to their daughter, but they never turned their anger against Alanna herself. They stood by her, taking David to raise for the first fifteen months of his life so that she could finish her education. Sometimes now, even though nearly seven years had passed, she found that fact hardest to forgive Professor Elliot Mayhew for—that he'd cheated her out of those first wonderful, never-to-be recaptured months of David's life.

Lunch was very informal and lighthearted, keeping Alanna's thoughts from turning too far inward, for which she was grateful. They sat on the low stone wall surrounding the Capitol grounds and ate hot dogs and drank sodas bought from a vendor's cart. Alanna basked in the genial warmth of the spring sun and watched the swelling crowds of humanity swirl by them in a flurry of sound and color.

She was staring, rather absently, at a group of Japanese tourists who were weighted down by a bewildering assortment of cameras, lenses and light meters while Kyle outlined some of the suggestions for changes at the winery that would make production and accounting more efficient. She was only half listening, enjoying the hustle and bustle around her, aware that Kyle would put all his suggestions into writing for her perusal on the flight home, when he stopped talking and leaned toward her, touching her arm in a light, tingling caress. "Look," he murmured, gesturing with his pipe. The subtle aroma of tobacco smoke filling her nostrils, Alanna followed the path of his gaze with her own eyes.

Standing on the corner, a small boy, no more than six or seven years old, had managed to dribble mustard from his hot dog all down the front of his Dukes of Hazzard T-shirt, much to his mother's dismay. Alanna smiled, seeing herself with Davy in similar circumstances as the young harried-looking woman dabbed at the stain and scolded softly.

"Being here probably saved him from the spanking of his life." She laughed up into Kyle's eyes and let the perfect opportunity to tell him about David slide away. Sunlight bounced in bright geometric patterns as it fell through the latticework of new green leaves but there was no sigh to tell her she'd made a fatal error, none at all. Indeed it felt mighty good to be alive in this time and place with Kyle by her side. Alanna could have stayed there forever, watching the world go by and might have, if not for Kyle's insistence that they had a great deal yet to see.

And they had seen so many things. Alanna stood up reluctantly, stretching cramped muscles, not really wanting to give up the warm enveloping remembrance of happiness her thoughts had conjured up. They'd gone to the Smithsonian after lunch, she remembered, switching off the desk lamp with a dreamy little smile touching the corners of her mouth, before catching the high points at the Air and Space Museum. After that they rode the elevator to the top of the Washington Monument where all the city lay spread out below them in the hazy light of a spring afternoon.

Later he'd inserted them deftly into a tour of the Capitol. Alanna had been entranced, gawking and staring at the Rotunda roof and Statuary Hall as eagerly as any of the hundreds of others jostling shoulders in the stately building. But for dinner she'd gotten her wish. The clarity of her inner vision faded. Alanna glanced sadly down at her sandwich, the crust already dry and unappetizing, as she picked up the plate and empty wineglass. She headed down the corridor to the winery kitchen, her footsteps making a hollow echo on the concrete floor.

Kyle had taken her to a quiet little Italian restaurant for linguini and white clam sauce before once more venturing out to see the city by moonlight. And during all that time they'd found interests and subjects in common. Alanna enlarged on her hopes for the winery and her father's return to health but still remained silent about her son. Kyle, in return, gave her small bits and pieces of himself, vignettes of his boyhood summers at his cousin's and grandfather's home in New York State, anecdotes of the famous and near famous who at one time or another had been connected with the Stafford Foundation. It wasn't until much later—when it was too late—that Alanna realized she really didn't know any more about what made Kyle Stafford who he was than she had a few days before when he was only a name on a grant application.

She stopped outside the kitchen door, her hand on the wooden panel ready to swing it open into the cavernous room, dark and silent now that the winery was closed. It wasn't any use fighting the pull of her memories. They were too strong. She let them tug her back. She could smell the flowers, feel the cool touch of the Potomac breeze on her skin. She had been pleasantly exhausted, content for the moment to let Kyle chart their course, concerned only that the lovely day would end too soon. They stood silently, hands entwined, alone even though they were surrounded by scores of others as the Army Band serenaded before the majestic columns of the Lincoln Memorial.

When the last notes had died away, and Alanna had had her fill of gazing on the poignant, stately figure of Lincoln, they made their way back to the car in near silence. "Thank you for a most lovely day," she murmured as Kyle handed her into the seat and slid behind the wheel. "I can't tell you how much I've enjoyed it."

"I don't want it to end either, Alanna," Kyle answered softly, taking her hand once more. He studied her fingers intensely, although surely he would make out little in the dim light from the dashboard.

"I don't think you said that only because we missed the Bureau of Engraving and the FBI building." Alanna's sleepy gray eyes flew open as she searched his face as she'd done so often in the last day. It seemed almost impossible that she'd known this man for only twenty-four hours. Her voice grated, sounding scratchy and tight in her own ears. She was frightened by the intensity of her feelings — feelings she'd worked so hard to suppress, to stamp out of her heart and her body.

"I don't want to take you back to that frumpy hotel and give you one kiss in plain view of Atilla the Hun's aunt," Kyle answered with the merest hint of a smile in his words. "You hate the noise and crowds of the city. I can see it in your face and pick up the vibrations in your behavior." He cupped her face in his big strong hands. His thumb traced over the curve of her cheek almost wonderingly. "Let me take you to a place I know, Alanna. It's secluded, peaceful; a lovely old colonial inn. It's in Maryland. It's also the perfect setting for you."

"Kyle... I don't know what to say." Alanna could feel herself being drawn into his spell. Should she even allow him to finish what he had to say? Why not? Who would she be hurting but herself if she agreed to go with him, allowed their relationship to move along a more romantic path, allowed him to make love to her? Because in her woman's soul she knew that was what he wanted.

And it was what she had wanted, too, Alanna admitted sadly, leaning her forehead tiredly against the cool stone wall of the hallway. She blinked back sudden hot stinging tears. A part of her still wanted that. She'd felt it the first moment she saw him, the first time she'd heard his voice on the phone this afternoon. She'd agreed to go with Kyle that night in Washington because she'd sensed his integrity, his honor and sense of purpose.

But she'd been mistaken in that trust, just as she'd been mistaken in loving David's father so impetuously and so unwisely.

And just as certainly, what was done was done and couldn't be recalled. There was no use shedding any more tears over what was past. As it was, she'd cried herself to sleep too many nights. Alanna swung open the kitchen door. Instead of hushed darkness she came on a scene of light and noise and boyish chaos. David and Billy were making sandwiches. Peanut butter and jelly, from the looks of things. "Hi, guys," she called setting her own plate and wineglass on the stainless steel counter alongside the dishwasher. She cut off the past with ruthless swiftness. "What's up?"

"We're starved, Mom," David stated, waving the bread knife for emphasis. A blob of peanut butter wavered on the end. "We came in for a snack before Billy heads home."

"Which he'd better do pronto or his mother is going to have a fit," Alanna warned.

"She's always having a fit," Billy mourned, his golden head nodding portentously. "It's because my goofy Aunt Leslie is making such a big deal of her stupid old wedding."

"Girls always do," David said with disgust. "They think of the yuckiest things." A big dollop of strawberry jam landed approximately in the middle of his piece of bread. He examined it critically, made one or two more swirls in the matching slice and slapped them together satisfied. Billy already had his mouth full of peanut butter and mayonnaise, a combination that Alanna had never cared for, and contented himself with a worldly nod. "Real stupid," he mumbled around his food.

"Weird," David agreed in an equally muffled voice.

"Don't talk with your mouths full," Alanna cautioned automatically. "Get this stuff put away and wipe up the counter or Mrs. Ackerman will have a fit in the morning." Mrs. Ackerman was Island Vineyards' chief cook and bottle washer and a crony of Alanna's mother. "And then Billy had better be on his way home."

David swallowed hastily. "Will you ride with us on the bikes so I can go along? Please, Mom, it isn't really dark yet."

"I have a lot of work to do this evening, David," Alanna hedged. She was tired, but the thought of possibly encountering Kyle Stafford, even in her own home was daunting. She'd succeeded in subduing most of her memories for the time being, but not the treacherous sensations of physical longing and loving, that had accompanied them. David looked crestfallen as only an eight-and-a-half-year-old can. "On second thought I don't know why not," Alanna backtracked, ruffling his short, red hair. He ducked his head. "I'll go get my bike and meet you outside. You should have this place shipshape by the time I get out front. Deal?"

"Deal!" The two youngsters shouted in unison. Alanna watched them out of the corner of her eye as she left the room. Peanut butter and jam jars flew back into the big institutional-sized refrigerator. Billy leaned far over the deep stainless steel sinks, his feet dangling several inches above the floor, to dampen a paper towel and swipe ineffectually at the sticky peanut butter mess on the counter. She'd have to come back and straighten up or Mrs. Ackerman really would have a fit.

They were such a pair. David was a great kid, even allowing for her mother's bias. She'd done the right thing in keeping him, loving him. It had been a hard decision but it had been the right one. She was done with looking back...at least for tonight.

KYLE STEPPED BACK into the shadows of his bedroom. It was large and simply furnished and he'd guess it was impossible to heat in the winter. The house was a treasure: three stories high with a square tower room and a wrought iron widow's walk, and gingerbread trim scrolling over every available square inch of roof and porch. White painted, with green shutters and green slate roof, it sat well back on the sloping lawn shaded by huge oaks and maples, every window on three sides commanding a view of the lake and other small islands. But now he wasn't interested in the view. He'd seen David and his friend sneak into the winery kitchen, probably for a snack, fifteen minutes earlier.

He wasn't tired, indeed it was scarcely nine o'clock, but the long summer twilight had just begun to darken into night. Cicadas shrilled, they were early this year, and several birds rustled to sleep in the trees with a series of trills and chirps. It was a wonderful, restful place. But Kyle couldn't rest. He was waiting for Alanna.

Almost on the thought, she appeared at the back of the winery calling over her shoulder to her son. Then she was gone again. Kyle moved back out of the shadows, his hand clenched into a fist as he rested it against the oak window frame. Where had she gone? The light went out in the kitchen. The boys galloped off across the lawn and reappeared a few minutes later on their bikes. They stopped, looking back toward the house. Again Kyle retreated a step into the shadows. This time he remained there, as Alanna joined the youngsters. He heard her laugh carry on the damp wind off the lake as they challenged her to a race down the dusty gravel lane to the road. He watched Alanna until she was out of sight, envying her relationship with her son, desiring her, loving her, but allowing none of those emotions to show on his face. He was very good at hiding his feelings. He was also very good at hiding his loneliness—but he had never grown used to being so alone.

Chapter Four

"Morning," David chirped, spreading butter on his toast with the concentration of a connoisseur. "I thought you'd be up a lot earlier than this. Don't you have to go to work in the morning in Washington?" His smile erased the rudeness from his words and the awe with which he spoke the city's name made it hard for Kyle not to smile in return.

"I did sleep well, thank you," Kyle responded. Irene's boys had been as devastatingly blunt at David's age, he recalled. And little girls? He hadn't been privileged to know his daughter at eight-and-a-half. He'd only been admitted to the fringes of her life four years ago when she was nearly thirteen. That was at his grandfather's funeral. And he'd remained on the fringes of her life, a shadowy "uncle" figure; that was Catherine and Derek's wish and he honored it. There was nothing else he could do. He had no claim on Kelly at all.

"I like to sleep in when it's icky and rainy out, but not on a great day like this," David revealed.

"Is your mother already at the winery?" Kyle pressed, scanning the kitchen with narrowed hazel eyes. It was a big, high-ceilinged room with white-painted cupboards, bright yellow Formica countertops and wildflower prints in rough-cut frames on the wall.

"She went over hours ago," David informed him while shaking cold cereal into a bowl. "The tour boat comes from Toledo today. It'll be a madhouse." The last phrase sounded curiously grownup and Kyle guessed correctly that David had culled it from his mother's speech. "We're always busy in the summer."

With a long hectic day in store for her, Alanna would be able to avoid him easily if she chose. A little of the optimism Kyle'd been feeling faded away.

"It won't be time for the first tour for a little while yet. Do you want some cereal and toast, then I'll show you where to find her."

"I think I'll just have a cup of coffee while you're finishing your breakfast," Kyle countered politely.

"Suit yourself." David shrugged at the strange way of adults who could turn down a heaping bowl of Fruit Loops without batting an eye. "Mom made coffee before she left this morning. It's over there." He tipped his head toward the counter where the coffeemaker steamed gently, filling the kitchen with one of Kyle's favorite aromas. "Do you like to fish?" David asked, suddenly shy, his eyes intent on his cereal. "I mean if you're not too busy. Mom said I shouldn't pester you."

"I used to fish with my grandfather when I was your age." Kyle smiled encouragement as he poured himself a cup of coffee. He straddled the back of a solid walnut kitchen chair. "Do you fish a lot?"

It was just the opening David had been hoping for. "You bet, Kyle. I can show you all the best places to catch walleyes," David beamed. "And I'm the cheapest guide on the lake. Only five dollars a day."

"Sounds like the best deal I'll ever get." Kyle laughed out loud. David was a Jeffries to the bone, a capitalist bred and born.

"Course I have to get Mom's permission to use the boat. Can you help me start the motor?" He looked worried that his needing assistance might jeopardize the outing.

"No problem." Kyle hid his smile behind the rim of his coffee cup.

"It's all set then. Wait till I tell Billy."

Half an hour later, the subject of fishing pretty much exhausted for the time being, David led Kyle into the huge echoing main room of the winery. Overhead its high vaulted ceiling and dark, old wooden beams were almost lost in the shadows. Stained glass windows of surprising beauty were set in arches along the west wall. Almost all the southern exposure consisted of double French doors set in arched frames, revealing a view of the harbor and marina as well as the Ohio shoreline, hazy and gray-green, in the distance. Alanna was right: it would make a beautiful restaurant with very little renovation at all.

But at the moment, as far as he could tell, the winery's menu seemed limited to deli items served in the tasting room or carried out onto the veranda. Picnic tables were scattered here and there under the big maples beyond. The lawn was emerald green and well cared for, sloping down to the small marina the Jeffries were in the midst of improving. It was another sound idea since the main docking facilities in town and at the small state park were filled to capacity from June to September.

"Mom'll show up here in a minute," David informed him. "I've got to go help my grandpa get ready to fly over to the hospital. He can't walk very well, you know." His impish face was suddenly serious.

"I know. And I'm sorry to hear that," Kyle replied softly.

"But he's getting better, slow but sure." David brightened. "He'll be able to come out fishing with me and Billy pretty soon, you wait and see. He's a great guy, just like you told me your grandpa was. See you later." David rocketed off, scampering away into the interior of the building, most likely heading for the back entrance he'd used last night. Kyle frowned briefly in bewilderment. He'd never thought he could enjoy a youngster's nonstop chatter so much.

He took his time joining the dozen or so tourists milling around the big room. Stationing himself against the cherry-wood bar, worn smooth by thousands of elbows rubbing over it, he picked up a cardboard menu but continued to study the others. Most of the women wore brightly colored sundresses or shorts and halters. The men were in shirts and baggy pants or jogging shorts. Alanna was right on the money in wanting to keep the atmosphere casual but comfortably elegant.

Several people were inspecting the display of souvenir hats and sweatshirts in the gift shop, wandering back and forth between the two rooms. Kyle was a little surprised to find twenty names signed up for the tour in a gold-edged ledger at his elbow. It was still fairly early in the day. Some of those twenty were studying the various medals and awards that Island Vineyards had won in competitions all over the East and Midwest. They fingered corkscrews and taster's glasses emblazoned with the winery logo, or chose postcards from the rack by the door. They seemed obligingly intent on picking and choosing from among the paraphernalia offered to entice vacation dollars out of their pockets.

Island Vineyards' wines were prominently displayed in a variety of gift packs. The prices were reasonable, Kyle noted, with the labels attractive and easy to read and identify. Alanna was probably on the right track promoting her wines as a regional delicacy. She and her father both knew it was the best course to follow with the generally sweet, unsophisticated wines of the area.

Still, Lake Erie wines enjoyed quite a following. In the last
century they had been world famous. They were well made,
light, visually attractive and moderately priced—all good
selling points in any marketplace. Alanna was branching out
aggressively with several new vintages of French-American
hybrid grapes that would interest the more discerning, ad-
venturous wine drinker. Her first limited pressing had
turned out well according to her concise, well-written re-
ports that found their way, somehow, from Irene's desk to
his own each quarter.

A door opened in the far wall and Kyle felt his chest
tighten with anticipation. None of the tourists in the room
seemed to have noticed the change in the atmosphere but he
did. Sunlight from the windows, stirred by her passing,
danced and fizzled with a sparkle like champagne as Alanna
advanced across the room. She hesitated for a moment, her
eyes searching and appraising the faces around her. Her gray
eyes met his, widened in surprise, held his gaze for a few
quickened heartbeats then slipped away. She nodded slightly
but gave no further recognition of his presence. She smiled
at one or two of the others and nodded a greeting.

Elation faded in Kyle; anticipation was tempered by his
more usual caution in dealing with his emotions. Last night
Alanna had made it clear she didn't want to resume any kind
of a more intimate relationship. This morning her reserve
was equally as clear. He wanted to change her mind, but he
had to go slowly, or lose this precious chance at a reconcil-
iation that fate had placed in his path. If he couldn't make
her understand, couldn't make her love him again, he would
lose her forever.

"Good morning ladies and gentlemen." A wisp of gauzy
forest-green scarf held Alanna's riot of auburn-tinged curls
in a soft swirl on top of her head. She seemed to like those
earthy vibrant colors: corals, golds and browns. They suited

her. She reminded him of an old print he'd seen some-where. A Gibson girl, that was it. Although Charles Dana Gibson had generally chosen models far taller and more willowy than Alanna, she still possessed the same heart-shaped features and engaging blend of innocence and slumbering sensuality that was evident in the old engrav-ings.

"Ladies and gentlemen, your attention please." Alanna repeated the call to order more loudly this time. "Right this way." She waited several more moments as last-minute purchases were completed in the gift shop and one or two stragglers were called in off the veranda. "Welcome to Island Vineyards." She smiled graciously, including them all, but her eyes never quite lifted high enough to single him out at the back of the group. Kyle felt a primitive and un-accustomed urge to shoulder his way through the crowd and force her to acknowledge him. But that kind of reckless grandstanding would only frighten her. Almost at once the fierce burst of desire inside him burned away, leaving a sweet aching glow of wanting and pleasure at just having her near, almost close enough to hold in his arms. He relaxed slightly against the bar and began to pay attention to her words as well as the sound of her voice.

"We'll begin our tour with a very short history of the building." Alanna went on to highlight points in the win-ery's century-old traditions in a light, carrying tone, inter-jecting anecdotes and innuendo as well as enough vivid description to keep her audience attentive and stationary. "At the end of the tour there will be a brief video presen-tation outlining the golden era of Lake Erie wines when the excursion boats from Chicago, Cleveland and points east made this a popular summer resort for the very rich and fa-mous."

She led the party out through a door into the sunlight and the ruins of a splendid flagstone patio that Kyle hadn't known was there. A dry fountain in the center depicted a German girl in native costume carrying a basket of grapes to the harvest. A gazebo leaned drunkenly in on itself, its doorway boarded shut. Alanna was explaining that the early German settlers who founded the island's wine industry and built the original cellars had used the terrace for dancing in the old days. A fire had destroyed the wooden dance pavilion at the turn of the century and twenty years later Prohibition had nearly destroyed the wine industry. Now the patio and the stone wall, behind which lay the modern processing facilities of Island Vineyards were all that remained of the winery's heyday.

"Except for our cellars, of course." She had the routine down pat, Kyle concluded. He tuned out the usual assortment of queries and shoptalk that amateur vintners in the group were inclined to indulge in. Alanna gave an abbreviated account of the picking, stemming and crushing operations carried on in the low, modern building behind the stone wall. She fielded all the questions expertly, keeping the technicalities to a minimum, moving the group steadily forward. Only Kyle lagged behind.

All around him ruler-straight rows of grapevines stretched off down a graded slope away from the lake. Here the huge gnarled vines with their heavy burden of leaves and new clusters of fruit grew almost to the edge of the building. Trained, tended, encouraged in the direction their stewards wished them to grow, the orderly abundance appealed to his methodical soul. These were Catawbas: old vines, heavy with the dignity of their years. The native American grapes were green now, not taking on their rich purple color until August. The plantings were widely spaced to accommodate the huge mechanical picker Alanna leased for harvesting.

All the plantings he saw were mature, well cared for and productive, though not as old as the grapes directly before him. A man could find a great deal of satisfaction working with these vines.

But the winery itself was another story. Kyle swiveled his head, putting vague fantasies of himself here out of his thoughts. The terrace wasn't the only portion in disrepair, but it was still a remarkable edifice. A gothic monstrosity, it was topped by an octagonal tower and a conical roof of beaten copper turned green with age. He wondered how long it had been since the clock on its face had struck the hour. Made entirely of native limestone quarried on the islands, it rose seventy-five feet above the cellars. The original excavations had been there since before the Civil War and might possibly have sheltered a runaway slave or two, since the islands were one of the last stops on the Underground Railroad, Canada's Pelee Island lying only five miles to the north.

Ideally situated, less than a hundred feet from the shore, the winery dominated the skyline along this section of the island. The wide veranda wrapped around two sides of the building, and already several patrons were seated at the wrought iron tables and chairs near the tasting room doors. They would do a brisk business in cheese and fruit platters and tasting trays on hot lazy summer days such as this. But Alanna wanted to do more. That's why he was here, not so he could build a dream of himself tending her vines, or imagine shadowy images of ragged fugitives escaping over the horizon to freedom in Canada in small boats; not because he wanted to make things right with her—but because Island Vineyards was the foundation's business.

Kyle followed the lilting sound of Alanna's voice, drawn to her like a thirsting man to water. She was leading her obedient flock past the open doors of the bottling plant where little activity was in progress this morning. She opened a low wooden door where the stone wall jutted out from the winery proper and motioned them down a steep narrow set of stairs into the cellars. Kyle ducked his head and followed.

The smell of old wine and new assaulted his nose. It took a moment for his eyes to adjust to the aromatic gloom. Then he saw Alanna poised beside a huge oak cask, one hand stroking its glossy surface like an old friend, or a lover. She had touched his body in just that way, lingeringly, wonderingly as though she couldn't quite believe he was real. It had been a heady intoxicating feeling, and at the same time he had felt humbled by her innocence and simplicity.

The cask was nearly sixteen feet high, dwarfing Alanna's small form. Her voice was also muted by the vast dimensions of the cellar, but her words were clear and strong. "At the turn of the last century my great-grandfather imported German oak and German craftsmen to build these vats. Red wine is aged here for as long as two years, picking up a hint of oak flavoring and throwing off impurities. At today's prices these vats, each of which holds approximately ten thousand bottles of wine, would cost over a thousand dollars a foot to replace." The crowd gasped and viewed the double row of vats with new respect. Kyle caught the tag end of a smile on Alanna's lips and guessed that the information had brought the expected reaction from her charges. "In the smaller casks to our left we store white wines, which take much less time to mature."

A tall gangling man with dark wavy hair and a beak of a nose raised his hand. "I understand these casks have to be cleaned periodically. Who does that?"

"The cellarmaster," Alanna replied without missing a beat. She raised a slender hand to point at her chest. "I inspect each cask personally."

"Even those small ones?" A heavy-set woman in bright pink squealed in horror. Her words echoed about the room, dying out in the far dim corners. While the small kegs were nearly six feet high and oval shaped, the opening in front wasn't large. Kyle looked at Alanna's softly rounded form intently as did most of the other males in the group.

"Every one," Alanna assured laughingly.

"Well I'm sure I could never do that," the woman in pink said, eyeing the vats distrustfully.

"Not for the last twenty years you couldn't honey." A balding man in a gray T-shirt, obviously her husband, patted her ample fanny and laughed aloud. The rest of the group laughed also and only Kyle noticed the faint telltale blush mount to Alanna's cheekbones yet again.

"I watch my weight religiously," Alanna quipped, but her color darkened a little more. She glanced quickly in Kyle's direction, directly acknowledging him for the first time. She caught his gaze, shielded though it was, then dropped her eyes and turned back to the group with a gracious smile. The light from the low wattage overhead bulb caught, and in turn was caught up in, the auburn streaks in her hair.

"I wouldn't do it on a bet," the woman in pink repeated with emphasis.

"Let's just wait till we can get it in a bottle," the balding man decided, giving his wife a hug.

"It's certainly no job for anyone who suffers from claustrophobia." Again there was a ripple of amused laughter as Alanna motioned her group forward. The heavy-set woman hurried on, shaking her head.

"At various stages in its aging, the wine must be racked," Alanna continued her lecture. "To do that we draw it off into clean barrels. It remains there until it's bottled." She had her back to Kyle as they walked on through the line of kegs but she could feel him watching her every step of the

way and her pulse tingled with mingled pleasure and apprehension at the sensation. "The gauges you see on each cask
measure the temperature of the wine and its sugar content.
Accurate record keeping is essential in wine making whether
you are doing vintages of thousands of gallons, or keeping
two five gallon jugs in your basement." She took a long
deep breath before launching into her next speech. She
couldn't go on letting Kyle affect her this way or she'd never
get through the next few days without betraying the confusion of her emotions. That she could never bear.

"Now, ladies and gentlemen, if you'll watch your step on
this ramp we'll go back outside for a look at our Solera
where we make a sherry that is comparable to the finest imported from Spain." If her voice was a little harsh and high
pitched she hoped no one would notice amid the babble of
comments underscoring her words. "Please let me caution
you to be wary of the bees. Those casks attract honey bees
from all over the island. And tipsy bees can be most unpredictable."

"But I bet they make swell honey." The balding man got
the last laugh.

"They certainly do. Our tour concludes in the tasting
room where I'll hand you over to one of my assistants who'll
be more than happy to help you with your choices of Island
Vineyards' wines. Thank you for visiting us, and enjoy your
stay on the island." She answered one or two more routine
questions in a daze. The faces around her were smiling and
interested so she realized she must have gotten through the
spiel without any major gaffes, but she couldn't recall a
word she'd spoken from the moment she'd spotted Kyle
leaning against the bar. All she could remember was Kyle's
lean silver-haired form in the back of the group watching
her, almost caressing her with his eyes

Or so she imagined. And that was by far the most upsetting part of having him there. She didn't want to feel like that about him ever again. She couldn't or she would be lost. Why did it have to be that way? The one or two times she'd run into David's father after the end of their heartbreaking affair she'd only-felt anger and remorse but never, never the slightest wish to have him hold her close and tell her everything would be all right, to make her believe there was a future for them—together. With Kyle all her daydreams would end that way if she allowed them to.

The tour broke up, the last of the amateur vintners who'd been plying her with questions drifted away with a final wave. She would have to face Kyle soon. She was running out of excuses to avoid him. And surely she could control her body's responses to his nearness if she only tried hard enough. It was just a question of conditioning, after all. Once she was used to having such a disturbing male back in her life surely the warm, melting longings he triggered deep within her would fade away. She would be herself again, in control, cool and aloof and mistress of her own thoughts and deeds.

She might as well start now. Alanna squared her shoulders in a habitual unconscious gesture and turned to face Kyle Stafford's unsettling countenance. He was nowhere to be seen.

KYLE DIDN'T HAVE a specific destination in mind when he broke away from the tour group. He only knew he didn't want to confront Alanna in a crowd of strangers. She'd looked too wary, too easily persuaded to fob him off with some excuse about her work or her family obligations back there. He wanted to catch her off guard, perhaps in the cool twilight under one of the big spreading maples on the lawn. They needed time alone and undisturbed to talk and to listen to what the other was truly trying to say, not just to trade more of the inevitable platitudes and fall back on shoptalk when the silence stretched out too long.

They'd talked so much in those first days when they met. But they had each left out important portions of their lives and that had been their undoing. Kyle's aimless distance-eating stride carried him toward the vitality and colorful holiday atmosphere of the town square. He stopped suddenly, not wanting to be caught up in the melee. He looked around. On his right the lake lapped against a concrete retaining wall, blue-green and placid at the moment. The sun was hot, the humidity stifling and the shade of several mammoth old pines looked inviting. He was almost directly in front of the Perry Column so he climbed several of the shallow steps to prop himself against the stone wall, shaded by those same pines, and let the long-suppressed memories flood over him.

They had spent time learning to know each other in Maryland. That had been a new experience for him, a man who kept his liaisons with women deliberately casual and always brief. And their loving had come naturally as a part of that learning process. On the morning of their second day at the old inn, they'd taken a walk into the restored Colonial village outside the low stone gates at the end of the drive. Alanna's hand was folded in his and he began making slow sensual circles with his thumb against her palm. Her grasp had tightened in response to the pleasurable caress and he felt his answering response deep within.

"Did you sleep well?" he'd asked with deliberate provocation. Alanna's ready blush fascinated him and he took every opportunity to bring that beguiling color to her cheeks. She'd looked so surprised last night when she found he'd made reservations for two rooms, as though she'd expected to be thrust willy-nilly into his bed, as well as into his heart.

And if he'd been thinking as usual with his head and not his heart he might have done just that, never noticing the little shadow of fear and unease that darkened her gray eyes. But he had taken extra care, because she was so very special, and he had made the right choice. Now thirty-six hours later he still hadn't done anything more than kiss her, but the need to be closer physically was growing very strong within him. And within Alanna if he read the signals correctly.

"I was very comfortable. The quilt on my bed is a Lafayette's Orange Peel." She hurried into speech as they stepped onto the wooden sidewalk that marked the beginning of the village shops. "My mother is quite a needlewoman." It was apparent she was aware of the excitement snapping and sparking like static electricity between them and wanted to gloss over the fact, but her hand remained in his and Kyle didn't stop the slow sensual caress of his fingers over hers. "Quilts are her passion. The pattern was named for the Marquis." Alanna's composure was crumbling. She flushed again, glancing at him from the corner of her eye but allowed her hand to remain in his. "He presented a young Philadelphia lady with one of them at a banquet. They were quite rare during Revolutionary times, you know. Oranges, I mean, not quilts." She smiled up at him with a question in her eyes.

"And?" Kyle prompted when she faltered and stopped speaking, stopped moving altogether. Her tongue came out to moisten the edge of her bottom lip but she didn't break the contact of their eyes and he knew all at once, and with exhilarating certainty, that she shared the delightful heavy warmth stealing through his limbs.

"And?" Alanna questioned, her voice low and throaty. She smiled but her manner was absentminded. "Oh, my story. The young lady took the fruit home and carefully copied the shape of the paring, working the design into a quilt she made to remember the event. The one in my room isn't that old of course, but I'm sure it's an antique, beautifully made.'' She looked down at their clasped hands as if seeing them for the first time.

"So are you beautifully made." His lips were only inches from her temple. She smelled fresh and clean and a little like flowers after a summer rainshower.

He'd waited so long, kept himself from blurting out how strong his feelings for her already were, to ruin it now by frightening her out of her wits with his passion. What they would share—perhaps for the rest of their lives—was too special to rush Alanna into before she was ready.

"Kyle...I..." Alanna's voice trembled like her fingers and died away into silence.

"I have a very special gift to choose for another woman who blushes as delightfully and as often as you do." He lifted her chin with the tip of his finger to make her face him. "Will you help me pick it out?"

"If you promise never to refer to my blushes again I'd be happy to," Alanna replied, her eyes gleaming darkly with a mixture of desire and pique.

"Agreed," Kyle said with a laugh.

"I should refuse, for most women would heartily resent such a request," she went on with unexpected spirit. "But since this is a toy shop, I assume she's a much younger lady." Her voice held a glint of challenge and a new strength as though in the last few moments she'd made a decision within herself.

"So much for hoping to make you jealous, my practical lady vintner," Kyle murmured in mock dismay, easing the sensual tension mounting between them. "It's for my cousin's child." He tried very hard to keep his tone ordinary and matter-of-fact. Kelly wasn't his child—legally or morally—it shouldn't be so hard to merely say the words aloud.

Alanna was quick to pick up on the shift in his teasing mood and answered swiftly. "Let's see what they have inside."

They spent almost an hour prowling among the hand-carved wooden soldiers, china dolls and antique cast iron mechanical toys that were interspersed with more modern childhood treasures. Kyle allowed himself the luxury of pretending they were shopping for their own children; a girl, perhaps, who would look far more like Alanna than was good for her; and a boy because it would be fun to have a son to share things with. He gravitated toward the dollhouses and miniature furniture since he wasn't really sure what a girl going on fourteen would like. He'd only seen Kelly twice in her life and both times had been within the last year.

He wondered if he should ask Alanna what to do. She, after all, had been a fourteen-year-old girl not too long ago herself. He said so and she laughed that enchanting, tinkling laugh.

"It's been longer than you might think. I'm twenty-six."

He noticed she'd been browsing through the mechanical toys and battery operated cars and trucks. Had Alanna been a tomboy? Was that why she looked uncomfortable when he found her there among the electric trains? She was standing before a smoke-puffing steam engine that rode an endless circle of track, pulling its tender, a pullman car and a small red caboose behind it through a tiny wooden village. Her expression was rapt and delighted, and more than a little chagrined when he called her back to the problem at hand.

"Do you think Kelly... my cousin's child... would like this doll?" Damn, he had to keep thinking, even in the most private corner of his soul that Kelly was Derek's daughter, not his. *She had been his cousin's child since before she was born.* He held up a china doll dressed in a long, embroidered, Victorian bridal gown. Its flaxen hair and blue eyes gave the finely molded bisque features a look of ethereal beauty. Alanna nodded but qualified her approval with a tilt of her head.

"If you really want to make an impression on the young lady I'd add something more grown up if I were you," she offered, pursing her full lips thoughtfully. "When I was fourteen most of my thoughts were taken up with trying to make myself look vastly older and more sophisticated. I'd have loved that doll, but not the idea that anyone thought I was still young enough to want to play with it. Get my point?"

"It's a good one," Kyle responded, but a dark cloud passed over his face. "What do you suggest?" He made a real effort to appear unfazed by the well-meant criticism. "I have to bow to your vastly superior knowledge of adolescent girls."

"Hmmm." Alanna made a great show of considering her answer but her gray eyes watched him seriously. There was no playfulness in their concerned, ebony-shot depths. Kyle couldn't return that gentle scrutiny so he studied the china doll in his hands. When he looked up again the darkness was gone from his face, hidden away with ruthless determination in the deep recesses of his heart.

"There." Alanna's face brightened too. She pointed out the window across the cobbled street to a very modern looking drug store masquerading behind a bow-shaped window and inaccurately signed as Ye Olde Apothecary Shoppe. His eyes followed her pointing finger.

"What's over there?" He was genuinely puzzled.

"Cosmetics, silly." Alanna grinned mischievously. "Unless you feel her parents, your cousins . . . ?" She hesitated slightly then went on when he nodded shortly, "... would object. I can't think of anything that would make her feel more grown-up than some appropriate makeup."

"Do girls that age wear makeup?"

"They certainly do." Alanna gave one last longing glance at the train set. While Kyle completed transactions for the delivery of the doll to the inn, her fingers traced lightly over the steeple of the small church set in a grove of those fuzzy, improbably green trees that always seem to sprout up around a model train set. When she moved ahead of him toward the door of the shop, Kyle impulsively added the train and its tiny village to his purchases.

"What does Kelly look like?" Alanna quizzed as they headed for the drug store. She sounded excited, truly caught up in their shopping spree. She unhesitatingly placed her hand in his when he offered it to help her step off the wooden sidewalk into the narrow street.

He handled it better this time. "She's dark like me..." Then halted abruptly when he heard himself say those words. A stain of dull color came up around the collar of his dark red sport shirt. "I mean she looks like her father, all the Stafford family is dark." He didn't volunteer any more information. He couldn't. Alanna didn't seem to find his silence unusual. She was making the whole project so sunny and entertaining he could almost forget some of the old pain and nagging remorse.

When the pale pink lipstick, dusting powder, nail gloss and other assorted feminine knicknacks had been packed into a small wicker basket lined with scented yellow tissue paper and topped with a silky lemon and white checkered bow, they were both laughing and relaxed. And very, very aware of each other.

"You're sure Kelly's parents won't object?" Alanna had asked with a pretty little moue of uncertainty when she looked at all the assembled paraphernalia one last time before the helpful middle-aged clerk whisked it into a box.

"No, they won't object. Catherine is a very indulgent mother."

"I'm glad. This was fun. Thank you for asking for my help. I don't often get to shop for girls." Alanna shut her lips tightly on the last word.

"Are you tired of walking?" Kyle was busy with his own thoughts and missed the nuances of her last statement.

"No, I love to walk." Alanna met his gold-flecked gaze head on. "I have two hundred and fifty acres of grapevines to keep track of. I do a lot of it on foot."

"There's a place I'd like to show you. It reminds me of you, as the inn reminded me of you." He could sense she was aware he was asking more than his words conveyed. "It has a kind of timeless peace about it, a serenity much like what I see at times in your eyes."

"I'd very much like to see this special place of yours." Their glances caught and held yet again.

Kyle kept her arm tucked near to his heart from that moment on. He let the sweet stinging tension between them build by slow degrees. He could feel her attraction to him; see it in the way she faltered as she shifted his hand to rest beneath the swell of her breast as they walked, and it pleased him a great deal.

He wanted to make love to Alanna, slowly, lingeringly, but only when the time was right. She looked up to him, the successful older man, the white knight who could take from her shoulders the burden of keeping her vineyards free of outside influences. He wanted to be that man for her sake. He wanted to find release and contentment within her, share the pleasures of loving with her. But he never wanted Alanna to know he had feet of clay, not until he could be sure enough of their growing love to tell her the secrets of his past.

Halfway up the gradual slope behind the town they came on a shady green clearing tucked into a small depression. Below them the village spread out like the tiny wooden town clustered around the train set. From farther away he could make out the faint sound of traffic on the highway as it wafted by on a fickle wind that just as quickly switched direction and eddied it away. Nothing moved after its passing to disturb the silence of the deserted glade. It was as quiet and peaceful as a watercolor. On the far side of the clearing stood the remains of an old gristmill. Remnants of the spillway created a miniature waterfall that burbled and danced over a fallen log.

"Oh, Kyle, it's beautiful. Like a fairy tale," Alanna breathed, dropping to her knees to run her hand lightly over a fragrant patch of pale blue violets nestled among ferns near the water's edge. Her coral blouse and slacks were a bright spot of color in the subdued setting of blues and greens. "The Garden of Eden must have looked like this." She laughed and looked up at him, suddenly shy. She held out her hand. Kyle dropped to his knees and folded her hand in his. "Thank you for showing me this place, for the days we've spent together ... for everything. I'll remember this time always."

"That's exactly how I want you to feel—as if this time we're sharing is very special. That this time is for always." Kyle cupped her chin in one strong, brown hand and tilted her face up to his. "Alanna." Her name, spoken quietly, mingled with the rush of water and the sound of wind high in the trees. He repeated it, liking the taste of it on his tongue, following it with the even more intoxicating taste of her skin.

He shifted nearer, his hands threading through her hair, positioning her to be claimed by his kiss and by his body. Alanna caught her breath on a sigh of pleasure, then melted into his embrace so naturally that wanting her, desiring her seemed as right as sunshine chasing away the darkness of a long, cold night.

Kyle had never felt so taken out of himself, so ready to give of himself, to accept intimacy with another human being as he did that day in the Maryland countryside. But he couldn't disregard the clamoring of his thoughts, the cautionary lessons he'd learned so harshly.

"Alanna, I find you so beautiful, so warm and sweet and desirable, but I can't make love to you. Not here under the sun and the sky even though I've never wanted anything more in my life. I didn't plan for this to happen so quickly. I'm not prepared to protect you. I won't allow you to be put at risk no matter how badly I want to take you in my arms and love you as you've never been loved before." He could recall even at this distance in time the tightness in his throat and chest, the difficulty he had even forming the words at all.

She'd smiled as he held her in his arms and the expression had been made even more blindingly beautiful when the faint shadow of anxiety he'd noticed lifted from her features. She'd been frightened of making love; then, he had thought it was because she was inexperienced. Later, later, he knew the truth. Alanna's lessons in the harsh realities of man-woman relationships had been even more traumatic than his own.

Kyle felt the rough edge of the marble ledge press into his palms as the lovely memories of their days together at the inn faded away. All around him the raucous sights and sounds of the busy tourist attraction intruded on his reverie. Later... Kyle tried stubbornly to hang on to the pleasure of his recollections but the memories refused to become clear. Individual voices and figures came into focus, further disrupting his concentration. All that lingered was a sweet glow of fulfillment as he felt again the joy of their love-making in the big four-poster bed at the inn. When Alanna knew that he would be responsible for protecting her from becoming pregnant she had been all he could have ever hoped to find in a partner, a lover. She had welcomed him, guided him into the soft secret places of her woman's body without reservation. She had loved him, given of herself and taken from him in return, answering his passion and allowing him to feel, for a little while, whole and free and worthy again.

He had to find some way to recapture what they had shared then; the spark was still there, the strength of his feeling was still as insistent as before; he could admit that now. But how to win back Alanna's trust; that was the problem he must deal with first.

A blunt object sailed through the air and caught him just below the rib cage, bringing Kyle the rest of the way back to the present with painful alacrity. He looked around, gasping a little, blinking against the bright glare of sunlight off the water and shook his head to clear the memories that lingered like alcohol fumes in his brain. His assailant, a bright red Frisbee, lay at his feet.

"Hey, mister, we didn't hurt you, did we?" Two blond, athletic youngsters in tight shorts, jogging shoes and not much else but fantastic tans came bounding up the monument steps. "Our Frisbee got caught in a gust of wind. We sure didn't mean to hit you like that."

"Yeah, we're awful sorry. Did it knock the wind out of you?" the darker of the two blondes asked worriedly, glancing at the Park Service ranger stationed outside the entrance to the column. The khaki-uniformed young woman was looking the other way. "You look kind of shell-shocked."

The two boys exchanged worried glances and Kyle didn't have any trouble reading their meaning. They were wondering how badly they'd hurt the absentminded old coot.

"I'm fine." Kyle waved off their concern. "I was day-dreaming or I'd probably have been able to get out of the way. Don't think a thing of it. Go back to your friends and your game." He waved toward two or three teens standing in a cluster on the lawn. Other family groups and young couples sunbathed or strolled around the grounds. He tossed the plastic circle back to the boys with a flip of his wrist and they ran off still mumbling apologies over their shoulders.

"That's what spending time rehashing what can't be changed will get you," Kyle mumbled to himself, rubbing his aching ribs. "If only... damn, I hate those words." If only he hadn't given in to that one suicidal impulse to tell Alanna the truth about Kelly on their last day together, none of what followed two years ago would have happened. They would have gone on living in their enchanted world, making love, learning to love more deeply with each passing hour, learning to need each other so completely nothing could have parted them.

But fate hadn't been so kind. Kyle couldn't even recall today why he'd taken his billfold out that afternoon as they shared a late lunch on the inn's screened dining porch. They had been making love all morning and were happy and sated and full of caring for each other. Perhaps he'd been going to leave a tip? Or confirm a date? It didn't matter. Kelly's picture had drifted out with the blizzard of notes and scraps of paper he always kept there. It was a school picture—a gift from Kelly when she'd sent him a thank you note for the first Christmas gift he'd ever dared send her.

Is this Kelly? Alanna had asked, her cheeks still rosy with a blush because he'd been teasing her that she'd rather play with her train than make love with him. *She's a lovely child.* She had picked up the photo to examine it more closely. *Does she favor her mother's family at all? She looks all Stafford to me.*

She's all Stafford all right. That was all he would have had to say, but the lovely languorous sharing of bodies and hearts they'd enjoyed just before coming down to the meal had combined to override his usual reticence. *She's my daughter,* he'd said.

I didn't know you'd been married. Why hadn't he noticed the trembling of Alanna's slender, ringless fingers then? The sudden paleness and stricken darkness in her eyes.

Strange but his next few simple sentences had hurt them both so deeply. *I've never been married, Alanna. But Kelly is my daughter.* He'd meant to go on and explain to her, as he'd never done for anyone before, the sorrow and remorse that had dogged him throughout the years.

But she never gave him a chance.

"Hey, Kyle, are you all right?" David's piping treble voice preceded him up the first few steps to the monument. "We saw the Bartley twins hit you with their Frisbee." His bicycle lay in the grass alongside the steps, watched over by the tow-headed youngster Kyle had seen with Alanna's son the evening before.

"They're bullies," the other boy called out. He was slightly taller and heavier than David, but it was easy to see which of the two was the leader and which the follower.

"They're not even twins," David scoffed. "Alex got passed over in the first grade. Now they think they're hot stuff 'cause they're the seniors this year."

"*The* seniors?" Kyle was quick to pick up on David's intonation.

"They're the only two this year."

"Last year there weren't any so we didn't have to go to stupid old graduation," the other boy chimed in. "Me and David are the only two third graders. Our school is real small," he added unnecessarily.

"He knows that, Billy. This is my friend, Bill Harmon." David recalled the manners Alanna had drilled into him. "Bill, this is Mr. Stafford but he says we can call him Kyle."

"Me too?" Billy asked ingenuously, and Kyle laughed down at him as he followed David down the steps.

"Any friend of David's is a friend of mine." He held out his hand. "Pleased to meet you Bill." He was careful not to use the diminutive.

"Me too, Kyle." Young Master Harmon preened and showed a grin that revealed two more missing teeth than David could boast of.

"Billy's dad is a charter captain in the summer. In the winter he just teaches school." David dropped back to the more familiar form of his friend's name. "If you'd rather, we could go out fishing on his boat instead of mine. It's lots bigger." David's offer was gallantly made but his reluctance sifted through to color the polite words.

"No way." Kyle's answer was emphatic. "Unless you want to back out of our arrangement?" He cocked his head and waited for the reply with a smile lurking in his eyes and at the corners of his mouth.

"No way." David beamed over at his cohort. "I told you he was an okay guy. Hey, Kyle, would you like to come with us? My mom and Billy's mom are too busy to cook supper tonight and we're going to eat at Grandma's." He made a face. "She'll probably cook something weird. She likes to experiment sometimes, so we're going to the Dairy Queen to get something to hold us over. Just in case."

"Supper won't be ready for hours," Billy chimed in.

"Then we're going to get in a couple of games of Star Invaders at the arcade. We got our allowances today."

So Alanna had already made plans to stay out of his way for the rest of the afternoon. It shouldn't be a disappointment. He expected it after all.

"My aunt Leslie is getting married pretty soon and that's all they can think about," Billy explained mournfully.

"Women," David added, with what his mother would surely decry as chauvinism if she'd been there to hear.

"There's no figuring them out, guys," Kyle assured them and grinned as the last of the past faded into dreams once more. "There's just no figuring them out."

"You can say that again," David nodded sagely. "Not in a million years."

Chapter Five

Alanna locked the door of the winery and stepped out into the muggy evening. Daylight saving time always made the night seem as if it might never come. The shadows were long but the sun was still some distance above the western horizon and the air was warm. She'd had a quick bite to eat in the winery kitchen before they closed. Her mother was feeding David dinner, but Alanna knew Phyllis Jeffries wouldn't be expecting her to join them. She gave the doorknob one last twist, satisfied the lock had snapped home. It seemed as if she and David spent more and more time in the old building. One of her favorite fantasies this past year was to imagine the huge second floor loft winterized and remodeled into a home for the two of them.

She wondered what Kyle's reaction to her broaching the subject would be, then brought herself up short. She had no business projecting Kyle into her dreams however casually. These stray, comfortable imaginings were the kind of thing she had to be on guard against. They happened too often, they felt too right, they were too easy to build on and elaborate in her dreams.

Where had Kyle gone when he left the tour group hours ago? She hadn't seen him since. Had he shown himself around the vineyards and the bottling rooms? She'd wanted to point out the new plantings of the hardy French-American hybrid grapes, Chelois and Seyval Blanc, introduce him to her parents . . . spend time with him.

But the yard was deserted and so was the house, she discovered. Alanna showered and changed into a cream-colored, cotton tank top and khaki green slacks. She found the kitchen unnaturally tidy. David must have spent all day with Billy and her parents. He was growing up so fast but she didn't have to worry about him wandering off. He always asked permission to leave the grounds.

Their private stretch of boulder-strewn shoreline and the road that ran behind it was deserted of even bicycle traffic. Hands on her hips, capriciously arched brows drawn together in perplexity, Alanna surveyed the quiet scene.

Laughter carried through the eight-foot-high spirea hedge that hid her parents' clapboard cottage from her view. It was David's shrill, high-pitched squeals of delight that first attracted her notice. Her mother's throaty laugh filled the pauses. Men's voices, deeper and more restrained, could also be heard. Stooping to squeeze through the opening that her brother had carved years ago into the living wall while a much smaller Alanna had watched in little-sister adoration, she stepped onto the lawn.

A lively game of croquet was going on, and David was beating the pants off his grandmother and Billy Harlan. Fireflies blinked Morse code-like messages in the lengthening shadows along the hedgerow, and a faint chill carried on the lake breeze as the sun dipped more quickly than Alanna expected below the horizon. Still there would be nearly an hour until nightfall. Twilight lingered a long time in the middle of summer.

On the porch contentedly rocking, his cane propped carelessly against the railing, her father sat in serious conversation with Kyle Stafford. Alanna's heart gave a funny little lurch that was far more anticipation than warning.

Her father looked animated. Alanna wondered fleetingly what the two men were discussing so earnestly. Malcolm Jeffries had the same dark copper hair as Alanna and David. He was thin and spare. All of his nearly sixty-eight years showed in the carved lines of his face. Pain and suffering were also evident in the depth of those lines, but the discomfort was downplayed and denied as much as possible. Outwardly gruff and opinionated, her father was also one of the kindest, most loving men Alanna had ever known. She was so very proud to be his daughter, to have his guidance to help raise her son. They were all Jeffrieses together. The Jeffrieses of South Bass Island in Lake Erie, as their labels proclaimed.

Swallowing an unexpected lump of emotion that had lodged somewhere near her windpipe, Alanna took a moment to ostensibly straighten her tank top and pat her hair into place. The familiar actions were camouflage for her real objective.

She wanted to watch Kyle with her family. He stood leaning against a porch post, laughing, and that was what caught her attention and held it so firmly. He laughed so seldom that she found the changes in his face fascinating to contemplate. His eyes darkened and narrowed, lines fanned out at the corners, and his mouth twisted upward almost reluctantly. She liked his laugh, it echoed her father's deep baritone and was infectious enough to bring a smile to her own lips as well.

And decidedly she liked his gray hair. The last of the sunlight set it shining as he bent his head to catch one of her father's acerbic comments. The older man gestured broadly, poking one long-fingered hand in the direction of Kyle's oxford-cloth covered chest. Alanna hoped they weren't arguing politics. Her father's views lay somewhere only slightly left of, and a centimeter more forward-thinking than, Herbert Hoover's. She'd better make her presence known before he pinned Kyle to the rail with his cane.

But Alanna hesitated a few seconds longer. Several late bees droned among the petunias in a nearby bed. The peculiarly heavy, sweet smell of the flowers almost covered the moist aquatic scent of the lake carried on the breeze. She needed this time to order her thoughts. She needed to try to make sense out of the jumble of conflicting emotions that lurked just below the deceptively placid exterior of her thoughts. Already, after only a single day on the island, Kyle seemed more the man she remembered from their magical time together that faraway spring and less the tired older stranger she'd met on the pier.

Why was it all her hard-won security and independence had evaporated the moment he'd reentered her life? Why was it she could be so easily swayed by the men who attracted her the most? David's father had also swept her off her feet, although she could understand now that any suave sophisticated older man might have done so at the time. She had only turned nineteen; she had been so homesick, so grieved for her brother and so needful of being loved. She had cared deeply for Elliot Mayhew, at least until she'd learned the truth about him. And she'd cared even more deeply for Kyle. She had been ready, willing, and very, very close to falling in love with him.

Her feelings for David's father had carried with them all the sincerity she'd been capable of at nineteen. Lord knows, she'd had enough time to dissect and examine her emotions during the last nine years. That conviction had carried her through great hardship but reality had cured her of what she could now admit had been more infatuation than true love. There had never been any question of not going through with her pregnancy—the consequence of passion and innocence, combined with Elliot's careless attitude toward birth control. She had considered long and hard the question of putting the baby up for adoption—for the child's sake; but the moment she'd seen her son she'd abandoned that course of action without a moment's hesitation. Her child was the product of a relationship that was very meaningful to her, if not to his biological father.

Yet Kyle Stafford must share some of Elliot Mayhew's baser qualities. He too had fathered a child out of wedlock. He too was guilty of deserting a girl, possibly as young and innocent as she'd been nine years ago. That couldn't be wished away. It had happened. It was fact. It couldn't be changed just because Alanna's feelings for the man had refused to die a decent death.

She began to turn away, recollections of half-forgotten pain dulling her fog-gray eyes. David spotted her as she moved in the shadows and dragged her forward. "Kyle doesn't know how to play croquet," David informed his parent, pleased to be able to demonstrate his own skill. "He's watching us play this game. Then he's going to give it a try."

"I'd advise you not to give away all your secrets then," Alanna warned, grinning down at David's mischievous upturned face. "Strategy's the name of the game. Get Grandpa to coach you before the big match. He's the best croquet player around."

"That's a good idea, Mom." David's face took on a crafty look as he glanced over his shoulder at the two men on the porch. "Kyle plays golf so he'll get the hang of it real fast I bet." He furrowed his brow in concentration. "We can't show him all our trick shots showing off. I'd better warn Billy." He hopped away to confer with his friend, dragging his mallet behind him, leaving a trail of darker green in the damp, lush grass. Two shots later they seemed to have abandoned their dissembling game plan as they argued vociferously over the best angle that would send his grandmother's ball spinning into the dense shrubbery. Phyllis laughed and made a face as her red ball careened away from the playing field.

She was a smaller, plumper version of her daughter, with jet black hair almost untouched by gray, and laughing blue eyes. She waved a preoccupied greeting in Alanna's direction as she bemoaned her predicament. The boys chortled in unholy glee and gamboled about her like young lambs.

"So much for attempts to instill a little chivalry in those two, Alanna," her father quipped as she climbed the three wooden steps to the porch. His speech was clear, the words distinct. Alanna was pleased. Some days the trip to Port Clinton for therapy tired him to the point of incoherency. The third and most recent stroke he'd suffered a year ago had robbed him of the use of his left arm, weakened the muscles of his left leg and for a time, severely affected his speech.

It hadn't deterred Malcolm Jeffries's spirit or his zest for life. Hard work and pure bullheadedness had brought him a long way. His speech had returned, he'd learned to walk again and was able to continue as much of his former lifestyle as was humanly possible. Although Alanna ran the winery full-time she still conferred with her father daily.

Kyle unfolded his rangy length from the porch rail as Alanna moved past his perch to give her father a quick peck on the cheek. She motioned him back to his seat without directly meeting his gold-flecked gaze. "I see you've already met my parents."

"Saw him walking down the road. Knew right away by the look of him he was a city slicker," Malcolm drawled. "But he was too damned interested in the test plot of Chardonnays to be a day-tripper. I figured he must be who he says he is.'' One of the compensations for his disability, he often said, was an excuse to cut out unnecessary words. Malcolm loved to talk in fragments of sentences, occasionally in single words fired off like commands from a drill sergeant. He played it to the hilt. ''Gave him a ride in the Woody on the way back from the airstrip. Your mother stuffed him. Veal scaloppine and brussels sprouts. Nasty things. And sour-cherry pie for dessert.''

Alanna's eyes widened in dismay.

''It was excellent,'' Kyle inserted with the smooth assurance of perfect manners. Phyllis Jeffries was a wonderful mother and loving grandmother, a good businesswoman in her own right, an expert needlewoman. But as far as housekeeping and culinary skills, they rated far down on her list of accomplishments. Alanna caught her father's eye and hastily stifled a chuckle, turning it into a cough that she smothered with the back of her hand.

''Kyle's been telling me he's got some ideas for marketing the new wines in the next few seasons. The De Chaunac is going to be worth the effort it will take to bring it to the public's notice. I think you'll be wise to hear him out, Lanny girl.'' The speech was a clue to her father's excitement in the project. He came closest to forgetting his limitations when he was involved in the business of making and selling wine. Alanna allowed herself a glance in Kyle's direction and wasn't altogether surprised to find him watching her father carefully, noting the same variation in speech and coming swiftly and accurately to the same conclusion.

''Of course, Dad.'' Alanna poured herself a glass of lemonade from the pitcher near his chair. Malcolm was allowed a single glass of wine a day and made it a bedtime ritual complete with tasting notes that often found their way to Alanna's desk with his suggestions for improvements the next day. The rest of the time he made do with fruit drinks. "Mr. Stafford's ideas will be given every consideration." She darted a quick saucy look at Kyle's averted profile. She saw his lips quirk in response to her pedantic tone. She found herself wanting to laugh out loud as she returned to her seat. Her hands were trembling and her thoughts tended to scatter too, if she didn't pay very close attention to the conversation. She curled her fingers more tightly around the frosty glass and decided the meeting was going much more smoothly than she'd dared to imagine it could.

Her parents knew nothing of her previous involvement with Kyle. She wanted to keep it that way. But both Phyllis and Malcolm were very perceptive where she was concerned. Alanna wanted to bring off this initial encounter on just the right light note.

"Bring Kyle over in the morning with the blueprints for the winery renovations, will you, Alanna?" Malcolm suggested, pushing himself up out of the heavy walnut rocking chair he preferred. "I'll be all stove-up tomorrow like as not. Always am when I've been to see those pesky doctors." With a practiced gesture of his right hand Malcolm tucked the thumb of his paralyzed left hand into his belt and accepted his cane from Alanna's outstretched hand.

"Thanks, honey. It's past my bedtime. More harm than good," he grumbled the familiar litany. "But I sure like those pretty young nurses. And don't tell your mother I said that. She'll be refusing me my conjugal rights again and that's about all the excitement I get out of life these days!"

"Dad!"

Malcolm winked at Kyle who was standing again, pleased with Alanna's reaction to his sally.

"Mum's the word, sir. It's been a pleasure to meet you in person at last. I'll be available whenever you'd like to talk business."

"Play chess?" Malcolm barked.

"Not very well," Kyle admitted with a wry twist of his lips.

"Good. Damnable priest has been beating me three games out of four all summer. Need a partner I can beat. Be here by ten."

"Yes, sir. Unless your daughter has other plans for me?" Kyle inclined his head in Alanna's direction. There was a faint, wicked spark in Kyle's hazel eyes that sent answering tingles up and down the length of Alanna's spine. He seemed a very different person from the tired, dispirited man of yesterday. He was so very much the old Kyle, the man who'd stolen her heart and her peace of mind.

"Oh, no, you don't." Alanna bristled facetiously, but the effort to appear only slightly amused was tremendous. She hoped her bantering tone hid her confusion. "Dad's still the president and CEO of Island Vineyards. What he says goes. If you'd like, I'll get the blueprints now so that you can go over them at your leisure."

"Smart girl," Malcolm approved with a growl. "Now go rescue your mother from those young rascals. We had a long day."

"Good night Daddy," Alanna whispered. "Sleep well." He ducked his head for a quick kiss as she held open the old-fashioned, sailor-blue-painted screen door.

"Good night, Kyle. Glad you came in person. Island Vineyards is worth your time and effort. And the foundation's money."

"We're well aware of that, sir. Good night."

Her mother stood at the bottom of the steps flanked by the two boys when Alanna turned away from the door. "They beat me so badly I offered them an ice cream cone to halt the massacre."

David waved two dollar bills triumphantly before Alanna's eyes. "Can we ride our bikes up to the Dairy Queen? Please, can we, huh?"

"If you hurry," Alanna gave her permission, squelching an urge to remind the boys they'd already made a trip to the ice-cream shop once that day. But what was summer vacation for if not to break routine once in a while? "Don't loiter, don't talk to strangers from the boats and don't keep Billy out until after dark. His mother worries so." She shifted position, pointing a warning finger at Bette's towheaded firstborn. "Go straight on home, William James Harlan or we'll both be in hot water with your mother. We just made it in under curfew last night, remember?"

"Yes'm," Billy responded as the duo pelted off toward the boy-sized hole in the hedge.

"Do you want something to eat, Alanna?" Phyllis asked looking at her daughter standing above her on the porch steps. "I doubt you've eaten. You never do when you close up."

"No thanks, Mom. I'm fine, really. And it's getting late. Why don't you make an early night of it too?"

"That does sound like a good idea." Phyllis sighed and leaned her mallet against the blue wooden lattice that screened the foundation of the porch. "It was so hot and muggy on the mainland today. I still feel like a limp dishrag. Good night, Mr. Stafford." She accepted Kyle's hand to mount the steps with gentle dignity.

"Make it Kyle, please. And I'll call you Phyllis if I may?" His smile was quick, slightly wistful and altogether charming. Alanna felt the power of it in the very marrow of her bones. Evidently her mother wasn't immune either. She laughed up into his serious dark face with girlish delight.

"Kyle it will be. There's Alka Seltzer in all the bathrooms of the big house. You were very polite about my cooking, but I'm no fool. Alanna has some wonderful plans for the winery. I hope you see your way to backing them." She held his hand for an extra second, her voice earnest, her eyes searching his.

"There's no question of that. Only of ironing out the details." Phyllis nodded and smiled. She turned to open the screen door and follow her husband inside the small cottage where they'd lived since Malcolm's first stroke had precluded his climbing stairs.

"Good night, Mom. Pleasant dreams." Alanna glanced down at her watch. "I think I'll sit out on the beach and wait for David to get back. I know he needs to be allowed to do things for himself. But..." she shrugged, letting her words drift off in confusion.

"Don't take a chill, dear. Good night."

"'Night, Mom."

"I'll walk with you if you don't mind the company." Again Alanna detected a hesitancy in Kyle's words, as though he waited for her to make the first move.

"I'd like that." She hoped the reluctance in her voice wasn't noticeable.

Kyle had been disarmed by his easy rapport with her parents into believing things might be different between them. Now that they were alone for the first time since he'd arrived his doubts returned with renewed vigor. There was an invisible wall of reserve between them, pliant and yielding to a certain degree, but very solid and real nonetheless. It would take perseverance and courage to bring it down to destruction.

They crossed the lawn, climbed the vineyard slope, skirted the winery and crossed the road to the lakeshore in silence. Kyle's nostrils were bombarded by an array of alien, aquatic smells. His ears picked up the sleepy buzzing of tipsy, hive-bound bees, and far away he heard the noisy revelry of weekend sailors at the marina in town. They were walking close enough for their hands to brush, and Kyle reached out to imprison Alanna's slender fingers within his own, as if that might keep her by him more easily. She didn't try to pull away but when she spoke, her innocuous comment set the frustrating tone for their conversation.

"There's just enough of a breeze to keep the mosquitoes away," she said, not quite meeting his gaze head-on. Her eyes kept slipping off to the horizon, as if she were merely watching the sunset, but Kyle wasn't fooled.

"Alanna, we have to talk." He tried again to penetrate the shell of reserve he could feel cloaking her like an invisible force. Alanna kept looking out over the water with a kind of fierce determination that was painful to watch. He looked away in his turn.

"Why? We said it all two years ago, didn't we, Kyle?" But they hadn't talked at all. She hadn't given him a chance to say anything. His fingers tightened around hers involuntarily as he struggled to keep from blurting those bitter statements aloud.

"It's deep enough to swim off those rocks, if you don't try diving at too sharp an angle." Alanna changed the subject abruptly, ignoring the pressure of his fingers although he was afraid he'd hurt her. He put his hands on her shoulders and turned her to face him. "Don't bring up that time, Kyle. Please," she said, and her words though hurried were soft, almost a plea.

"Thanks for the warning." Alanna couldn't be sure which of her statements he was answering. She prayed he wouldn't bring that last terrible confrontation up again. She didn't think she was strong enough to handle it tonight. He released her shoulders and offered his hand as they stepped up on a pitted limestone boulder. Beyond them lay a small spit of land sheltered from the wind and waves where a tiny half moon crescent of golden sand was brushed by the gently tossing leaves of a weeping willow.

Kyle remained standing until Alanna seated herself on a wide stone shelf, half screened by the trailing branches, before he dropped into a crouch beside her. He rested his forearms on muscled thighs in a stance that was totally masculine. He turned toward her and waited, composed and seemingly at one with his surroundings.

"Our boat is moored beyond those cottonwood trees." Alanna tried once more for just the right inconsequential note and failed to find it. They weren't going to be able to pretend they were merely two old acquaintances sharing an evening stroll.

"David's offered to take me fishing. Does that meet with your approval?" Kyle asked abruptly.

"Certainly. There's going to be a full moon tonight." She digested his remarks pertaining to her son. She must be more cautious about allowing David to spend too much time with Kyle. The boy would only be hurt in the end. Wouldn't he? She drifted into silence, her eyes riveted to the pale, almost transparent white moon, a mere shadow of what it would be in a few hours. Her hands twisted in her lap. She was running out of subjects. What would she say next? What should she do next?

Suddenly, illogically, she longed for the easy camaraderie they'd shared in Maryland. It seemed, then, as if she could talk to Kyle about anything. Now they were truly strangers again, separated by time and circumstances beyond their control. And surely that was for the best.

The breeze sent waves crashing rhythmically against the base of the rocks. Alanna lowered her eyes to the rise and fall of coral-gilded white caps, resting her chin on her bent knees, wrapping her hands around her legs. Kyle stood, picking up a handful of pebbles, pitching them out into the lake. The muscles of his arms rippled under his light blue shirt. Alanna found it hard to ignore the grace and strength of his body. She dragged her eyes away, all too aware of him as a man, of herself as a woman; a lonely woman. She stared sightlessly at the pleasure craft and fishing boats making their way to safe harbors in the channel between South and Middle Bass Islands.

"Alanna, why didn't you answer any of my letters or return my calls?" Kyle's voice was even, as detached as her own had been, as though they were only continuing their conversation about the weather. In reality they were probing the fragile chambers of their hearts where the most hurting of memories were stored away. Only the sharp, almost violent movements of his hand and arm revealed Kyle's inner agitation.

"There wasn't anything more to say." Alanna shifted her position a few inches. Her voice was soft, sad and resigned, almost a sigh. Kyle winced at the note of detachment but didn't let the uncertainty he felt show on his face.

"I wanted to explain everything..." *Damn!* He was going about this all wrong again. What was it about this small, determined woman that tied him up in knots, made him sound like a lovesick idiot when he tried to speak his thoughts in plain English?

"Kyle, don't..." Alanna moved farther away, aware, as she'd been since the first moment she'd set eyes on him, that she could so easily be swallowed up by the solitude that surrounded him, be drawn inexorably into the calm eye of his storm, be lost forever in the swirling golden depths of his eyes. "I don't know if I can explain after all these months," she admitted at last.

Kyle was silent in his turn. "I missed you," he said. The words were simply spoken. He turned and dropped down onto the sand, reaching out a hand to Alanna.

She hesitated. "Kyle..." Now was as good a time as any to try an explain her sorrow and anger that last day. She had to make him understand at least part of the wrenching sense of betrayal she'd felt. How earth shaking it had been for her to find he was no better or worse than any other man.

"Did you miss me?" There was nothing boyish about the figure of the man before her, but nonetheless his tone reminded her of a small boy, eager to know, but worried, unsure of what he may hear. The illusion of vulnerability faded as Alanna accepted the touch of his hand to step down onto the sand beside him.

"I missed you." *There, she'd said it.* His arm came around her and she didn't move away, couldn't move away, but no more could she had stepped forward into his embrace.

"Do you know how often I've wished we could change the past?" Kyle's voice was low and rough, his breath warm and moist against her hair.

"I don't think there's a person living or dead who hasn't wanted the very same thing at least once in his life." She tried to smile but she wanted more to cry out against the great tide of longing that washed over her. When she started to tell him they couldn't change anything that had gone before, his mouth lowered to cover hers. His tongue slipped past her teeth to probe gently for the tip of her tongue. Her arms slid around his lean hard waist as she answered the caress with her own hungry seeking kiss.

Alanna felt her knees start to buckle; lowering her gently Kyle followed her down onto the damp coarse sand. "I've dreamed of you so many nights." His voice was rough with longing and a great need. "So many long, lonely nights."

"I know." Alanna found it hard to speak pressed so closely against the hard wall of his chest. Her breasts ached to be free of the confines of her tank top. She wanted to feel the rough gentleness of his fingers soothing her, his lips and teeth and tongue bringing pleasure and excitement to every inch of her body. "But it doesn't . . ."

"Don't talk, Alanna." Kyle's words were almost a plea. His finger traced the curve of her mouth, sealing her lips. "Don't spoil these moments. I've had so little time alone with you. Will we be disturbed here?" He raised himself on one elbow to look down into her cloud-gray eyes.

"I don't think so. But this doesn't change . . ." Again she faltered and let her words trail away into silence. What was it that she was fighting against? Kyle making love to her? Or that Kyle might stop making love to her? Alanna couldn't recall when she'd been so confused about her own feelings.

"So beautiful." Alanna could feel his arousal strong and hard against her thigh. Instead of moving away she ignored her clamoring intellect and pressed tighter against the heat and strength of his body. One hand cradled her head, pillowing her, keeping the sand from her hair. The other lowered the strap of her tank top and bared one small ivory breast. "So beautiful." Kyle shifted against her, lowering his head to taste the ripe fullness of her nipple. He sighed, deep in his throat, a sound so satisfying, so erotically charged that Alanna felt the pull of answering desire in every cell of her being.

"Kyle." With adroitness she didn't know she possessed, Alanna made short work of the buttons of his shirt. She parted the soft cotton material with trembling fingers, her palms tingling from their contact with the crisp curling hair on his chest. His lips left her breast to place a line of tiny stinging kisses across her throat. Alanna's hands glided up to frame his face as she pulled him back up to taste his mouth. The kiss was slow and satisfying and she draped her arms around his neck to hold him close. Her breasts pushed eagerly against his chest, and she shifted in his arms to mold herself closer still. His hands skimmed over the curve of her waist, fitting their bodies more intimately together. Alanna moved with him in a dance of timeless, ageless pleasure, the rhythm of their caresses overruling her mind's cautious objections with a swiftness that left her breathless and dizzy.

"I've needed you so long, Alanna," he whispered against her lips. "I've fantasized about making everything come right between us so often over the past two years. I've dreamed of holding you in my arms like this so many times that I'm afraid to close my eyes, because if I do, when I open them you might be gone and I'll be alone again." Kyle threaded his fingers through her hair, tangling them in the fine silken mass as though to anchor her to him. He moved her head, turning her face so that he could read her expression in the faint light of a rising moon. He kissed her again, a wondering caress that traced the curve of her brows, the bridge of her nose, and touched fleetingly on the velvet skin of her eyelids. "Do you know how worried I was after you left me? You never answered any of my letters, returned any of my calls."

It wasn't easy to say the words, to humble himself enough to ask for an explanation she didn't seem willing to give. His body yearned to find release once again in the silky heated mysteries of her softness. He made himself remain relaxed, cradling her head in the hollow of his shoulder, searching for the best way to explain, to make Alanna understand the seething jumble of emotions and feelings he could barely make sense of himself.

"Kyle, please don't bring that time up, not tonight. Can't we just let the past be the past?" Alanna pulled a little away from his hard, comforting warmth and placed her hands flat on the sand, digging her fingers into its dampness. She tried to repress a shiver when the cool night air touched her skin. She tugged at the straps of her top, pulling them back onto her shoulders. She had so desperately wanted to ignore the past, to let the present and the future wash away all that had gone before. Now that was impossible.

"What if something had gone wrong? What if you'd become pregnant as a result of our time together? Would you have told me?"

Alanna resented the unbelievable amount of pain his remark caused even as she recognized the remorse and tension that had prompted it. "I...I...don't know what I would have done in that situation. I don't even want to think about the possibility," she replied in all honesty. She couldn't meet his eyes or the stark agony she saw there would have halted her words completely. "I wouldn't have made love with you in Maryland if I hadn't trusted you to prevent that from happening." She rose to her knees. The coming together they'd shared in those days, that first expression of physical caring she'd allowed herself since David was born had been so perfect, so right. She felt released from deeply ingrained anxieties because Kyle had considered her, considered her position and accepted his responsibility for providing a means of protecting her. It had made all the difference, all the difference in the world. But telling him that would mean telling him about David's father and his callous betrayal of her innocence, and that she wasn't ready to do.

"As deeply as we cared for each other...then," Kyle's voice roughened on the qualifying words, "would you have refused to make love with me, not have told me the true reason, walked out of my life with no explanation?" The words were harsh and he regretted it. He pushed himself up to a sitting position and attempted to take her hand in his, tried to make her see the point he was trying so hard to make clear. Alanna pulled away, still unwilling to meet his eyes.

"Is that so difficult to understand? I wasn't thinking very clearly at the time. And my relationships with men haven't been exactly noteworthy." Alanna wanted him to stop pulling bits and pieces of her private torment up out of the darkness to where she had to analyze and defend them. "I have an illegitimate child, Kyle. I love my son, more than life itself, but I don't want to go through that kind of nightmare experience again. Surely you, of all people, should understand why I would be so wary of a physical relationship."

Kyle rose from the sand slowly, stiffly, with none of his usual grace. He didn't bother with the buttons of his shirt but thrust his hands into the pockets of his black cords. His face was harsh and unrelenting in the fading light. Alanna shivered involuntarily, a combined result of chill air and emotional shock. "You never answered my question," he persisted. "If the improbable had happened, if for the sake of argument you had become pregnant, would you have told me about the child?" His voice was taut with suppressed anger.

Alanna jumped up from the sand, angry now in her own right. She paced the small beach like a caged animal. Her hair had come loose from its soft topknot and hung down over her shoulders, catching stray winks of moonlight as she whirled to face him. She reached up to strip the leaves from a branch of weeping willow in her path, biting back a sharp reply. Her gray eyes had darkened to the twilight shade of the eastern sky where the moon hung low and gleaming. "No," she said as calmly as she could manage. "I don't think I would have told you."

The pupils of her eyes were huge and distended with tears, Kyle noticed. Nothing about this reunion was going as he'd planned. He'd meant to tell Alanna he would have stood by her, cared for her and his child if that had been the conse-

quence of their brief loving time together. They were both
too scarred by their experiences to be able to listen and to
communicate their feelings easily. She didn't seem to understand what he was trying so clumsily to say. She hadn't
lost any of that protective armor she encased herself in so
efficiently. Or any of the pent-up misdirected passion she'd
unleashed on him when she learned about his daughter.
Underneath that competent, serene exterior Alanna was still
an abandoned, unwed teenage mother, and he . . . he was no
better than David's father.

"You don't pull your punches, do you, Alanna?" Her
words had hit him like a blow, but they were no more cen-
suring than his own thoughts. "Your welfare is very important to me. I wouldn't have allowed you to shoulder all the
burdens alone." Kyle strove for a mild tone, biting off the
three simple words he longed to finish the statement with. *I
love you.* That was all he needed to say, but he couldn't take
the risk that she would respond the way he prayed she
would. "I thought you knew me that well at least."

Alanna shook her head sadly. "The problem is that I still
don't know you well enough to put myself in your power
that way. Certainly I didn't know you well enough two years
ago. I'm sorry, Kyle. But you asked for the truth. With a
baby to be responsible for it would have been even more
frightening to allow you into my life. I would have carried
the child, but I wouldn't have welcomed it, I couldn't, cir-
cumstanced as I am." Alanna was afraid he must think her
a terribly cold and unfeeling woman, but she had to tell him
the truth. "Please don't think too badly of me for telling
you this. It's only a hypothetical situation, after all. But
does it explain to you why I would have run away rather
than face it? If by some cruel quirk of fate I'd have become
pregnant after those days in Maryland, I would have carried the baby . . . but I would never have told you." She

turned and started walking back to the house, then stopped, unable to keep from saying the words in her heart. "But Kyle, never think that I wouldn't have loved your baby as much as I love my son."

"I would have loved a child we created together every bit as much as you, Alanna." The sincerity in his deep tones was unmistakable. So was the misery. Alanna shut her eyes against a white-hot shaft of painful regret. Why had she spoken so militantly? She had made no excuses for her life choices to anyone; why should she expect Kyle to behave differently? Was it because she knew there *were* no more babies for her; that all the love and caring and nurturing she longed to lavish on another child would have no outlet, would forever have to be locked away in her heart? "It doesn't matter anymore," she said woodenly. "It never happened."

"It does matter," Kyle insisted stubbornly. "I love my daughter even though I can never have her with me. I respect her mother's wishes about my involvement in her life, but that doesn't mean I wouldn't welcome a chance to be a real father to her, to any child. Do you believe me when I say that?"

Alanna couldn't find the words to answer him at once. This ability of his to disarm her, to shoot down her most potent arguments against any renewing of their relationship was his most devastating weapon against her, far more powerful than the sensual attraction that sparked between them so strongly. She hesitated too long because Kyle continued speaking before she could frame her answer to his moving declaration of vulnerability.

"I think I hear David calling you." He shifted his stance to hold out a helping hand. She didn't take it. "I think it's better if we end this discussion before we cause each other any more pain." He looked at his empty outstretched hand a long moment then lifted it to trace a fingertip along the clear line of her jaw. Alanna's lips softened in a sweet sad smile.

"It's too soon for us," Kyle said quietly. "Maybe the time will never be right. We can't seem to be objective about our past. And at any rate, it's over and done with. We can't go back and change any of it. And without changing it we can't seem to move ahead."

He looked so tired and his hands trembled slightly as he lifted them to rebutton his shirt. Alanna couldn't absorb the multitude of sensations bombarding her. There was the familiar but unwelcome bitterness when she thought about David's father and what he'd done to her; new questions, new conclusions forming about the fascinating man beside her that Kyle's candid disclosure of his deepest feelings had brought to the foreground. She didn't know the true story behind Kyle's fathering a child outside of marriage. She didn't want to know, Alanna reminded herself gratingly. *Let it die, let what never was and never could be fade into oblivion. It was best. It was best for all of them.*

"Your hearing must be very good. It is David calling me," Alanna replied at last, ashamed of her cowardice but unable to conquer it. "I have to oversee his bath or he only manages to rearrange the dirt." Her voice caught on a tiny sob. It was even sadder somehow, to have descended to such commonplace subjects. Would it really be of interest to this brooding, distant stranger to learn the complicated strategic ploys necessary to keep an eight-and-a-half-year-old boy reasonably clean? She wished with all her heart that it was so. Because she still cared too much for him; she couldn't deny it. That fact made Kyle's presence on her little island world so very dangerous emotionally for both of them. Even disillusionment couldn't shut out the appeal he held for her. Another heartbreak was more than she felt she could stand right now. Her spirit would bend only so far, surely sooner or later it would snap and her innermost hopes and dreams would die of exposure.

"Mom, where are you?" David was silhouetted by the porch light as he hung over the railing, watching Alanna and Kyle walk side by side toward the house, not touching, not speaking. "I got a chocolate dipped cone with sprinkles. I'm not tired either. Can I stay up and watch the late movie on TV?"

"I don't think so, we have so much to do tomorrow. The wedding is only a few days away."

"Aw, come on Mom," he wheedled with a gap-toothed grin. "Hi, Kyle." David broke off his rapid fire requests to greet his new friend.

"Hi, fella." Kyle tried to form a smile but his lips were stiff. Thankfully the youngster didn't seem to notice.

"Do you want to stay up and watch the late movie? I'll keep you company." David shot his mother a swift assessing glance as he tried this new diversionary tactic.

"Not tonight," Kyle begged off. "Sorry, old sport, but I think I'll go up to my room and turn in right now."

"Sure, that's all right." David was disappointed and showed it.

"And it's into the tub with you, young man," Alanna ordered, trying and succeeding not to look in Kyle's direction again.

"Good night, Kyle." David bounded down the hall as Kyle ascended the stairs. Alanna remained at the foot of the oak steps, watching for a long moment.

Kyle never looked back.

Everything is such a mess. Alanna sighed and started toward the sound of gushing bathwater and David's bright little-boy voice commanding a fleet of rebel destroyers into battle among the stars.

Chapter Six

"You must be Kyle Stafford."

Kyle turned at the bright, vibrant sound of a woman's voice. It took a moment or two to shake the almost hypnotic rhythm of Alanna's champagne bottling mechanism from his optic nerve. The steady humming sound of machinery filled his ears but he sketched a polite smile of greeting in the direction of the blurred female outline before him.

"I always love it when they run pink champagne on this line," she went on without seeming to stop and take a breath. "I know this is bulk processed wine, strictly mass market stuff, but it's very showy cascading down off those cooling units, don't you agree?"

"Wholeheartedly," Kyle said politely. His rare smile became genuine as he put an identity to the decidedly pregnant female form. "You must be Alanna's friend..."

"Bette Harlan." She pushed a pair of red plastic sunglasses up into the mass of dark brown curls on top of her head. "I'm sorry I forgot to introduce myself right away. I'm afraid that's what comes from living in such a small community. You just assume because you know everyone that everyone knows you." She held out her hand and Kyle took it without reservation.

"I'm very pleased to meet you, Mrs. Harlan."

"Bette, please. Mrs. Harlan is my mother-in-law, bless her. Could you tell me where Alanna is this morning? I would like to talk to her."

Kyle watched in fascination as a small, blond, fairy child danced from behind Bette's pant legs. The variation triggered the almost magical change in his rough-hewn features that so intrigued Alanna. Bette caught the change in his attitude and her skin tingled pleasantly. He was the kind of man that made a woman stop and look twice: calm, controlled, maybe even a little dangerous if you didn't handle him correctly. The evaluation popped into her thoughts unbidden. Bette usually didn't make snap judgments about people, but she knew instinctively that this one was correct.

The little girl who looked to be about three or four—it was hard for Kyle to judge small children's ages—walked forward and tugged on the knee of his dark slacks. "Up," she demanded in a high clear voice, reaching out her hands as she smiled up at Kyle blindingly. "Up!" she repeated the command for emphasis.

"Would you mind taking her up, please. She's such a handful for me these days, and this really isn't the place to be running around loose for a child who's as nosy as Tracie. Believe me, I know." She lifted her daughter into his arms before Kyle could form a polite refusal. "The moment she heard I was going to look for her 'Aunt Lanny' there was no holding her back."

Kyle's arms closed automatically around the small body. Tracie immediately placed a wet sloppy kiss on his cheek and popped her thumb into her mouth, smiling contentedly all the while. "What's your name?" Kyle asked softly, at a loss for a subject of conversation.

"Tracie," she answered, removing all but the tip of her thumb from her mouth. "Where's Lanny?" She eyed Kyle unblinkingly, waiting for his answer.

"I believe she's in the vineyards, evaluating the sugar content in the *De Chaunacs*." Kyle directed his answer to Tracie's mother. His still-dark brows pulled together and a thick lock of silver-gray hair dipped onto his forehead. Bette found his frown almost as charming as his smile. He shifted Tracie's weight onto his left arm and pushed at his hair with an impatient gesture of his strong square hand.

"*Brix* and *Twaddle*," Bette said, as if her words should make perfect sense to him.

"I beg your pardon?" Kyle apologized.

"Sounds like something from Lewis Carroll, doesn't it?" Bette gurgled, not a bit put off by his puzzled reply. "I'll explain if you like." She cocked her head, surprised at herself for the almost flirtatious tone of her voice. She was thirty-one years old, happily married, nearly eight months into her third pregnancy, but she could still appreciate the charm of a very sexy male.

"I'd be obliged if you would," Kyle answered with another half smile, but this time Bette felt he was regarding her as a personality in her own right, not just as Alanna's friend.

"In America, sugar content in wine and grape juice is measured in terms of degrees *Brix*," Bette began in a lecturing tone. "I ought to know, I've heard Alanna carry on about it often enough: 'Too much sugar in the grapes is as bad for making wine as too little.'" She stopped and drew a breath, smoothing the thin material of her smock over her distended stomach absently as she spoke. "In Britain, however, we could use the term *Twaddles*. Reduces winemaking to a child's game, doesn't it?" she said with a laugh.

"And what about the French?" Kyle allowed himself to be drawn into the bantering conversation despite his preoccupation with his own thoughts.

"In French I'm positive it's something very romantic," Bette sighed. "I'll have to ask Alanna sometime."

"Ask Alanna what?" She was only a few feet away, standing in the doorway beyond the conveyor belt where dark green bottles of champagne, sealed with plastic corks, but without their wire cage or gold foil collars as yet in place spun by in a seemingly endless march.

"I'm giving Kyle my minicourse in viniculture," Bette answered irrepressibly, narrowing her eyes against the glare of sunlight that outlined Alanna's figure in fiery gold. "Everything you've always wanted to know about wine-making in . . . about thirty seconds . . . actually." She smiled over at Kyle and was gratified to see the corners of his stern but well-shaped mouth relax into another faint smile.

"Is that all the information you've picked up after following Dad and me around this place for more than twenty years?" Alanna laughed, feigning chagrin. The merriment was slightly forced. She'd seen so little of Kyle over the last day or so, since their argument on the beach, that she couldn't be comfortable in his company.

"Lanny!" Tracie launched herself out of Kyle's arms as Alanna walked out of the sun's glare. "Aunt Lanny, give me a kiss."

"That's the best offer I've had all day, Tracie," Alanna laughed unreservedly this time, and Kyle caught the faint alteration in the sound. He frowned slightly, watching Alanna receive Tracie's wet exuberant kiss and return it along with a hug.

Kyle's arms felt uncomfortably empty without the small but wiry body nestled in them. Had Kelly ever been this tiny, this precious? He had never known his daughter when she was small. Catherine and Derek hadn't permitted it. It wasn't until after his grandfather's death that he'd made an appearance on the fringes of Kelly's life.

And how did Alanna feel about holding Tracie in her arms, all the while knowing she would probably have no more children of her own? He sensed intuitively she had a great deal of mother love to share. Some of her angry reaction to his disclosures on the beach must have sprung from that reservoir of frustration. It was evident, to anyone who cared to notice, that she tried very hard not to smother her son in that abundance.

And in the end, it only pointed out once more his own limited vision. Surely, when they'd been together in Maryland, there had been physical signs that Alanna had borne a child. Why hadn't he discerned them? Or had his subconscious mind blocked out any hints that would have shattered the illusion of the precious fantasy world they'd created in those few lovely spring days.

Kyle ached to hold her again, to have her close within the circle of his arms, to discover all the enchanting secrets he'd failed to unravel before. The inability to resolve their conflict ate at him like acid on metal. Alanna had avoided him so skillfully these past two days that it was as though they existed in separate dimensions, parallel worlds that were identical but never touching.

"What brings you out here so early in the morning?" Alanna asked, breaking into his thoughts as Tracie hopped up and down, giddy with delight at being suspended from Alanna's hands like a puppet on a string.

"I came to tell you that, believe it or not, all the wedding plans are on schedule." Bette sounded marvelously pleased with herself, Alanna decided. "The silk flower arrangements are coming this afternoon; the tuxedos and Leslie's wedding gown will be ready to pick up tomorrow, so we can bring them out with the cake Friday morning." Bette finished ticking off the points on her fingers and made a flicking gesture with her hand in the air as if to indicate every task had been accomplished just as easily. "It's all coming together. I can hardly believe my luck."

"It's not luck, it's good planning," Alanna replied a little breathlessly as she bent to take Tracie into her arms once again.

"Luck has something to do with it. Everything my family plans from a picnic in the backyard on up always encounters enormous glitches," she informed Kyle laughingly. "It's karma or some genetic defect or something." Bette shrugged in a lighthearted manner that belied the dire tone of her words. Despite her attempted gaiety, Alanna caught the carefully repressed note of anxiety in her friend's voice.

She looked closely at Bette for the first time that morning, noting the circles under her brown eyes and the tired droop to her usually sunny smile. Bette talked blithely of having everything under control, but the upcoming festivities were stressful for her nonetheless.

"The rehearsal is set for seven on Friday evening. Would it be too much to ask if Billy stayed with David for the afternoon? Our place will be a mad house—or Grand Central Station—or something between the two."

"We'll be glad to have him," Alanna assured Billy's mother.

"Good, I'm glad that's settled. If your stay on South Bass is going to extend until the weekend, we'd be very happy to have you attend my sister's wedding, Kyle." Bette used his name as though she'd known him for years, and Kyle was surprised to find he was glad she did.

"Why, thank you. I am planning to remain somewhat longer," Kyle answered carefully. "Alanna's been too busy to spend much time discussing the renovations with me.

Perhaps you could persuade her to let me see the plans at least." He caught and held Bette's eye conspiratorially for a brief second before switching his gaze to rest on Alanna's discomfited expression.

Bette almost snorted in disgust. It was going to be harder than she thought getting these two to talk about their differences. She studied Kyle with new interest. He looked as if he could handle Alanna's crotchets. She'd like to give him some advice about finding his way through the thorns and prickles to her friend's soft but bruised heart. Still, she'd promised herself not to interfere, even though she'd suspected from the very beginning that there was something more exciting than winery business between these two.

"I'm sure Alanna won't expect you to be reading blueprints and checking estimates all through a lovely July weekend, will you, Alanna?" she asked pointedly, her smile sparkling with good natured mischief.

"No, I suppose I can't." Alanna answered uncomfortably.

"That's good news. I'll count on both of you being there." Bette gave a satisfied nod of her head.

"I wouldn't miss it for the world," Kyle said with a slight nod of his own, a silent acknowledgement of her assistance.

Bette smiled back. "Come on, Tracie," she ordered as Alanna lowered the child to the floor. "We've got to be off or we're going to miss the ferry into Port Clinton." With a wave of her hand they were gone. Alanna remained just inside the doorway of the bottling room, her back to Kyle, unable to turn and face him immediately.

"Your friend is one of a kind," Kyle said with a grin, shaking his head in awe before running the flat of his palm over the thick gray layers of his hair. "Is she always wired that high?"

"Actually, she's remarkably subdued this morning." Alanna admitted, turning toward him at last with an answering grin that was only faintly self-conscious. These were the first private words they'd spoken since that evening on the beach. She felt awkward, tongue-tied and wished he'd go away. But she also wanted him to stay, to prolong the conversation, so she went on talking. "Wait until Friday and the day after. By the time the reception is over Saturday afternoon she'll be ten feet off the ground."

"That should be quite a sight," Kyle agreed.

"Are you sure you want to expose yourself to a small-town wedding?" Alanna asked, not attempting to temper the uncertainty in her voice. "It won't be what you're used to."

"You haven't any idea what I'm used to," Kyle reminded her more sharply than he wanted to. She wasn't going to give an inch. He shut his mouth abruptly. He put his hand on the stone wall that Alanna had pointed out to the tour group his first day on the island. "I wouldn't miss this shindig for the world. You won't desert me, leave me to blunder around among your friends by myself, will you, Alanna?"

His voice was suddenly so warm, so cajoling that Alanna found a smile growing inside her and was powerless to resist it spreading across her face.

"No, I won't abandon you to the mercies of the populace of South Bass." The sunlight in the doorway where they still stood was blinding. Alanna narrowed her eyes to block out the glare. Somehow this narrowing of her field of vision made her feel very much alone with Kyle.

"Will you dance every dance with me?" He was very close. Alanna could feel the heat of his body through the thin linen weave of her blouse, smell the clean spicy scent of his after-shave and the faint evocative muskiness of his skin.

"No, Kyle. Please don't do this to me again." She was almost pleading and didn't care. "I have to go now. I have a million things to do yet this morning." Alanna changed the subject with a nervous quiver in her voice. "I haven't had a chance to take a look at the grape picker since it arrived. My field man thinks it needs to be readjusted before harvest. He's probably right." She couldn't be sanguine when he was so close that she could reach out and straighten the collar of his shirt.

"I'd like to see the picker, too," Kyle said with authority, "in the interests of the foundation." Even in denims and a casual shirt he had that innate aura of command that couldn't be hidden, or even ignored, as far as Alanna was concerned.

"Certainly, if you're interested in farm machinery; it's right this way." Alanna was trapped by her own sense of duty to the vineyards and Kyle knew it.

"Later I want to go over the plans for the restaurant," he added pointedly. "Where are they? You never brought them to the cottage. I had to make up a song and dance routine to put your father off the other morning."

"I know. I'm grateful you did that." She didn't elaborate. "The plans are in the loft." Alanna gave in without firing a shot in her own defense. "I'll take you up after dinner." She tried to resent his power over her but she couldn't. He made her feel jumpy, skittery and at the same time wonderfully alive. She relished the sensations: the pleasure of his company was growing steadily stronger, overshadowing the hurt and unease she'd felt in the beginning. He was taking up a great deal of time in her thoughts and in her dreams, and there didn't seem to be anything she could do to stop it.

IT WAS WARM AND SULTRY in the big loft above the main wing of the winery. As always, Alanna didn't see the unfinished bare stud wall, the wide splintered plank floor or the dusty cobwebbed ceiling. Instead, in the corner near the outside stairs, she saw a galley kitchen, with wide butcher-block counters, done in sunny yellows and warm browns. There would be a big open space, where she now stood, and a cozy fire in a Franklin stove against the far wall. The bedrooms would be furnished with huge brass beds covered with bright examples of Phyllis's quilting expertise.

She intended to have two fully tiled baths. Maybe even a hot tub for long soaks on cold winter nights. The double wall of many-paned windows that faced south and west, corresponding to the stained glass windows in the main hall below, would require sun screening in the summer. That would have to be accomplished from the inside, as well as insulating the walls, because the landmark status bestowed on the winery by the State Historical Society precluded changes to the outside architecture of the building. But that was all in the future. Now there was only her worktable and the partitioned space David called his train room.

Alanna fidgeted with the mother-of-pearl combs holding her thick coppery hair. It was loose but she didn't have time to go back to the house and fix it. It had been a busy afternoon. The crowd in the winery had been good, the tours full and noisy. Her throat ached with the exertion of keeping their attention focused on herself and what she had to say.

She wished she had a glass of wine. She needed something, anything, to do with her hands. Kyle would be up at any moment. The tension between them had been growing all day until it sang along her nerves like a current between points. Bette's visit to the vineyard seemed to have changed the momentum of the relationship. Alanna was aware she no longer controlled the game, could no longer sneak around corners, shut herself alone into her office, keep David as a buffer between her and Kyle Stafford.

He'd made his intentions apparent by staying with her almost the entire day. Now, he insisted on seeing the blue-prints for the winery renovations and she'd run out of excuses to deny him. She spread the architect's drawings out on the rough worktable, holding down the corners with a stapler, a cup of pencils and her brother's old slide rule. Finding nothing else to serve her purpose, she allowed the fourth edge to curl back on itself. She was too nervous to stand there holding it down. Anyway she knew the drawings by heart. She didn't need to look at them to see them.

Alanna heard a firm rubber-soled tread on the stairs and whirled to face the man silhouetted against the glory of a summer sunset. He'd changed his clothes. A crisp white shirt set off the bronze of his skin and made his gray hair appear even brighter than before.

"Here they are," Alanna blurted out, speaking the first words that came into her mind. He stood quietly at the top of the stairs studying her amber-gold sundress and the ornamental combs that held her hair back off her face. "Everything's set and ready to go. Would you like a few minutes to study the plans before we discuss them?"

"That won't be necessary." Kyle's gaze had moved past her to the model trains set up across the partitioned space near the stairway. He bypassed the worktable and stopped before the display that now included her brother's old Lionel 2-6-2 engine and freight cars, two tunnels, three bridges, a manufacturing complex for the small village and a farm complete with a dairy herd that Alanna had given her son for Christmas a year ago.

"I thought perhaps you'd left this behind in Maryland." Kyle reached out to touch the buildings in the little village with the tip of a long, blunt finger.

"I wouldn't have done that Kyle. I hope I wasn't that petty a person, even then." She remained near the worktable, her fingers digging into the beveled edge with painful intensity. "David adores it. I was thinking of him that day in the toy shop."

"I realized that . . . later." What he left unsaid hovered between them like a long dark shadow.

"I remember the balloons you tied to the tender when you put it in my room at the inn," Alanna said unexpectedly. The spring-bright helium spheres had proved to her that the sense of gentle whimsy she'd suspected lurked beneath Kyle's button-down, businesslike facade had indeed existed.

"And I remember how beautiful you looked, kneeling on the floor in only that ivory-colored teddy thing and very little else. I remember how we missed dinner that evening and breakfast the next morning." He was very close to her and Alanna felt herself drifting back against him, pulled by the magnetism of his body.

The next morning.

The day he'd told her about Kelly and ruined it all. Alanna straightened her spine and pulled her scattering thoughts back into line. "I think you'll find these drawings quite easy to figure out," she said too loudly and too abruptly. "The kitchen will have to be enlarged, of course, but Dad insisted we replace the major appliances a few years ago, and we bought institutional sizes with just these plans in mind."

"Alanna, we can't go on like this, avoiding what's between us." Kyle's hands came around her, cutting off her escape to the left and right. She pushed her hips against the table to avoid any contact between them. "I want to apologize for what I said to you the other night on the beach. It all came out wrong, it stirred up all the old pain, brought back the old conflicts. That was hard on both of us. I'm sorry."

Alanna shook her head and brushed aside his hand. He made no move to stop her as she walked toward the windows. The view out over the lake and tranquil harbor was magnificent. From the clock tower, directly above, you could see the lake for miles in every direction, fiery and coral-gilded in the sunset light. Out there lay Ohio, and far to the west, just a smudge on the horizon, was the Michigan shoreline. Behind her to the north was Canada. "Kyle, there's nothing more to apologize for. We just got caught up in something that neither one of us had any control over."

She was painfully aware that she shouldn't have allowed herself to be alone with him, to indulge in any of her fantasies that were still so strong and insistent where he was concerned. Already her heart beat a rapid unsteady tattoo in her breast, which couldn't be blamed on the heat.

"Two years ago I was a different person, I think. I was a girl really, not a woman. I wasn't prepared for our affair, or its aftermath. I've always been terrible at relationships. But I *have* changed since then. And I don't want to go back; can you understand that?" She whirled to find him still studying the drawings, but Alanna suspected he saw no more of them than she did of the view beyond the window. "I don't think it's possible to go back," she added with a sad little catch to her words. "You're part of what I've put behind me. That's all there is to it."

Kyle took the toneless, unemotional words like so many pellets from a scatter gun. He even looked down at his chest to see if there was blood, the pain was so real. Each tiny missile seemed to have lodged itself around his heart. He clenched his fingers around the slide rule he found under his hand. The sharp edges bit into his palm, but the pain was so slight it went unnoticed in the larger torment of his soul.

He wanted Alanna to love him. If nothing else, he'd admitted that truth to himself these last few days. He wasn't sure she could understand the reasoning that caused him to run away from his responsibilities to Catherine seventeen years ago. He'd never tried to put that in words before, even for himself.

"We have to speak of it." His words were almost a growl, the tone low and somehow dangerous to Alanna's sensitized ears. "I don't know when we'll have another chance. You seem determined to keep something, or someone, between us all the time, Alanna." He came up behind her so quietly she never heard a footstep, yet she knew he was close. So close that if she turned from the window she'd be in his arms where she longed to be. She held herself stiff and unresponsive even when his fingers slid under the loosened fall of her hair at the nape of her neck and began to massage the tension away with warm tranquilizing strokes.

Alanna bowed her head, willing her resistance to stay firm in the midst of his sensual assault. "You're here on business, Kyle, why can't we keep it on that level?"

"Because it isn't possible," he answered reasonably. "We haven't been able to keep it on a business level at any time since we met."

She couldn't deny the statement and didn't try. "I can't see where our rehashing the same personal problems over and over again will do anything but complicate matters further."

The tantalizing play of his fingers ceased. He swung her around to face him. "Alanna, I don't have any excuse for what happened to Kelly's mother. Is that what you want to hear me say? I abandoned her. She wasn't any older than you were when David was born. My draft card said I was twenty-one but I was a hell of a lot less mature than that. I panicked and ran away."

"Don't." The words came out all tangled and breathless. "Don't say anything else." Alanna covered her ears with her hands just like the frightened child she felt inside. "I don't want to hear any of this."

"I want you to." Suddenly Kyle was as angry as she tried to be. Damn her stubbornness. Why couldn't she see he was only a man who'd made mistakes that he'd regret for the rest of his life? That he'd made all the restitution he could for his sins; that he wanted to start again, to have what every man was entitled to, a loving wife and family of his own. "I have a daughter who hardly knows I exist. She's sixteen, almost a woman, starting out on a great adventure—a life of her own—and she will never know who I am, what we are to each other. Does that make some amends for what David's father did to you?"

"No! I can never make up for what he did to me." Alanna spoke with savage certainty, but she bowed her head, unable to meet the anguished hazel eyes that stared down at her. What was wrong with her? She'd put the trauma and disillusionment of her first unhappy love behind her years ago, hadn't she? Why should it rear its ugly head now? She couldn't stop the tears that dripped steadily onto her clasped hands. She'd never been so ashamed of her own shortcomings as she was at that moment. Kyle was reaching out to her. And because she was so dismayed at her own emotions, at her own response to his halting attempts to explain his behavior, she couldn't find the right words to speak.

"Alanna, let's try to put the past behind us for the sake of what we could have together." Kyle didn't plead but spoke the sentence as if the facts were plainly evident—any more passion, unchecked emotion, might send her racing off into the twilight and he didn't want to risk that.

"I'd like that, to start over as if there was nothing to keep us apart." There was no more anger, only a trace of whimsy in Alanna's words. "I'd like to put all the bad times out of my head and just talk, ask you all the things I haven't been able to say."

"Like what?" Kyle cocked his head slightly to one side and watched her color fluctuate from ivory to pale peach and back again.

"Silly things," Alanna shrugged. "When did you stop smoking a pipe? And telling you how very distinguished I find your gray hair." She bent her head, refusing to meet his eyes. Kyle lifted his hand, cupping her chin, following the path of a crystal tear with the tip of his finger.

"I didn't even think you'd noticed I don't smoke anymore." He held her face in tender bondage until she no longer resisted meeting his dark, gold-flecked gaze.

"I notice everything about you." Alanna opened her mouth for his kiss reluctantly. Kyle knew she couldn't resist him physically and the realization tempered a little of the anguish inside him. She wanted him as much as he wanted her. She tasted so good, sweet and flowery and salty with tears all mingled together. "I missed the scent of smoke on your clothes," Alanna whispered against his lips. "And the feel of your pipe in your pocket when you hold me in your arms." She slipped her arms around his neck. "I wish I couldn't remember anything but those lovely days we spent together in Maryland." Her voice was strained, a little desperate.

Kyle rested his chin on the top of Alanna's head. Her hair smelled good, too, like sandalwood or some other exotic scent. The cinnamon strands wrapped themselves around his fingers, glowing with living fire in the late afternoon light. "We can start over, Alanna. We can't forget, either of us, but we can start over. We can begin again." It took all the willpower he possessed to keep from deepening his kiss to a ritual penetration, not to move his tongue in cadence with the deep slow beat of passion building within him. He held himself tightly in check. She was frightened, confused, unsure which way to turn, what to do next. He wanted to soothe her, to comfort her and arouse her all at once.

"Starting over would be very nice, but it just won't work." Alanna sighed and shook her head, capturing his gaze with her cloud-gray eyes. Tears sparkled on her lashes and Kyle bent his head to kiss them away. She turned her head to meet his lips. "The past is always there, it becomes part of us."

Alanna sounded as if she wanted to be convinced otherwise. There was hope, Kyle decided as she began to kiss him back with little hungering moans of desire. If only he could be patient, if only he could wait for her to come to him. She wasn't ready, not yet, he could feel it in the taut lines of her curving form as she nestled closer to him.

Kyle raised his head. "Forgive me, please." He could give her everything she wanted, physically, materially, but spiritually she found him lacking. Would she ever trust him completely or had David's father effectively killed the innocence and trust within her, the ability to love completely and without reservation?

"You don't have to ask for my forgiveness for anything, Kyle. You didn't deliberately deceive me any more than I did by not telling you about David. But I'm sorry, I just can't forget." She wanted to add *not yet* but she couldn't make herself speak the words. Tears glistened on the spiky dark brown tips of her lashes. Kyle still held her head cradled between his strong lean fingers. He released her slowly with great reluctance. "I'm sorry, Kyle. I just can't forget."

MIDNIGHT. THE WITCHING HOUR. Alanna curled her arms around her before stepping out into the dewy summer night, the silken skirts of her robe and nightgown brushing over each other with soft whispers of sound.

Midnight. The moon that had been so large, so touchable a few nights before, when she'd sat on the rocks with Kyle, now sailed high above her. It was so far away, brilliant and ethereal, beautiful and unobtainable like the stuff dreams are made of.

Tears welled up behind her eyes, making the moon's trail on the lightly ruffled surface of the lake break up into a myriad of tiny diamond chips. All the time she'd spent putting David to bed, intentionally dawdling to straighten his room; all the time she'd been showering and changing into her night clothes; the past had tugged at her with its siren call. And not the memories she expected; that was what was so unsettling. It wasn't those last bitter words that had passed between her and Kyle but the quieter moments of passion and happiness at the inn: more pictures in her mind's eye of pastel-colored balloons dancing above the tender of the steam train, the desire in Kyle's eyes when he'd stepped around the open door of the connecting rooms to find her kneeling in the lace teddy, the joy with which she'd launched herself into his arms, the passion they'd then shared in the tall four-poster bed, and later, again and again.

Alanna had tried to sleep, willed herself to mentally review the accounts due at the winery, even childishly pulled the pillow over her ears to block out the sound of water running in the shower, doors opening, Kyle moving around on the floor above her, but nothing worked. So here she was, standing on the porch hoping the cool moist night air would blow the cobwebs from her mind and let her sleep.

She shivered convulsively, moving toward the wooden bench swing beneath her grandmother's large white clema-

tis bush, reliving those lovely and precious days with Kyle
yet again. She was chilled. Several large star-shaped white
petals drifted down on her head and shoulders and she
shivered again. The screen door banged back against the
wall then slammed shut, the spring reverberating for a long
time after David's pajama-clad figure, outlined by the
moon's cold silver light, moved out onto the lawn. Her son
bounded across the grass, dragging behind him the big geo-
metrical-patterned quilt that Phyllis had made for him for
his fifth birthday.

It was his security blanket, Alanna liked to tease. The
coverlet with its startling arrangement of primary colors was
showing wear and tear from constant use. But the bold
bright squares of padded wool set off the rather stark simplicity of the off-white walls and pine-green painted wood
floor of his room, so she hadn't suggested that it was time
to retire it to the cedar chest at the foot of his bed. Now the
sight of the quilt brought a lump to her throat. David must
have awakened and found her gone from her room next to
his. That he'd brought his quilt out into the night, searching for her, told her that David was far more upset than he'd
ever admit.

"Why aren't you asleep?" She spoke quickly but kept her
voice low. Kyle's window was directly above their sheltered, trellised alcove. She couldn't take adding his presence to the midnight foray, not while her body still burned
with memories of his loving touch.

"Something woke me up." David shrugged off her query.
"I couldn't find you. I was scared... a little bit."

How long had it been since he'd come searching for company in the night? Quite a while. He was growing up so fast,
too fast for Alanna. "Don't ever be frightened of that. I'll
never leave you, but I couldn't sleep so I came outside
to... watch the moon." Alanna gathered her son into her

arms for a quick hard embrace that David returned with special fervor.

"I don't like to wake up at night alone," he stated emphatically. "I don't like being alone in the dark."

"No one does, sweetheart. That's why God gave all of us mommies, and grandpas and grandmas and other people to love. So we won't ever have to feel we're alone in the night."

"God has good ideas. Are you coming back to bed?" David asked, apparently satisfied with her words.

"In a little while. I have a lot to think about," Alanna hedged. She couldn't face her cold, narrow bed just yet. The warm cloud of recollection was evaporating like mist before the wind. She was afraid if she went back to her lonely bed her sleep would be troubled by less happy dreams.

"Business?" David sounded so grown-up Alanna had to smile despite the lingering ache of memory.

"Yes, that's it. Business."

"I think Kyle will like our ideas for the restaurant," David answered importantly, trying to pull the folds of the heavy quilt up out of the dewy grass. "Have you told him we want to sell the house and move into the winery?"

"No. That's our secret for the time being, okay? The foundation proposal doesn't cover remodeling living quarters for the two of us," Alanna warned.

"Don't show them all our tricky shots first thing. Right, Mom? But I bet Kyle'd like it. He already likes *everything* here. He told Grandpa so this evening, when he came over to say good-night. I heard him."

"He was just being polite I imagine," Alanna answered more harshly than she intended.

"I don't think so," David objected, shaking his dark red head. His hair was all tousled and stood up in spikes on his forehead and around his ears. "I like Kyle. He's an okay guy." For an eight-year-old, that said it all.

And it gave his mother pause. What if David became so attached to Kyle he began to ask questions about his own father? So far her simple explanations that they couldn't live together like Billy's family had sufficed. David's environment was so limited on the island, so sheltered that few people ever mentioned his lack of a male parent. It had been one of the small blessings Alanna thanked her Maker for daily. But someday soon she'd have to tell him the truth; that his father cared so little for his welfare he never bothered to inquire about his son at all. Would Kyle's intrusion in their little world precipitate that day?

"I'll tell you what. Let's make a snack and then camp out," Alanna suggested with what she hoped was genuine enthusiasm in her voice. David was hard to fool. "Come on. I'll make cocoa and you get some pillows. We'll sleep in the swing."

"And don't forget the marshmallows, those little ones that melt real fast. I'll get the bug spray." Alanna held back a grin. He was always so practical. "I bet I can stay awake until the sun comes up," he boasted on their way back to the house.

"I expect you will." Alanna chuckled softly and the echo of golden bells floated upward on the night breeze to the ears of the wakeful man above them. "I expect we'll both do just that."

ALANNA'S PREDICTION WAS ONLY half correct. David had gone to sleep within minutes of finishing his cocoa. Now he snored faintly in gentle little puffs of breath, his head in her lap, but Alanna was wide awake. The siren song of remembering, the call of past events, was drawing her slowly and irrevocably back into its net. This time her memories were not happy ones. Even the warm sleeping body of her son curled up beside her couldn't keep her thoughts from slipping back to another time and place.

A faint echoing of sound came to her ears. A loose shutter somewhere probably, banging in a gust of wind off the lake. Or was it the ghostly remembrance of a fist banging on the locked door of her room at the inn? Kyle's fist, insistent, his voice angry, concerned, questioning her irrational behavior through the thick wooden panel.

She hadn't bothered to answer him, couldn't answer him through the thick choking ache of tears in her throat, so she'd gone on flinging clothes into her suitcase, brushing frantically at her eyes to keep back treacherous, defeating tears.

"Alanna, let me in! What have I done?" One last reverberating thump on the thick oak door and then silence. "Alanna, please, are you all right? Tell me that at least."

"I'm okay, please just go away. I don't want to talk." It had taken all the stubborn will she possessed to get the words out in a half normal voice.

"No," Kyle came back equally stubbornly. "I need to talk to you about Kelly. About my daughter." The last words were spoken so quietly Alanna almost missed them.

His daughter. Kyle had a daughter, a child fathered out of wedlock. He was no better than Elliot Mayhew. But he'd seemed so much more to her wary inexperienced heart—until he'd taken a child's picture out of his wallet and brought her new and fragile dreams crashing down around her feet. *Why did you have to be like David's father?* The pain was so intense she nearly screamed the words aloud. Outside the door Kyle was silent. Alanna didn't know what to think, so distracted that she couldn't imagine where he'd gone until he walked into her room through the connecting door.

"You didn't lock this one," he said unnecessarily.

"I..." Why bother to answer? she thought. It was obvious she'd forgotten to lock the door that connected their two rooms. Kyle still had a yellow luncheon napkin clutched in his hands. His knuckles were white with strain.

"Alanna, you have to let me explain." His voice was hoarse, rough with emotion, but it gentled when he saw the look of stricken anguish on her face. He took a step forward.

"No!" Alanna held out her hand to ward him off. "No, don't say anything." She shook her head so hard it made her dizzy. "You see, it isn't so simple anymore. It's not only that you have an...illegitimate daughter. I...I have a son." She met his eyes then, head-on, trying valiantly to keep her tears at bay, her face so stiff not a trace of expression showed.

"A son?" Kyle looked stupefied, his eyes dull and lifeless, his face carved from stone. She looked that way too, she knew, as if only part of her was left living.

"I've been keeping secrets too," she managed to say, although her words sounded hollow and wooden to her ears. "I have a child of my own."

"I don't give a damn if you've been married before. It's none of my business, for God's sake." Kyle crossed the small room to stand at the foot of the rumpled bed.

"I've never been married." Alanna blurted it out to dull the image of his hands caressing her in that bed, loving her, teaching her to love him in return. She closed her eyes against the pain. "I have an illegitimate son." The crystal shell, which she'd fashioned around her heart after Davy's birth to protect the last of her illusions and her dreams, began to form once again, sealing off her emotions. She'd never thought she'd welcome its protection again. The sense of detachment that she'd been shedding more confide_.tly each day she spent in Kyle Stafford's company and that she'd hoped never to experience again, was coming back, unexpectedly comforting and familiar. She welcomed it.

"Oh, God." Kyle dropped his hand onto the carved foot of the bed, his open palm hitting the wood with a crack like a pistol shot. "I . . ."

"It's a ghastly coincidence, isn't it?" She went on with pathetic dignity drawing her numbing cloak tighter around her. "What do you suppose the chances of something like this happening really are? A million to one . . . or more?"

"Stop it, Alanna," Kyle commanded roughly. "Tell me . . ."

She cut him off. "My son's father wouldn't marry me, Kyle, it's as simple as that." She watched him take every word like a blow. "And you're the same kind of man. You have to be." She had begun crying helplessly then, despite her determination not to. "I don't want to talk about it any more. I want you to go. Now! I don't want to see you ever again." Her tears had been hot and salty and had stung her cheeks.

Alanna stared up at the dark velvet of the night sky. The stars were high and bright and cold like splinters of ice and diamonds. She was crying again, as she'd cried that day in Maryland, but she wasn't alone now. She had her son and her vineyards and they would sustain her. She could let the rest of the dark memories of that day flow over her like eddies of smoke.

She hadn't been able to stop crying, not for hours, but when she did Kyle had been there waiting. He had wanted to talk, to explain, to try and work things out, but she'd cut him off brutally and completely. She couldn't even recall the things she'd said to him, but they had been cruel and hurting because she was hurting so badly herself.

After a while he'd stopped trying to break through the hard crystal shell to touch her. There had been no more hysterics on her part. She'd packed her bags, called a cab, gone straight to the airport and booked a flight home. She hadn't seen or talked to Kyle Stafford again until this week. Two years ago she was certain that was the way she wanted it. That was the way it had to be. But now... now she was no longer so sure.

THE SCREEN OPENED and closed behind Kyle without a sound. He was barefoot and the porch steps were slippery with dew. He could make out the dim figures of Alanna and David in the large covered swing. Her head was bent over the sleeping figure of her son, a big blanket of some kind tented over their heads to keep off the dew. It was much cooler than he expected. Kyle quietly moved closer. He wondered if he should leave them both sleeping out here unprotected. Alanna answered the question for him by lifting her head and smiling sleepily.

"I must have dozed off. What time is it, do you know?" She didn't seem alarmed to find him bending over her, barefoot, with his shirt hanging open, the tails not even tucked into his slacks.

"Almost four. It will be light soon. Let me carry him inside for you."

"I promised we'd watch the sun come up but it is chilly. And damp." Alanna brushed surreptitiously at the tear stains on her cheeks. Kyle's jaw hardened at the new evidence of her distress as he lifted David into his arms.

"I've made you cry again." Kyle waited to speak until she was standing before him. Alanna reached out and tucked a fold of the quilt more closely around the sleeping child. David sighed and turned his head into Kyle's shoulder the way Alanna wished she could do. The trusting gesture loosened the guard she'd put on her tongue.

"No, it was only a dream. A bad dream." And it seemed just that. Alanna smiled and for Kyle it was as if the sun had come up hours early and straight over his head. "It was only a bad dream. I don't think it will ever trouble me again."

She allowed her hand to rest momentarily on his. What she said was true. She couldn't forget the past completely yet. But together could they put it behind them and go on? Alanna led the way into the house, holding the door for Kyle to carry her son inside. All around her the people she cared for were caving in to his charm. Perversely, then it had been easy for her to avoid him, to wallow in the hurt of the past, recall each and every painful moment, to feel superior and so sure of her solitary course. His quiet sadness whenever they spoke about his child, her child, had stripped away her sophomoric disguise. Tonight's reminiscence had tipped the scale. She had fallen head over heels in love with this man. That revelation, although not truly surprising, left her at a loss for words.

"Kyle . . ." Alanna believed with time she could put aside her pain, completely, with no regrets, no misplaced empathy for the mother of Kyle's child. The way seemed so much clearer now. Alanna wanted to tell him what was going through her mind like overloaded computer circuits but when she opened her mouth to speak she yawned instead. Her body was exhausted and didn't intend to let her mind overrule its needs any longer.

"Get some sleep, Alanna." Kyle's smile was rueful as he laid David on the boy's bed and pulled the quilt up under his chin. "Tomorrow's going to be another busy day." His lips brushed her forehead in a butterfly-light caress that left her skin tingling and very much alive where he touched her.

Alanna looked down at David curled under his blanket, unable to say the simple declarative sentence she wished to speak aloud. She took a deep breath and tried again. "I love you, Kyle." The words came out so softly she wondered if he could hear her at all. "I love you," she repeated again, more boldly. It didn't matter. When she turned away from David's bed she was alone.

She hadn't even heard Kyle leave the room. There was no one but a sleeping little boy to hear her long-delayed declaration of love.

Chapter Seven

Once again it seemed that the tables had turned. It was Alanna's turn to scheme and plan. She began proposing and rejecting ways and means to bring Kyle under her sway. The most logical alternative she discarded out of hand. How could she walk up to him, the man she'd just discovered she loved, had loved for hundreds of lonely days and nights, and demand to know the most carefully guarded secrets of his heart? From the moment he'd set foot on the island she'd been avoiding just such an encounter. She wouldn't blame him if he turned his back and walked away.

Yet their time together was finite. She couldn't let nature take its course to bring them closer gradually. It wasn't all that different from making wine she decided. When nature failed, or was lacking, the vintner had to step in and enhance the vintage with skill and love.

Kyle could leave them at any time. Alanna didn't want to think about that but she had to. He could be called to New York, Washington, California, or to his family home in upper New York State, a place called Dutch River. She might never be given another chance to confide all the things she'd worked through so painfully in her heart and in her mind. Alanna felt that she was close to finding happiness at last, and nothing must be allowed to cheat her out of the wonder of being truly loved by a man she loved wholeheartedly in return.

But matters seemed to conspire against her. Before the sun was fully over the tree tops the new bottle line was down. It was Alanna's pride and joy. She wanted to have Kyle see it at its most efficient. Instead, the innovative, lightweight, plastic-lined boxes with easy-pour spouts, destined for restaurants and commercial use, were punched full of holes by a runaway press.

There was absolutely nothing state-of-the-art about soggy perforated cardboard boxes. To add to the frustration, hundreds of dollars of wasted wine poured out onto the concrete floor before the machine could be shut down. It took the whole crew, Alanna included, until lunchtime to remedy the glitch.

She saw Kyle only once during the whole long day. He had paused in the doorway of the bottling wing on his way to confer on the winery renovations with her father. She thought he might volunteer his help, but he didn't. He was polite and guarded, obviously recalling her tear-streaked face when he found her asleep in the garden. Alanna almost lost heart then but rallied her forces. First things first. Her duty was to the vineyards, her inclination was to Kyle. This time duty won. She put the coming, interesting battle of wills from her mind and concentrated on her work.

But the evening was as disappointing as the day. Kyle, David, Billy and her father spent it fishing for perch and walleye on a lake as placid as a lily pond. They came back late loaded down with their catch and tired and hungry. By the time Phyllis had fed them sandwiches and cake, and David had been bathed and put to bed, Alanna was feeling the effects of the long day herself.

Kyle gave her a quick, brotherly peck on the cheek at the bottom of the stairs and took himself off to his room as soon as the fish were cleaned and packed in ice. Alanna fell asleep frustrated but determined to carry the day.

The sun had climbed high in the achingly blue sky, beating straight down on her uncovered head by the time she left the winery Friday morning. Alanna rubbed a twinging shoulder while she tucked her hair back into the soft coil that added not only to her height but her self-image. A whimsical wish that Kyle be near was answered by the sight of his tall, bronzed figure rounding the far end of the hedge. Alanna suspected he'd disdained the shortcut more from an excess of inches than a lack of adventure. He looked relaxed and casual in a yellow cotton shirt and dark slacks, less intimidating, more approachable. Alanna felt her heart beat a little faster with anticipation at the thought of having him all to herself, even for a little while. This was her best chance to start rebuilding their relationship and she was determined to make the most of it. "I'm starved," she declared with a smile so brilliant it rivaled the sun. "But I promised Bette I'd bring the Woody up to the docks at noon to help load the cake and Leslie's wedding gown to take to the church. Would you care to come along?" Her bright facade shriveled in the face of his stern, preoccupied manner but Alanna shored up her confidence with another blinding smile.

Kyle didn't answer at once, unknowingly causing Alanna another sharp pang of doubt. He scuffed the toe of his suede loafer in the grass, disturbing a fluffy dandelion that released its feathery seeds into the wind. He wanted as badly as Alanna to resume negotiations in an atmosphere of trust and understanding. When he'd found her and her son asleep in the garden, she'd been crying over the past, he was sure. But yesterday she seemed different somehow, and he hoped he hadn't been imagining the change in her attitude. Yet he hadn't had the nerve to test her so he'd taken the easy way out, spending the day with David and Alanna's father. Avoiding her, if the truth be told, but knowing that wouldn't solve anything between them. You didn't complete a merger by keeping the principal parties apart.

Somehow that's the way he'd come to look at his unconventional wooing of this stubborn, beguiling woman, as a negotiated merger of two slightly hostile entities. Twice they'd come very close to bridging the chasm. But both times old miseries and present uncertainties had held them back. He didn't intend to allow that state of affairs to continue. "I'd like that. If you let me buy you lunch," he countered. "It's deductible that way, Foundation business." A muscle twitched along his jaw and his eyes lightened with amusement.

"Fine. And I'll spring for dessert. Just to keep it official. Would you like an ice-cream cone? They have butterscotch-dipped ones at the Dairy Queen. With sprinkles," Alanna added coyly with an exaggerated batting of spiky brown lashes.

"How can I resist?" Kyle's smile broke through the barrier of habitual studied reserve with stunning results, triggering the alchemy that sent Alanna's senses reeling. "Butterscotch?" he questioned. "It's been years since I had a butterscotch-dipped cone."

"With sprinkles." Alanna put as much meaning into the nonsense statement as her courage would allow. Did he understand that she wanted to try again? Make another attempt to push past the reinforced perimeters they both had erected around their battered emotions?

"It's a deal. I'll drive," Kyle offered, holding out one long tanned arm as Alanna fished in her pocket for the key to the pre-World War II Ford station wagon. He felt suddenly lighthearted and lightheaded with her so near. He wondered what she'd do if he caught her hands and held her still long enough to drop a kiss at the corner of her rosy mouth. When she dangled the keys before him his fingers closed over hers, refusing to relinquish their prize.

Alanna felt her color rise. Her skin burned with pleasant heat whenever his eyes touched her.

"Does everyone on this island own a vintage car?" He took pity on her evident confusion. Rushing her was the last thing he intended to do.

"Quite a few," Alanna managed to answer with an attempt of lightness that was every bit as determined as Kyle's. "It's something of a status symbol. And most of us walk or ride bikes a great deal of the time so they tend to last longer that way." His hand felt so good curled around her fingers that she didn't even try to retrieve the use of her hand as they crossed the parking lot to the car.

"I could get used to this life very quickly."

"You'd die of boredom in the winter," Alanna warned in all seriousness. "Then it's just islanders, bass and minnows, as the oldtimers say." Kyle bent to open the passenger door for her and the subtle spicy aroma of his aftershave wafted over her. "Some days we don't even get the mail; the newspapers are late. The bank is only open on Wednesday from nine to one. Can you believe that?" She itched to bury her fingers in the layers of his steel-gray hair. Her eyes followed the curl of it at the nape of his neck with hungry greed.

Kyle bent nearer still, resting his arm along the roof of the car as he watched her through gold-rimmed hazel eyes. "There you go again, Alanna, jumping to conclusions about me. If I say I'd enjoy living here, I'd enjoy living here; no mail, limited financial services and all. Understood?"

"Yes, Mr. Stafford. I understand you very clearly." Something tight and aching jolted loose inside Alanna as she slid onto the leather seat with her heart pounding high in her throat. She didn't really understand with her intellect, but with her woman's heart, and that was an organ she intended to place more reliance on in the future. He did want to try again, she was certain of it. He didn't want their botched attempts at communicating to be the end of their relationship any more than she did. Dear Lord, why did language have to be so imprecise, so ambiguous. Why did she have to be so reticent about speaking her needs. If she got the chance to try again, to make him understand her, to understand him, she'd grab at it with both hands.

But not even lunch came off as planned, although the Dairy Queen was only a few feet from the ferry dock. There seemed to be a great deal of commotion in the small crowd of people gathered on the concrete pier. David's red head appeared smack in the middle of the noisy group.

"What the devil's going on?" Kyle asked, sliding the Woody skillfully into a miraculously untenanted parking space.

"Something must have happened," Alanna surmised, not waiting for Kyle to open the door on her side of the station wagon. She stood on the running board to get a better view of the altercation. She slammed the door before Kyle could switch off the ignition and exit the car. She made herself walk at a reasonable pace. The facts, Alanna, get the facts before you leap to the defense of your son.

She wiggled her way past two tall young men she recognized as members of the wedding party to find Leslie with angry tears sparkling on her long blond lashes as she held the two wriggling boys firmly by the collars of their lightweight windbreakers. David's was black, sporting the emblem of his favorite football team, the Pittsburgh Steelers. Billy's was bright orange, decorated by a Cleveland Browns logo. Their fierce loyalty to two rival football clubs was the only thing Alanna could ever remember them disagreeing on.

Leslie was blond and petite, her round face and snapping brown eyes very much like Bette's. Her wheat-blond hair and slender form were a grown-up version of Tracie. She was very pretty—when she wasn't crying. Alanna couldn't begin to imagine what had happened to set off such a brouhaha with her son at its center. She only knew for certain she didn't like any other woman chastising her child.

"You little monster," Leslie scolded. "I told you to sit still on the boat when it's this choppy. But no, you had to be jumping up and down. Now look what you've done." She stamped her foot in a spasm of temper.

Alanna's heart sank. She knew it wasn't a good idea to let David spend another day with Billy, but Bette had called early this morning and insisted it would be fine. Alanna had been so busy and so preoccupied with her thoughts about Kyle that she'd ignored her instincts to deny the plan and had let David go.

She glanced past Leslie's weeping figure to catch Father Timothy Juskevice's eye. His pleasant good-natured face wore an amused but flustered expression. Alanna attempted to relax. It couldn't be anything that awful if Father Tim wasn't alarmed.

"I believe Billy was demonstrating Hulk Hogan's latest wrestling hold. Not such a good idea on a boat I'll admit, but hardly a hanging offense." The priest held a Saran Wrap-covered box in both beefy black-clad arms. Long and flat, Alanna guessed that it held one of the cakes destined for the festivities. Or had held a cake. It was decidedly lopsided now.

The agitated bride, however, wasn't ready to bestow any Christian charity on the two small culprits. "I don't care what you say, Father. They've ruined my wedding, the little monsters. They were acting up during the whole trip over. They simply would not behave. I told my sister they should be locked up, not sent along on the boat." She glanced at her friends for confirmation and spotted Alanna. She blushed furiously but held her ground. "I'm sorry Alanna, but my nephew and your son are incorrigible brats."

Seeing his mother for the first time, David squirmed away from his captor and rushed to Alanna's side. He didn't reach out and touch her for assurance, but he stood as close as he could manage, his soft gray eyes dark with hurt and wounded male ego. "It wasn't our fault, Mom," he avowed, striving manfully not to cry. "We hit a big trough and the cake slid over where Billy and me were sitting. None of them were watchin' it like they should." He indicated Leslie's groomsmen and they refused to meet Alanna's stormy gray eyes. "We didn't mean to hurt it—it just got squashed."

By this time Bette had come hurrying up, for once without her toddler in tow. "I'm sorry I'm late, I couldn't find a place to park the car. Damn golf carts clogging up the streets—" she broke off. "Oh dear, what's happened now? Father Tim, is anyone hurt?" The priest shook his head and looked around for a place to deposit the battered cake box.

"I think the boys had better explain, Mrs. Harlan. I only came in on the aftermath of the disaster," he answered in a carefully noncommittal tone. One of the young men took pity on the elderly priest and removed the mutilated confection from his arms.

"Leslie, for heaven's sake, stop crying," Bette pleaded in an exasperated tone. "Boys, what did you do?" She rounded on the two youngsters impatiently as she handed her sniffling sister a tissue from the pocket of her skirt.

Two young voices began a noisy chorus of denials only to be drowned out by Leslie's passionate words. "Everything is going all wrong. Look at all of you standing there smiling behind your hands while these little brats ruin my wedding. It's awful. I wish I were dead.''

"Of course you don't wish any such thing," Bette answered heatedly. "Alanna, what's happened?" She looked completely at a loss to sort out the details of the mishap.

"The boys evidently sat on the cake coming over on the ferry. I gather it was a pretty rough ride." Alanna tried to make the explanation brief and to the point. David nodded sullenly and Billy only scowled harder at his young aunt's weeping form.

"She's been acting real crazy ever since she decided to get married. I don't care if we did squish her dumb cake. She pinched me, didn't she, Dave?"

"Yeah. And she just about jerked my arm off," David aired his own grievance. Leslie held no adult terror for him. She had been his baby sitter for as long as he could remember. Behind Alanna, Kyle made a strangled sound deep in his throat. He was enjoying this. Alanna bristled. It wasn't a bit funny to her.

Most days when David misbehaved she threw off her concern. Boys would be boys, and for the most part he was a loving, caring child who would outgrow his selfish ways as he matured. But today she felt his misbehavior keenly, as a stricture on her performance as a mother, as an unmarried woman trying to raise a child alone.

"David." She spoke more sharply than she usually did. "You'll apologize to Leslie for that remark."

"No." Stubborn gray eyes looked up at her. They didn't waver or slide away. Alanna felt her authority challenged as never before. She couldn't back down in front of so many others. The whole episode had been blown out of proportion but she saw no easy solution. Why did this have to happen today of all days?

"David Harris Jeffries. I want you to apologize to Leslie. I mean it."

"No!" He hunched his shoulders deeper into the windbreaker. It was a size too large and made him look small and very vulnerable as well as being too warm for such a hot day. Alanna felt like a cad.

"Me neither," Billy piped up as Bette added her command to the tense atmosphere.

"William James, just wait until your father gets home," she retorted sharply.

Silence from both culprits. Alanna could feel David's shoulders go rigid under her hands. At any other time the age-old phrasing of Bette's remark would have sailed over his head, but not today. She squeezed his arm reassuringly. He didn't relax under the pressure. If anything, he became more tense.

"William, you'll go to your room until you can learn to behave yourself. Leslie, for heaven's sake, stop crying," Bette pleaded in distraction. She put her hand on her stomach unconsciously. She looked pale and very tired. The wedding was taking its toll. Alanna felt another guilty pang for having allowed David to be added to her responsibilities on such a busy day.

"Bette, perhaps we should settle this in a less public place," Alanna ventured to point out.

"Oh, yes, good idea. Leslie, where's your gown? Where are the tuxes? They did make this boat, didn't they?" She looked completely distracted for a moment until she spotted the long plastic-covered wedding gown on its hanger and one of the groomsmen with his arms loaded down with the tuxedos. "Thank God. Now, let's get this settled. Father Tim's a busy man; we can't stand here all day making a spectacle for the rest of the town to enjoy."

"I'm afraid you'll have to suffer the same punishment as Billy until you can remember your manners, David," Alanna rebuked more softly than Bette. She'd hear his side of the story at home where there wasn't so much confusion. The crowd began to disperse and Alanna became aware once more of the sounds of happy voices, sails and rigging slapping in the freshening breeze from the southwest, and the sound of birds in the trees overhead.

"Oh, good grief." Bette raised her hand to her forehead. "I just remembered. Aunt Theresa is staying in Billy's room. Seventy-year-old Sisters of the Blessed Sacrament aren't used to sharing their bedrooms with eight-year-old miscreants. Now what do I do with you, you little imp?" Bette scolded, stepping away from her still-tearful sister to pull Billy close for a quick hard hug that belied the aggravation in her tone.

"Why don't you incarcerate them together," Kyle suggested without a hint of irony in his honey-rough tone. Bette glanced appraisingly at his darkly handsome face.

"Let the punishment fit the crime, you mean?" she asked straight-faced. "Alanna, what do you think about that?"

"I think an afternoon in solitary confinement, with no TV movies and no Popsicles would see justice served."

"Then it's all settled. Come on, Leslie, when we get home I'm seeing to it that you get a good long nap. That's what you need." Alanna wondered if Bette knew she was talking to a twenty-year-old woman as if she were her three-year-old daughter? "We'll see you at seven, Father Tim?"

"On the dot. The Indians and the Tigers are playing tonight. The game's on TV at eight-thirty. I don't want to miss it," the priest responded pointedly. He hurried off, his cassock flapping in the warm gusty breeze as he headed for his ancient Schwinn bicycle waiting in its customary place at the ferry office.

Ten minutes later Alanna stood at the foot of the stairs, her face carefully composed. "David, Billy, you will stay in David's room until supper is called at five-thirty. I think it's best for everybody if you don't attend the rehearsal this evening. I'm disappointed in both of you."

"But Mom," David interrupted, righteous indignation bursting out all over him. "It wasn't our fault. Nobody believes us, not even you."

"No buts, young man," Alanna insisted, wearying of the entire episode, stung by his last outburst. "If you can't apologize to Leslie for your rudeness before the wedding ceremony, we'll have to reconsider your going to that party also. Is that clear?"

"You don't even care if we were right or not," David repeated mutinously.

"That's enough, David. Do you understand me?" Alanna held on to her temper with a real effort.

"Yes, ma'am," came the reluctant answer in chorus. Both boys trailed down the hall with lagging steps. "I bet she wouldn't even care if we ran away," Billy grumbled over his shoulder, but Alanna missed the remark when she turned back to confront Kyle.

"And you told me it was dull around here," he laughed, abandoning his carefully neutral position. His laugh sounded rusty but genuinely amused.

"I stand corrected," Alanna responded with a lopsided grin. "But don't think we're this lively every day," she warned.

"No, but you have to be on your toes for the days you are. Especially those January Wednesdays when the bank is open and all."

"We do have our share of excitement, I can't deny that." Alanna made a face and laughed in return, appreciating the humor of the incident at last.

The rest of the day was anticlimactic. Alanna didn't have any tours to lead in the winery. She spent the afternoon quietly checking the progress of several vintages in the cellar and conferring with her father on the results. Kyle tagged along, listening to her explanation of vinicultural techniques that had been handed down through the generations, many of which, even today in the age of computers, high technology and men in space, couldn't be duplicated or improved.

Kyle was a stimulating, alluring companion. He complimented her skill as a vintner and her expertise with the 'wine thief.' The oddly named apparatus was in reality a long glass tube inserted through an opening in the top of a keg to siphon off a small quantity of wine with the least disturbance to the contents.

He watched intently as she tested the clarity and bouquet of the young wines. When she offered him a glass, Kyle accepted with alacrity, studying the robe, or color, savoring the sharp astringent aftertaste before agreeing with her opinion that this particular vintage could do with another season in the dark, quiet cellar.

By five-thirty, when the boys were to be released, the wind had settled into a steady whining keen. The lake was a churning, undulating mass of towering whitecaps. "It's going to storm," Alanna predicted, pushing wind-whipped strands of hair from her eyes.

"How can you be sure?" Kyle queried, searching the sky for signs of storm. Towering cumulonimbus stacks reached high into the firmament, but as yet they loomed far in the distance.

"I've lived on this island all my life, remember? It's a feeling you get more than anything concrete. And Dad's been listening to the marine forecast. Gale warnings can go up on this lake in a matter of minutes." Her worried gray eyes searched the rolling waters for any stragglers caught far from a safe port. "You can't trust Erie an inch. They don't call this lake the most unpredictable of the Great Lakes for nothing." Alanna was deadly serious and Kyle respected her wary attitude.

"What do you suppose the detainees have been up to all afternoon?" he asked, trying to divert her mind from the tension the deteriorating weather had produced in her. Alanna glanced at the open window of David's bedroom. Maternal experience distrusted the too-peaceful quiet. Usually the boys punctuated even the simplest conversations with engine noises, animal howls and artillery fire. "I can't believe they're taking a nap," she divulged with a graceful shrug of softly rounded shoulders. "Still, they've been up late every night and unusually active for the last few days. I'll leave them alone until supper is ready."

"You're a hard woman, Alanna Jeffries," Kyle said in a light, teasing tone. He brushed his fist carelessly along the line of her jaw and Alanna laughed in reply to the sensual bantering.

"You know, I think I am."

How had it happened? It was one of those nightmare situations that came to torment her dreams. It couldn't have become reality. David and Billy hadn't been in the room when she went to call them to the evening meal. When the boys didn't answer she used her mother's privilege to swing the door open. Then the nightmare began in earnest.

They weren't in the loft playing with the trains; they weren't in the winery kitchen or with her parents. They were gone. A quick check of the boat house revealed the two-man skiff that the boys had only that summer learned to sail was missing. Other clues began to come to light. Their favorite snack items had been pilfered from the kitchen. David's sleeping bag was missing from the shelf in his closet. It looked like he'd even considered taking his quilt before Billy had evidently talked him out of the idea. The blanket was pulled most of the way off his maple spindle bed and lay discarded on the hardwood floor. Alanna was all at once horribly certain the two boys were lost out there somewhere on a lake known for its dangerous, fickle temperament.

Kyle stayed close to her side as they hurried into the small church where Bette's family had gathered for the wedding rehearsal. As she feared, the boys weren't with them. Alanna could hide her agitation only because of her equally great concern for Bette's welfare. As quickly as possible she drew Jem Harlan off to the side, introduced him to Kyle with scant ceremony and confessed her dismay. He didn't question her deductions as she almost wished he might. She could see the fear quickly masked by stoic pride enter his clear brown eyes.

"Alanna." Jem spoke low so as not to disturb the instructions of the priest at the altar of the small church. Mother of Sorrows: the name had never seemed so ominous to Alanna before this very moment.

Bette, thankfully, was fully involved in the ceremony. She only looked back once, smiling, and waved at Alanna and the men before returning her attention to the priest. "We need to have some idea where they've gone if I'm going to get help to find them," Jem said, tugging at the knot of his tie.

"I haven't a clue." Alanna bit her lip to still the tremor in her voice. "They're always threatening to run away. All little boys do that. But with the wind blowing like this, they shouldn't have taken the skiff. I don't think either of them is skilled enough to run against the wind." She closed her eyes, trying unsuccessfully to blot out a terrifying picture of

the small skiff capsized in the unforgiving waters of the lake.
Alanna swayed unsteadily and immediately felt Kyle's arm
around her, strong and comforting.

He spoke for the first time since greeting Jem. "David has
told me several times of his plans to camp out on one of the
small uninhabited islands. I'm afraid I can't tell you which
one it was he mentioned, but it would seem like a logical
conclusion since we're pretty sure they took the skiff." He
wanted to hold Alanna so close that he blotted out all her
fear but it wasn't possible among so many people. And it
wasn't advisable for Alanna's sake or for Bette's. He sensed
instinctively that too much sympathy would send Alanna
over the edge, undermine her courage to deal with the situation as it developed.

"They couldn't have made it to Starve," Jem cataloged
aloud. "Alanna's right, they aren't strong enough to sail
against the wind. It must be Green. Far enough to prove
their point by running away and close enough to have made
it before nightfall."

"Yes, David has pestered me to camp out on Green Island
all summer. I'd forgotten until Kyle mentioned it." She
smiled up into his eyes with a shaky attempt at bravery.
"I'm so glad you remembered, that you've paid attention
to all his little boy chatter."

It felt so good to have her turn to him to share her heavy
burden of solitude. Kyle returned her smile but no one was
fooled. Alanna's expressive gray eyes fairly burned with silent agony for her son's safety.

"I'll slip out to radio around," Jem decreed. "See if
anyone's still out on the lake who can take a look for them.
I'll do it quietly." He glanced at Kyle as though seeking male
confirmation for his next words. "Alanna, I know it's asking a hell of a lot, but can you keep Bette occupied? Not let
her know what's happening until the rehearsal's over at

least? She's got so much on her mind already.'' He broke off, entreating her with his eyes to understand what he was asking.

Both men saw her falter under the weight of the request, then square her soft shoulders and give a determined little shake of her auburn head. "I'll do my best. But hurry, Jem, it will be dark early tonight. It's going to storm. I can feel it..." Alanna tried to swallow the lump of pure terror in her throat, but was only partially successful. Her words came out hoarse and barely audible. "David is afraid of the dark..."

And so was she.

Chapter Eight

"Alanna." Kyle's voice behind her in the darkness of David's bedroom was almost a growl, comforting and exasperated all at once. "It doesn't do any good for you to stand at the window all night."

"I can't see anything from here." Alanna shrugged and turned away distractedly. "It's still raining too hard. They'll be soaked through unless they found some kind of shelter. Did we make the right decision, Kyle? Were Jem and I right to urge the others to wait until daylight to rescue Billy and my son?" She needed to hear him say aloud that she'd made the only possible choice. She couldn't completely trust her own judgment any more: the stakes were too high, the decisions she'd had to make too difficult. "Did I do the right thing?" She wrapped her arms more tightly around herself, trying to contain the terror within.

"There was no alternative, Alanna," Kyle said with conviction. "It's suicide for anyone to be out on the lake now. No man could take a boat out there and live." He pulled her against him and held her there. She was still wearing the pearl-colored sundress she'd put on for the wedding rehearsal and her shoulders were bare. Her skin was cold to the touch. "Let's get you a sweater or a jacket," Kyle said with a note of self-recrimination in his words. "I should have noticed sooner how chilly you are."

"No, I'm fine, truly." Alanna pulled away from him, unable to stand still for any length of time, even to remain in Kyle's arms where she longed more and more to be. "I think we finally persuaded my parents to get some sleep." She sounded distracted. Kyle didn't like the way she kept plucking at David's jewel-toned security blanket, straightening it on his bed. At her side was the slim cordless telephone she'd kept within arm's reach since they'd returned to her home an hour earlier.

"They're resting, that's what counts, and so are Jem and Bette. So should you," he added sternly. "Daylight comes early."

"Not soon enough." Alanna's tone was brittle. "If I could only be sure they're not...hurt." She couldn't say drowned. Wouldn't even allow herself to think the word. Both boys could swim, thank God, and from the time they were little it had been a cardinal rule that they not go out in a boat without their life vests on. "If I only knew where they were. If I could just explain to David why I've left him out there in the dark."

Kyle reached out to enfold her once again, trying to share the warmth of his body, the strength of his conviction that she had acted in the best interests of all concerned. "Don't torture yourself this way, Alanna. You've done what's best for everyone, remember that." The decision hadn't been hers alone, although she wouldn't allow herself to believe that. It had been made reluctantly by all those involved, friends and neighbors included, strong and caring men and women who knew when to do battle with an unforgiving giant like Lake Erie, and when it was best to hold back and wait out her fury.

"They are both safe and well." Alanna had been repeating the words over and over in her head, now she said them aloud.

"Alanna, do you recall what Jem said to us, just before he took Bette home?" Kyle turned her in the circle of his arms so that she had to look at him, had to acknowledge his presence and accept the comforting warmth of his embrace. Alanna closed her eyes for a long moment as though fighting against any softening of her inner solitude, the core of solid steel that was keeping her upright and tearless.

"He said we couldn't ask our friends and neighbors to risk their lives." She broke off, unable to finish the sentence.

"No. He said you couldn't fight the lake, Alanna; he was right." Kyle shook her a little to emphasize the importance of his words. "The night isn't cold, thank God. In the morning, at first light, the Coast Guard will be out with boats and helicopters, whatever it takes. We can't do anything else tonight." He gentled his tone and pulled her closer. "I'll stay with you."

Alanna couldn't speak normally around the lump of anguish that had risen up from the very depths of her soul to lodge in her throat. Her words came out small and forlorn sounding. "But it's so very hard to wait."

THE HOURS CRAWLED BY so slowly Alanna couldn't believe the clock on the kitchen wall was still working. She walked over and lifted her hand to feel the vibrations of the tiny whirring motor within. The house was quiet, as quiet as an old house can be near midnight on a windy, rainy night. The sound of rain hitting the windows seemed less violent, less like splatters of BBs rattling the panes, more like a heavy summer shower.

Alanna stood quietly a moment listening to the mutter of thunder—surely it was more subdued, the rumbling drum rolls less frequent. Was it possible the storm was passing at last? She poured the rest of her cold coffee down the sink. The rain *was* letting up. She rushed through the swinging door into the long hallway that bisected the house. On her right the dining room lay in darkness. To her left, soft light came from the living room where Kyle waited for her to return. She kept on running, pulling open the heavy walnut front door with its oval of frosted, beveled glass.

"Alanna, where are you going?" Kyle stood in the doorway but she didn't stop to answer his question. She ran across the high wooden porch and out onto the lawn. She couldn't stand the loneliness inside anymore. Bette was surrounded by her loving husband and caring family. Alanna's parents had each other and a lifetime of sharing to sustain them. She had only an empty, silent house and it was all at once too great a solitude to bear. She rushed headlong toward the lakeshore, the pounding agony in her breast pushing stinging tears and choking sobs past the last barriers of her control.

But Kyle had no intention of leaving her to face the rest of the night alone. He followed Alanna, his quiet reassuring words helping to stem the torrent of her fear. "Alanna, wait for me."

She halted at the unintentional tone of command in his words. When she turned, the skirts of her dress lifted and swirled in the wind. Her eyes were dry but drops of rain traced wet paths down her pale cheeks. "He's all I have in the world, Kyle. I fought so hard to keep him. God can't take him from me now."

The words went straight to Kyle's heart and buried themselves deep within. He would give everything he possessed in the world to help restore Alanna's son to her, but he

found it hard to tell her that in so many words. The senti-
ment would sound merely trite, not a promise and a vow
that he meant from the bottom of his heart. "You're not
going to let this thing beat you now, are you, Alanna?" he
said forcefully, hoping to stem the hysteria he felt rising in
her. "It's only a few more hours until daylight. You can't
give up now."

"I won't." She whirled away from him to look out over
the wave-lashed rocks that were dimly visible in the light of
a street lamp a hundred feet away. "So dark and so angry," she murmured so quietly that Kyle strained to hear the
words. Just as quickly as she'd spun away from him she
turned back. Alanna raised her hand to cup his face as she
tried to communicate the urgency of her fear, oblivious to
the wind and flying spray from breakers pounding at their
feet. "He's so small . . . he tries so hard to be grown up, and
I try so hard to let him but he's not grown up. David's just
a little boy. They both are."

"They'll be fine," Kyle whispered against her hair as
tendrils caressed his face and neck in the fitful gusts of wind
that the branches of the huge cottonwoods above them
could only partially tame. The herbal scent of her hair en-
veloped him, eclipsing the smell of rain and the curious
mixture of life and decay that clung to the shoreline. He
could feel the distress in every tense muscle of her body as
Alanna fought to keep upright against the force of the wind.
He longed to take all her pain inside himself and leave her
free to rest and renew.

Spray from the breakers continued to mist over them with
each pounding rush. Alanna began to tremble again and
Kyle maneuvered her unresisting form until he sheltered her
from the onslaught of wind and waves. Far off in the distance thunder grumbled, a deep reverberating undertone,

felt more than heard, while lightning sparked from behind an inky mass of clouds.

Alanna leaned into Kyle's embrace, quieter and more controlled as his calm strength fed her own reviving courage. "Don't leave me alone, Kyle. I'm so very tired of being alone."

"Let's go back inside," he urged, not caring for the way her skin continued to feel cold and clammy even though she'd put on a long-sleeved shirt he'd found hanging by the kitchen door. She needed him. It wasn't the declaration he wanted to hear from her, but it was enough for now. If she admitted she needed him, could learning to love him be far behind?

"No, not back inside." Alanna broke out of his entwining arms with surprising force. "I can't see anything from the house." She looked over his shoulder at the dark bulk of the winery. "I'm going to the clock tower." She lifted her face to search his bewildered hazel gaze. "I'll take the portable phone and a lantern. They can see the light. I'll hold back the dark for my son. David will know I'm waiting for him to come home. He'll know he isn't alone in the night."

Kyle did nothing to dissuade her. She was almost at the limit of her endurance. If being in the clock tower high above the island could make her feel closer to her lost child, then he would be there for her also.

THE COLEMAN LANTERN gave off a warm yellow glow that reflected off the panes of glass ringing the small tower room just beneath the conical roof of the old building. Alanna stood on tiptoe, making a bracket of her hands on the glass, and stared out over the lake for a long time before lifting the lantern to the wide sill. "I can't see a thing. It's so dark. I hope there won't be fog in the morning; it might delay the search party."

She stood quietly a moment, watching Kyle spread a blanket, which he'd grabbed off the back of her living room sofa, over the dusty cover of the old daybed her brother had dragged up to the tower years before. The only other furniture the room boasted was a splintered wooden table and two straight-backed chairs. The portable telephone lay on the very edge of the table, inches from her hand. It was silent, as silent as it had been since her mother had called hours before to report they were safely home.

"I can't tell you how many tea parties Bette and I attended up here," Alanna remarked, running her hand lightly over the chair back. Kyle slid the other chair around and straddled the seat, his hands folded along the back. He watched her closely but said little, hoping Alanna would talk herself into exhaustion and quit fighting his urging to get some sleep.

"Most kids dream of having a place like this for make-believe. It's even better than Dutch River, and I thought that was the greatest house in the world to be a kid in." Kyle kept his voice matter-of-fact, his tone inconsequential, hoping she'd continue talking about happier times.

"I don't allow David up here to play. The stairs just aren't safe any longer. I'm sure you noticed that coming up. But it has to be included in the renovations, don't you agree? I mean, we can't have the tower coming down on the roof some evening when we're serving a hundred customers in the restaurant, now can we?" She tried for a clear, light laugh and failed miserably. "What time is it, Kyle?"

"A little after two."

"Time goes so slowly when you're in a hurry for something to happen." Alanna sighed. "It was only a few minutes ago when I asked you last, wasn't it? I can't imagine what became of my wristwatch this evening." Kyle was tugging at the knot of his tie. Alanna stepped around the table and reached over to pull his hands away. "Let me do that. Men always just start jerking at the things. You have to coax them loose," she scolded, working at the knot in the damp silky material.

"I'd forgotten I was wearing it," Kyle admitted with a quirk of his lips. "I'm not too sure what happened to my jacket either."

"You put it around Bette's shoulders during the storm, remember? There, is that more comfortable?" She stared down at her hand holding the strip of fabric patterned in muted grays and black. "I have to teach David how to tie a Windsor knot someday soon." Alanna's voice cracked with strain, but she didn't give way to tears. "Oh, Kyle, hold me for a little while, please."

Kyle pulled her close, smoothing her hair with his hand, gentling her, massaging away the tension between her shoulder blades with the palm of his hand. She needed him. And he wanted to make everything right for her. It had been so long since he could give of himself to another human being in that way it took him a long moment to recognize the emotion. And hard on its heels came a less welcome thought. Was it truly him she wanted here with her tonight? Or was it another, faceless shadowy figure, the lover who'd betrayed her. David's father.

Alanna's head was resting on his shoulder. Kyle wrestled with his new demon for a long time before speaking. When the doubt inside him had swelled so much he couldn't keep it contained any longer, he put a finger under her chin and lifted her head. He needed to see her expression so that he could judge her response to his question. "Do you want to notify David's father, Alanna?"

"David's father?" The query caught her off guard. She'd been drifting in a world between sleep and waking where nothing was as important as it appeared with open eyes. The lantern did indeed seem to be holding back the night, wrapping them tightly in a small self-contained world where they were growing closer, comforting each other. The wind moaned fitfully around the tower like a giant angry beast trying to gain entry to their private domain. Now she felt the touch of its cold sharp claws on her breast.

"Is he close by? Won't David's father want to know what's happening to his son?"

"No!" The negative came out tight and strangled. Alanna stiffened in Kyle's arms. She stepped away and he didn't try to stop her. She moved toward the window with quick jerky steps that betrayed her renewed agitation.

"Alanna, I'm sorry," Kyle began haltingly. He searched for the right words to make her understand why he had asked. "Do you still love David's father?" His voice was rough with emotion. It took more courage for him to say those few simple words than anyone could ever know.

"Love . . . David's father?" Alanna gave a cracked little laugh that held no amusement at all. "No, I don't love him," she continued softly, lifting her hands to shut out the light once more as she stared out into the rainy night. "And what's more important, I don't hate him anymore."

"I'm sorry, Alanna. It's none of my concern." Kyle stayed by the table, leaning his weight against it, his back to the window where she stood.

Alanna turned to face him and encountered the broad sweep of his shoulders beneath the damp fabric of his shirt. "Do you think David's father is someone I'm still close to? Someone who cares for his child . . . . as you care for Kelly?" she added very softly. Kyle didn't seem to hear, at least he didn't turn his head to look at her. She let all the emotion she'd denied for so long, all the pent-up longing she felt for him shine from her gray eyes for a moment, brilliant and unshuttered, then blinked it away.

"I know without your telling me that David's father was your first love." Kyle's voice remained carefully neutral. "Was he a childhood sweetheart, Alanna?"

"No. He was a professor at Davis. My Psych prof actually. I was nineteen," Alanna began. He could hear her take a deep breath as if preparing to recite a lesson by rote. "I'd gone there to study because that's where my brother went. But he was dead and I missed him so terribly. I wanted my parents to be proud of me and assured that the vineyards and the winery would go on..." She was silent a moment, sorting through her memories. Kyle waited patiently for her to continue.

"Elliot Mayhew was what every young girl fantasizes about. At least what I dreamed of. He was handsome, witty, very Ivy League. He even wore tweed jackets with suede patches on the elbow." Her words were wispy, far away. Alanna moved away from the window, skirting the edge of the table to pick up the small cordless phone, holding it in her hands like a talisman until Kyle lifted it away and took her cold fingers within his strong, comforting grasp. She refused to meet his eyes and Kyle didn't attempt to break in on her introspection.

"I fell for the man like a ton of bricks. Somewhere along the line, God help us both, he began to notice me. I was very flattered. It never occurred to me it was my naiveté, my innocence, my virginity that intrigued him. He became my lover so quickly I couldn't believe it was really happening." She laughed the self-mocking little laugh that always tore at Kyle's heart. At least for all his sins he hadn't been Catherine's first lover, or she his.

Kyle tightened his clasp slightly to stop the unconscious writhing of her fingers. He linked them with his own warm ones, stilling a little more of Alanna's inner turmoil with each passing second that their hands remained entwined.

"Did he hurt you, Alanna?" Kyle asked, drawing her back into his arms. He was sitting on the edge of the surprisingly sturdy old table and she rested her forehead against his a moment before replying.

"No, only my heart. He was thoughtless and selfish, not cruel. Our affair lasted two months and seventeen days. I know exactly because my roommate suspected I was pregnant almost as soon as I did myself. That's when she told me he was married. I can shut my eyes and see every detail of that afternoon as if it were happening now. But at the same time it all seems so long ago, almost as if it had happened to someone else." Alanna turned her face up to his, trailing her fingers over the faint stubble of beard that darkened Kyle's chin. The yellow light from the Coleman threw the strong planes and angles of his face into bold relief and beckoned her touch.

"You don't have to go on, Alanna." Kyle cursed the inane words under his breath. Her link with him had never seemed so fragile, so tenuous as it did at that moment. As fragile and fleeting as the unconscious touch of her fingers on his cheek.

"There's not much more to tell. It's an old story really. I ran to him like the terrified nineteen-year-old adolescent I was and blurted out the news. He was so angry at first. I'd never seen him that way. At the beginning he'd told me to go to the campus clinic and see about birth control. He didn't question me again. I thought it was because he respected my judgment. It was really because he didn't care enough to take any more responsibility. And I...I had lost my nerve and never made an appointment with the doctor. Somehow it spoiled all the romance...made it seem tawdry and ordinary...not the great and passionate love affair I'd built up in my dreams," Alanna said bitterly. "He stopped ranting after a while and offered to pay for an abortion. He didn't seem to feel he needed to defend himself for not telling me he was married. He said he thought there wasn't a coed on campus that didn't know. And he made it very clear that he wanted nothing to do with the baby. It was my fault . . . all of it was my fault."

Alanna was too restless to remain in his arms. She pushed away, moving to the window to turn down the lantern. The room faded into twilight all around them. "I don't want it to go out. I forgot to check the oil." Kyle hadn't said anything and her thoughts jumped from the dull ache of her past to the sharp hurting anxiety of the present. Why didn't he say something, anything to break the silence? Chair legs scraped on bare wood floor as Kyle pushed the nearest chair back under the table. He moved to stand beside her at the window. She leaned against the hard wall of his chest, savoring the warmth of his body. Her eyes were still fixed on the far distance, but her senses were alive to the rough texture of his skin and the faint lingering aroma of lime aftershave that rose to her nostrils.

"David's father has never tried to contact you?" he asked wonderingly. "Never asked you for permission to see his son?"

Alanna shook her head, her attention no longer completely focused on his words so that she missed the regret in his tone. She continued to stare out over the lake as she spoke. "No. Elliot applied for a sabbatical after I returned to school. My parents kept David, raised him until I graduated. I can never repay them," she added in a pathetically dignified tone that Kyle knew hid tears of love and gratitude behind its cool facade. "He's teaching in a small college in Oregon, I believe. He never tried to see David; he's never contacted me. That's the way I want it to remain." Her fingers tightened within the comforting circle of his hand. "Kyle, do you see it? A light. There's a light shining out on the water!"

Swiftly Alanna dimmed the Coleman even more, plunging them into near darkness, bringing the elements closer. The rain had nearly stopped but the wind still raged around the tower. Kyle released her, stepping up to the glass to peer out. "Where should I be looking?" Here and there small pricks of light were becoming visible as the rain retreated behind the storm front.

"Out there." Alanna reached up on tiptoe and turned his head slightly to the left. "That's Green Island. It's the place you heard David talking about. The place he planned for his camping trip." She was trying not to sound too anxious, too hopeful, Kyle realized, but her voice came out breathless and excited despite her restraint. "Can't you see it too?"

Kyle strained his eyes to see through the darkness. Was it a small brave dart of light low on the horizon he saw, or only wishful thinking? It was about the right position and height above the ground . . . only a few feet higher than the slashing waves. A small spit of land that David had pointed out to him when he'd gone fishing with Alanna's son and her father. "Were you able to discover if they took some kind of light with them?" He didn't want to disappoint her but he couldn't be sure, not yet.

"A flashlight, I think. A big one. You could see its light from here if the batteries were strong." Her voice faltered, then took on new strength, convincing herself. "I'm sure you could see a light from Green Island." She was peering out into the darkness, standing so near to him that their shoulders brushed. "There it is again. It is the boys. They're safe, I know it."

She spun away from the window and caught his arm, reaching up to wrap her arms around his neck so naturally that Kyle could do nothing but catch her and hold her close for a long precious moment. "You are very certain, aren't you, Alanna." He didn't need her answer, her faith was shining from her clear gray eyes as she turned the flame higher in the lantern once again.

Obviously she hadn't come to the same conclusions he had; the possibility that he didn't want to consider but couldn't stop himself from thinking about. How could they be sure that both boys were safe? He wasn't even positive he'd seen the light; he didn't have Alanna's familiarity of a lifetime of reference points to go by. It was still raining, blowing, visibility was limited, but he couldn't dash her hopes. "I think I saw it too, Alanna."

Her laugh was genuine and bright with relief. "We'll stay up here the rest of the night. They'll know they aren't alone as long as they can see the lantern. That flashlight is David's signal to me. He knows he's not alone in the dark. That's so important to him. We were talking about it just the other night...."

Her voice broke on the last words and she dropped her face into her hands. A sob shook her shoulders. "Oh, Kyle, I'm only fooling myself, aren't I? How do I know they're both safe out there? I can't be sure that there isn't only one of them...that David isn't hurt, or Billy." Her voice wavered and almost died away. "Or that something terrible... Why is waiting so hard?"

She began to cry in earnest then and Kyle felt his heart splinter inside him. It had been so long since he'd allowed himself to feel as deeply about another person as he did about this small brave woman and it hurt. Alanna had been a breath of healing, renewing beauty in his life, and his reawakening emotions, as well as his growing regard for her son, were causing him to suffer along with her. Kyle swept Alanna up into his arms. She didn't protest but let him carry her across the room and lay her gently on the daybed. She kept on crying, small reluctant sobs that were somehow harder to deal with than a fit of hysterics.

"He might be hurt." She grasped his arms so tightly Kyle winced. "What if one of them has fallen on the rocks and twisted an ankle or broken his wrist?"

He made low murmuring sounds of comfort, unclenching her fingers, sitting down beside her on the blanket. He propped his shoulders against the cold stone wall so that he could support her head and drape the outside edges of the blanket over her back and shoulders to keep out the worst of the chill damp air. She curled herself trustingly into the curve of his body, pulling her legs up beneath the full skirt of her dress.

"Try and sleep, Alanna, please," Kyle said, smoothing his hand over her hair, gentling her, cradling her close.

"I can't sleep. I won't," she replied stubbornly, but her sobs were almost under control. "I can't close my eyes and let the darkness win. Talk to me, Kyle. Help me stay awake," she begged, her hand moving restlessly across the folds of her skirt. "Tell me about yourself, about Catherine and Kelly." Her voice sounded small and faraway as though she didn't really hear what she was saying, didn't fully understand how painful her request was for him to comply with.

"You won't leave me to my misery, will you, Alanna?" His voice was no more than a harsh rasp of sound.

"No, never again. I said once, in anger, that you were like David's father. I know now how very wrong I was. But, Kyle, I do need to know, so that I can understand why you didn't marry the mother of your child." Alanna slipped her hands up over the broad expanse of his chest, resting her palm against the slow steady beat of the pulse in his neck. She felt his heartbeat quicken slightly under the gentle pressure of her fingers and she smiled to herself. Later, when

David was home and safe, she could concentrate on these feelings that floated just out of reach of her consciousness. She could concentrate on Kyle, on teaching him to love and trust again, as he was teaching her.

"I didn't marry Catherine because I was young, thoughtless and a fool," Kyle answered bluntly. "I don't have any valid excuse to take away the guilt, Alanna. I gave her a child and I refused to accept responsibility for it." He looked grim and foreboding in the fitful light of the lantern. He gazed off into the distance, refusing to meet her eyes.

"I don't think it was that simple." Alanna relaxed against his side, unknowingly infusing Kyle with new hope by her trusting gesture. She fit so perfectly into the curve of his arm, her soft feminine body complementing all his sharper lines and angles. She might have been made for him; the missing part of him that would make him whole. She rested her head on his chest and he felt the acceleration of her heartbeat as it echoed the syncopated cadence of his own. Perhaps it was time to tell her what had passed between Catherine and himself all those years ago. Alanna had told him about David's father, a subject she'd always refused to discuss before. These dark, anxious hours of waiting and worry had brought them closer, polished smooth some of the jagged edges of their relationship. Perhaps this was the last great hurdle he had to cross before he could ask her to be his?

"Catherine was the girl next door, an only child: happy, vibrant, a little spoiled, like I was myself. She had loved my cousin Derek since she was a little girl. I, on the other hand, never noticed her until the summer she was sixteen. From then on I couldn't seem to get her out of my mind." He broke off to smooth his hands over the bright softness of

Alanna's hair, the gesture an eloquent, silent plea for understanding.

Kyle's voice was a low rumble in her ear, firm, cool, without heat. How long ago had he learned to hide all his pain behind the courteous impenetrable shell he presented to the world, and at what price to his emotions? She wondered how many other people could see past the facade to read the pain in his gold-flecked eyes as she was learning to do. His sister, Irene, perhaps. But very few others, she was certain.

"You and Derek were rivals for Catherine's love?" Alanna asked the question from a deep, timeless feminine need that defied rational explanation.

"No, not rivals. It was always Derek first, but when he came back from Nam the autumn after Catherine turned eighteen he was a changed man." Alanna felt his muscles tense and flex under her fingertips when he shrugged. "His withdrawal hurt us both, but especially Catherine. Derek just needed time to readjust, but Catherine and I were both too immature to understand. They fought often, broke up, reconciled and fought again. Then one day in late winter she showed up at my apartment in New York."

"And you became involved."

"A classic case of romance on the rebound. It was my first semester at NYU. I didn't know what I wanted to do with the rest of my life, and I used her to satisfy some restless longing I couldn't explain even to myself. And Catherine...Catherine tried very hard not to pretend I was Derek. The physical resemblance between us is pretty striking. At least it used to be. He's aging much more gracefully than I am." Kyle didn't put an ounce of inflection in his voice but Alanna knew the effort it took to form the offhand words.

"I like gray hair," Alanna interrupted without thinking what she said, colored slightly, and went on. "Did you love Catherine?" Kyle had asked the same question about Elliot. Now Alanna could understand why it was so important for him to know. She held her breath.

"She was special, Alanna, always taking on new causes, trying out new ideas." He took her by the arms and stared deep into her eyes. "I didn't love Catherine. I wasn't wise enough to do that. But I was learning to care. Then she got pregnant. She was very big on natural things at the time, I remember. She started experimenting with some kind of back-to-nature, herbal birth control without telling me. When the inevitable happened...well, I felt trapped and our very fragile relationship fell apart."

"Did you...did you suggest she have an abortion?" Alanna was glad he wasn't looking at her when she voiced the question.

Kyle didn't resent the inquiry, knowing the pain that lay beneath; the courage it had taken for Alanna to choose to bear her son out of wedlock and raise him alone. "I didn't have the right to ask her to terminate a life we'd created together. In my clumsy way I was trying to tell you the same thing when you argued on the beach."

"I'm beginning to understand so many things...." Alanna let her words fade away into silence.

After a moment Kyle went on. "Maybe if Catherine had stopped loving Derek somewhere along the line, and I could have stopped feeling trapped and resentful...I don't know. I've gone over it so many times in my thoughts, but I still can't come up with an answer. The bottom line is that I panicked and took off. I wasn't gone long...I knew we had to work something out, but by then Derek had come to New York to take Catherine home. I'll never know if we might have made a go of it, if she might have tamed my wild streak."

"Your wild streak?" Alanna couldn't repress a gurgle of shaky golden laughter. "I don't know anyone more level-headed, less apt to be described as wild."

"I had it knocked out of me a long time ago." There was no bitterness in Kyle's words. "Derek beat me to a pulp when he came to New York. Then the army got hold of me and completed the transformation."

"Vietnam?"

"Just like every other guy my age." Kyle nodded and she felt the tip of his chin brush her hair ever so lightly "Most of those guys just wanted to get the job done and get home to marry their girls and raise families. A lot of them never made it back. And I ran like a damned coward from the responsibilities of being a father to my own child."

"It's not so unusual to do foolish, regretful things when we're young and uncertain of ourselves."

"It's never excusable to hurt other innocent human beings."

"Are Derek and Catherine happy now?" Somehow that seemed very important to Alanna. She stretched and shook her head to clear it of the clinging tendrils of sleep. She was becoming too warm and too comfortable in the secure haven of Kyle's arms. She couldn't give in to her longing and physical weakness now.

"Very much so. They have two boys of their own. And Kelly is growing into a beautiful young woman. I wish you could meet her...."

The phone went off in a series of small metallic beeps. It was the sound Alanna's senses had been attuned to hear for several long hours; the sound she kept imagining during every pause in the conversation, during every lull in the howling of wind and rain. For a moment she couldn't believe it was actually happening. She stared at the phone, then at Kyle, then sat up straight, dropping the edge of the blanket so that cool damp air swirled over her skin. They both stood up.

"Kyle...do you think...I can't, I can't answer it," Alanna whispered, momentarily overcome by dread. Kyle reached around her and picked the instrument up off the table, flicking the switch that completed the connection. Jem's voice floated into the air between them.

"Alanna?" She took the phone when Kyle held it out to her.

"Yes, Jem. Is there news?" She listened quietly for several moments, nodding her head in unseen agreement. "Yes, at first light we'll be ready. Oh, Jem...it is going to be all right, everything will be fine." She set the phone back down on the table with exaggerated care. When she lifted her head her eyes were once again bright with tears, but these tears were tears of joy.

"Oh, Kyle, they're safe...as safe as can be at least. There was a boat...a charter?...I don't know, I forgot to ask," she giggled in nervous relief and made a fluttery gesture with her hands. "They saw them, before the storm, on the island, exactly where I saw the light! The charter boat had engine trouble; they couldn't outrun the storm and it knocked out their radio. They only made it into port a few minutes ago and called the Coast Guard. The search and rescue station notified Jem."

"And your parents?" Kyle let his own smile grow and move upward to include his eyes.

"Jem called them first. He thought I might still be there. They said to tell us they're going to get some sleep. They'll be ready when the rescue team gets here."

Alanna moved to look out the window one last time. Now she knew she wasn't imagining that the wind and rain were less heavy. That if she stood here long enough she might see again the small shining point of light above the horizon.

"Kyle, I can't thank you enough." She turned to find him directly behind her. He opened his arms and she turned into his embrace, content at last. His lips touched her forehead, then her eyelids, her cheek and the corner of her mouth. At the slight pressure Alanna turned her head to search out his mouth. Their lips touched, hesitated, then returned to linger in a long sweet melding.

"Kyle, hold me as if you'll never let me go, please."

There wasn't anything he wanted more in the world. He pulled her close, soothing her with his hands, cradling her against the hard ache of his love. She needed him. She wanted him, and for tonight it was enough. Kyle lifted his hands to cup Alanna's face, letting his feelings guide his actions for the first time in far too long. "I'll be here, Alanna, for as long as you need me."

Their mouths met again, tentatively at first, then more deeply as he coaxed her lips to open with the tip of his tongue. Alanna's arms wound around his neck as she answered his growing passion with a response that was almost as strong. "I don't ever want to leave your arms, I know that now," she whispered against the skin of his throat.

"Alanna." He shifted so that she had to look at him. Kyle searched her eyes for a long moment, hoping for a clue to her true feelings for him. "I want more than anything to love you, to keep you safe and happy. But I won't take advantage of your distress. You need someone tonight. But what of tomorrow and all the days after that?"

"I'll always need you," she said. "I didn't want to admit that before tonight, before all the fear and anxiety of these hours burned away my reservations. I'm not saying this very well but I don't have time to compose a pretty speech. Do you understand?"

"Yes, I understand. It's what I feel, too."

Alanna's dress fell away from her shoulders with the hiss
of a descending zipper. The buttons of Kyle's shirt parted
under her fingers with painful slowness. As it had been in
Maryland all those months ago, she could no longer bear to
be separated from him by layers of garments, hampered by
artificial restraints. Their clothes soon made a dull heap of
color against the dusty wood floor.

Kyle's fingers tangled in her bright silky hair, scattering
pins and combs, freeing the shining mass to lay in curling
waves across her shoulders. He buried his face in the herbal
sweetness. "How I've missed holding you like this, Alanna,
as a woman should be held. Will you make love with me?
Let me hold you and keep you safe until dawn?"

Her face was buried against the sweep of his shoulder. She
didn't answer with words, nuzzling closer, nipping lightly at
the tanned column of his throat, inhaling the dizzying scent
of soap and skin and the very essence of Kyle. She felt giddy
and light-headed with relief and growing passion. Passion
so long held ruthlessly in check, subjugated to worry and
fear, would no longer be denied. For tonight, for Alanna,
the time for words was past. She arched her body closer to
his, glorying in the instant response of his manhood. She
drew her hands up the angled lines of hips and chest to circle his neck with her arms. "Love me, Kyle, please," she
whispered brokenly. It was too difficult to find the words to
tell him how much she needed him to hold her, touch her,
caress her and banish the night, hurry the daylight and all
their tomorrows.

Alanna had no idea how beautiful she looked in the soft
yellow glow of the lantern. Kyle burned with his own fire of
longing, yet it was tempered as always by caution, by lessons so harshly learned.

"Alanna..."

She pressed a finger to his lips, reading his mind because for her, too, making love could never be casual or spontaneous. "There's no need to worry, not tonight." Sadness dimmed the brilliant gray of her eyes for a moment. She didn't want to think about the timing of her body's cycles, about having babies or, more to the point, not having babies at all. But physically the chances were very slim and tonight she felt strong enough within herself to deny the odds.

"I trust your judgment," Kyle said quietly. "Everything will be fine." He guided her to the daybed, lying down beside her. "We have tonight and all the rest of the nights of our lives." His lips trailed a fiery line of kisses across her throat and down over her breasts. There he lingered, teasing the peaks to rosy buds, linking his fingers with hers, blotting out all the terror and fear of the past hours with the magic of his hands and lips. Alanna arched against his palm as he traced a path over the gentle rise of her stomach, over the curve of her hip, down to the creamy inner surface of her thighs, coming to rest on the warm, mysterious triangle between her legs. "You are lovely, Alanna, even more lovely than I remember, and I've thought of no one else for almost two years."

Alanna smiled up into his eyes, seeing her own flushed and happy face reflected there. She began her own exciting exploration of his hard lean body, skimming the smooth jutting angles, seeking out the trip points she had no trouble remembering that sparked his passion. She moved in concert with his seeking caress, reveling in the enjoyment his quickened breath and low moans of pleasure brought to her. For Alanna, to give as well as to receive made the joy of this coming together even more special.

Kyle moved above her, positioning her more intimately beneath his familiar bulk. His right hand was entwined with hers. Alanna felt the weight of it on her hair, tugging at her scalp when she tried to move her head closer to more deeply meet his probing kiss. He shifted his arm, freeing her hair. The movement pushed their lower bodies together, and Alanna parted her legs in a sensual, erotic movement that brought them closer still. Kyle groaned and nipped at the pale skin of her throat until she linked her arms behind his head to hold him tight against her while their mouths and tongues returned once more to sweet reunion.

His entry into her body was strong and deliberate but gentle and pleasurable beyond even her memories of their love-making. Kyle thrust deep into her warmth, and the joining of their bodies filled Alanna with sensations too tenuous, too evocative to analyze or catalog; they were only to be savored and enjoyed.

No words were exchanged between them. They had said all that needed to be said this night. Their coming together was silent, punctuated only by Alanna's breathy moans and Kyle's deep encouraging murmurs as they moved closer and closer to the fulfillment they desired. He continued to move strongly within her, matching her pace, allowing Alanna to establish her own rhythm, find her own path to the top of the mountain.

Kyle stayed with her, always in control, yet in concert, letting Alanna's excitement, her breathless little cries carry him along with her until a last fusing kiss sent them over the precipice together. They plunged headlong into contentment with a mutual groaning sigh of release and completion.

The silence in the tower room seemed even more intense as the echoing drumbeat of their hearts slowed once again. It was so very quiet now. The storm had spent itself, as they had spent themselves in each other. Only the sound of angry waves still pounding the shore intruded on the lovely sense of peace that filled Alanna like sweet drugging wine. Kyle lay with his hand on her shoulder, their bodies still molded together in the aftermath of love.

He was quiet, but she knew he wasn't asleep. Alanna didn't want to think that despite their sharing of a passion so great as to be almost beyond description they hadn't spoken of love. A delicious drowsy lethargy was stealing over her, making it impossible to keep her eyes open, diminishing the importance of telling Kyle in words how she felt. Tomorrow would be soon enough to talk of love. Hadn't he told her they had all the tomorrows in the world?

Alanna struggled against the cloud of sleep drifting down over her because David needed her, her thoughts, her life force renewed and strengthened by Kyle's love. She had to fight to keep her child safe because Kyle had given part of himself into her keeping for David's sake. She struggled valiantly for both of the men she loved but exhaustion and the aftermath of so great a passion took its toll.

Beside her, Kyle was aware of her losing battle with fading consciousness. She had held nothing back in their lovemaking despite her preoccupation with David's plight. It was so like her: generous and giving. He loved her so much he wasn't sure he could ever find the words to tell her. Somehow it frightened him to have to put his feelings into three such simple words. And possibly it wasn't even the right time to overwhelm her with speeches of love. Her enchanting, fog-gray eyes had fluttered closed. Her breasts rose and fell quietly. Her breath was warm and sultry against his skin. He studied her from narrowed eyes. Her mouth was full but delicately formed, the lips moist and sensually curved. The nails of her hand were tinted a warm coral where they lay outside the cover of their makeshift bed.

What would she say if he asked her to marry him, now, tonight? Would she turn away in surprise and stumble over her excuses? Would she resent having her concentration pulled even farther away from David's plight? Or would she say yes because she sensed his need for her and her heart was too soft, too full of caring, to turn him back out into the cold?

He couldn't be sure. He was thirty-eight years old, and he couldn't judge with any accuracy the feelings of the one woman in his life he had fallen head over heels in love with. Kyle reached out and traced lightly over the slight bump at the bridge of her nose. Had she broken it once upon a time? He'd like to know more about her girlhood. He wanted to know all about her life, to have the luxury of lying beside her every night, waking beside her every morning, to be part of her future. The feathering caress of his finger brought her back from the hazy edges of sleep.

Alanna opened her eyes with a guilty start. She looked around blankly for a second as though she'd forgotten where she was. She focused on his chin, blinked, then smiled up into his eyes with a brilliance that transformed her face and settled in Kyle's heart with a fierce warming glow. But even as he watched, the smile faded away.

"David?"

"Shhh," Kyle soothed. "You've only been sleeping for a very few minutes." He brought her hand up to kiss the tip of each finger.

"And we made love." Her voice was wondering. "It wasn't just a lovely dream?" A tiny smile of purely feminine satisfaction curled the corners of her mouth. Her eyes gleamed momentarily with fulfillment and sated desire.

"It was wonderful and it wasn't a dream." Kyle placed a tingling kiss on the edge of her hairline just above her ear.

"I'd better get dressed." Alanna trailed her fingers down the indentation of his breastbone. She flattened her hand against his warm skin, pushing to be set free, but at the same time remembering her haste to get his shirt off and was amazed at her own sensual boldness. Her fingers tangled in the silvery mat of curling hair and she let them linger for another long moment. She sighed and pushed again. "Someone may come looking for us. And it's far too comfortable lying here with you." She stifled a yawn with the back of her hand. "I can't stay awake and I have to." She sounded a little desperate as she held his gaze with her own mica-gray eyes.

"Don't try," Kyle comforted, making his voice a calm monotone, lulling her back to sleep. "Lying beside you is a habit I could easily become addicted to."

"I can't sleep," she repeated obstinately. Didn't he understand that David was counting on her to keep back the night? "I have to stay awake for David."

Life with Alanna would be an endless series of just such small battles of will, Kyle surmised. And each and every one of them could end as delightfully as he intended to end this one. He lowered his head, capturing her mouth for a long, exciting yet tender kiss that choked off his breath, but also silenced her resistance.

"Sleep, Alanna." His voice was husky and honey rich as he tucked the edges of the blanket around them, sealing out the chill of the summer night. "Daylight will come so much more quickly if you can rest. I'll stay awake and keep back the darkness for your son."

Chapter Nine

Sunrise was nothing more than a pink glow along the horizon but already a quietly waiting group of people stood in knots of two or three on the winery lawn. Gusts of wind, more feisty than frenzied now that the storm front had moved past, tugged at straggling wisps of Alanna's hair even though she'd twisted it into a French braid at the back of her neck and fastened it with a clasp after she'd showered and dressed.

Kyle had kept his promise but didn't waken her until the first gray light of dawn had slipped through the tower windows. She was grateful now that she'd had so little time to consider what lay ahead. Lights had already been on in her parents' cottage as they'd hurried through the early morning chill toward the house. Fifteen minutes later Jem and Bette and various relatives and townspeople had also arrived on the scene.

The Coast Guard Search and Rescue helicopter was already on its way. Alanna strained her eyes for a glimpse of it in the still-cloudy sky. The lake was a boiling mass of waves. Pushed along by the sheer weight of the water behind them, they would make a rescue of the two children by boat nearly impossible until well into the afternoon. That would mean more long, miserable hours of waiting and Alanna couldn't face the prospect of more delay.

Time was dragging again, miserably, each minute stretching out, stretching her nerves almost to the breaking point. "I'm going along when that helicopter gets here." For a crazy moment Alanna was afraid she'd spoken aloud. But it was Bette, her voice shrill with anxiety and the obstinacy of fatigue who was demanding to go with the rescue team. She gestured toward the sky. "Billy's going to be scared silly by that thing. How can they land it on that miserable little speck of scrub and rocks?"

"I don't know the drill exactly, Betts," Jem hedged. "They'll get the boys off. It's their job. They're good at it." Alanna turned a little to her left to face her friends directly. Out of the corner of her eye she could see her father leaning heavily on his cane, talking to the mayor and the island paramedics. Her mother stood beside him, straight and composed, her hands wrapped around a Styrofoam cup of coffee for warmth in the damp chill air. And Kyle. Kyle was just behind her. Alanna could feel the heat of his body through the long sleeves of her shirt and took comfort from his closeness as she had since the nightmare began.

"I'm going along. That's my baby out there." Bette's words were cut short by the beat of rotors filling the air with sound. The Coast Guard helicopter came in low and fast. In only a few more seconds it was hovering above the wide open spaces between the winery and the road, stirring the tree branches along the shoreline in a whirlwind dance. Jem and Bette were still arguing but Alanna could no longer make out their words. She glanced back at Kyle one more time and found strength in the sight of him so near, so dear.

Two jumpsuited coastguardsmen emerged from the open side of the aircraft, starting across the lawn in a half crouch. Alanna went forward to meet them along with Jem and

Bette. Kyle was no more than a step or two behind her. Alanna didn't even have to turn her head to know he had followed her.

"Mr. Harlan, Ms. Jeffries." The taller of the two men looked vaguely familiar and Alanna recalled she had seen him once or twice at different community affairs around the area. She relaxed a little, assured now that everything possible would be done to return David to her, safe and sound. The man didn't waste time in preliminaries.

"We saw the boys as we came out. Looks like they're pretty wet and miserable, but okay. I think it would be best if you accompanied us. It's going to be a little tricky getting them off that hunk of rock. No place to land this bird." He shifted his flight helmet from his left hand to the right and glanced apprehensively at Bette, who'd started to cry again.

"I'm going, Jem. You heard the man. I won't leave my baby out there alone one more minute." She was past reasoning with. Jem looked helplessly down at his sobbing wife, and then beseechingly at Alanna.

"Alanna, can't you make her see that what she's asking is impossible?"

The coast guardsman in charge answered before Alanna could speak. "I'm sorry, ma'am. We can't allow you to fly in your condition. It wouldn't be safe."

"I'm tired to death of hearing about my condition," Bette retorted sharply, her tears disappearing in a spurt of anger.

"Let Jem and me go, Betts. The boys will be easier to handle with him along." Alanna tried for a smile. Bette sniffed again, mimicking the gesture, but her lips only managed to twist into a grimace.

"I'm acting like a hysterical pregnant woman again, aren't I?" she asked forlornly.

"You're acting like a mother," Alanna whispered close to Bette's ear, giving her friend a hug.

"You stay with me, Alanna, please," Bette pleaded suddenly, grabbing Alanna's hand in a grip so tight she winced. "Let Kyle go with Jem. I need you. Please stay."

"I . . . I can't ask Kyle to do that," Alanna declined.

"Yes you can." Despite the noise from the helicopter's rotors, his voice was low and composed.

"No, Kyle . . . I . . ." Alanna wanted to sob in frustration. She'd been separated from her son for so long. She thought she might start screaming like a madwoman at all of them in another moment if they didn't let her go on the helicopter. But she didn't succumb to the impulse. Instead, she balled her hands into tight fists and fought down the urge to run to the helicopter and order the pilot into the air. She took a deep breath and let it out slowly. When she spoke, there was a only a slight catch in her voice. She knew she was being practical and expedient, but the words nearly choked her anyway. "Would you go in my place, Kyle, and watch over David for me . . . just a little longer?"

"Only a little while longer," Kyle promised. His eyes looked deep into hers and gave the words far more meaning than the simple assurance the others heard in them. "The night's over; the sun is coming up and it's the beginning of a bright new day." He didn't say anything more, but sprinted for the helicopter with Jem hard on his heels.

For Alanna, nothing about the last few moments had seemed quite real. There was an almost nightmarish quality about everything that was happening just as there had been last night before Kyle took her in his arms and banished her fear. Her feet felt mired in concrete. She couldn't move closer to David no matter how hard she tried. Now the awful heaviness that had impeded her brain and her limbs be-

Tomorrow's Vintage

gan to melt away. Kyle was taking her place; he was going to care for her son and it felt right and good, so very good.

Kyle climbed into the open door in the middle of the aircraft and watched the ground recede in a spinning rush. He fastened the safety harness the younger of the coastguardsmen handed him around his waist and watched the other man hook one end of the short tether line into a metal ring beside the door. He listened as the man explained the rescue procedure in short, clipped phrases, barely audible above the roar of the engine, but all the time he was watching, searching ahead with his eyes.

It didn't take them more than a minute or two to reach the place where the boys had been spotted. Leaning forward against the harness Kyle could see the skiff, pulled as high out of the water as two frightened small boys could manage. It was half sunk, its colorful rainbow-patterned sail draped over the boulders and torn in several places. Two forlorn figures sat huddled together under a bright red sleeping bag.

Kyle found he'd been holding his breath and let it out in a long, slow sigh of relief. He hadn't been able to quite believe they were truly safe, despite all the evidence. Now he knew why the look of haunted frustration hadn't left Alanna's eyes. She wanted to see for herself, to be able to hold David safe in her arms again and convince herself he was well and whole. Every moment their reunion was delayed must be stretching out into an agonizing eternity for her.

Below, David dropped the sleeping bag and stood up, waving when he recognized Kyle's face peering down at him. Billy sat hunched over, still crying, his forehead resting on his bent knees, but he managed to lift his head and wave when he saw his father appear beside Kyle in the open doorway of the helicopter. The two men moved back out of the way and with few wasted movements the two guardsmen tested their harness and the seemingly fragile nylon rope attached to an electric winch above the doorway. Soon the one who had talked to Alanna back on the island disappeared out the opening.

When his partner was safely on the ground, the second man unrolled a rope ladder and lowered it. Kyle watched as the man on the ground explained the procedure to the two dejected Robinson Crusoes. He motioned Billy to step into his harness after adjusting its straps to fit the small boy. Billy was crying more loudly now, his wails audible even above the ceaseless beating roar of the rotors.

Billy refused to budge from the spot where he was standing. Kyle could see David urging his friend on, but to no avail. With a consoling pat on Billy's hunched shoulder, David stepped forward and allowed the harness to be fastened around him.

David's face was white and frightened but his eyes were dry. He waited quietly while the electric winch began to take up the slack of the rope. The coastguardsman followed him up on the rope ladder, steadying him for about twenty-five feet, then returned to the ground. David looked so small and helpless swaying sixty feet below the belly of the helicopter that Kyle had to shut his eyes a moment against the razor sharp pain in his gut. God, what if something had happened to this marvelous product of Alanna's love, this small, mischievous center of her life? She would never have forgiven herself.

"Come on David, you're almost here," Kyle yelled encouragingly, and was rewarded with a wavering smile. David's hands were clenched so tightly on the harness straps that Kyle could see white knuckles and blue veins etched plainly under the skin. The winch stopped; David swung close and two pairs of helping hands hauled the wet, disheveled child inside the aircraft.

"Kyle! Boy, am I glad to see you!" David's voice shook with emotion. He was shivering and Jem handed Kyle one of a pile of heavy khaki-colored wool blankets from a nearby locker. Kyle wrapped it around David's shoulders and pulled the little boy close to his heart.

"I'm glad to see you too, sport." And he was. He'd never thought he could feel so close to a child, be so caught up in his needs that he could forget the ache of losing Kelly, but when he was with Alanna's son he came very close. He knew, without having to think about it at all, that he could come to love David as deeply as he loved his mother.

Big tears began to roll down David's cheeks and he mopped at them with his grubby fist. "I'm glad to see you, really I am Kyle, but where's my mom? I thought she'd be here. I saw her light. I watched it all night." He gulped and hiccupped on a sob.

"She had to stay with Bette and your Grandpa," Kyle explained, resting his hand on David's cheek for a fleeting moment before remembering that eight-year-old boys didn't always want to be cuddled. "She's waiting for you back on the lawn at the winery." He wanted nothing more than to hold Alanna's son in his arms and make everything right in his world again, but they could hear Billy's terrified yells coming closer with each turn of the winch.

"He's been crying like that all night," David disclosed, leaning out of Kyle's arms to see if he could catch a glimpse of his buddy. "And it was his idea to run away," he added disgustedly in a penetrating whisper that brought a tight smile to Jem's face even though all his attention was centered on his son's ascent. "I didn't cry...much..." David amended his final statement with the same innate honesty his mother possessed.

"Your mom told me you're brave." Kyle pulled David back into the interior of the helicopter as Billy arrived at the opening to be folded into Jem's waiting arms. The coast-guardsman followed a few minutes later. David had so forgotten his fright that he became very interested in the proceedings, and even managed to coax Billy to take a look down at their deserted camp and the skiff.

"Jeez, it's a mess," Billy sniffed, still holding very tightly to his father's hand. Wrapped in identical khaki blankets, the boys looked like refugees from a natural disaster of great magnitude.

"My mom will make us pay for getting it fixed," David announced fatalistically, and Kyle knew from that moment on that everything was going to be just fine. He settled back for the short ride home.

"DEAR FRIENDS, to bring this round of toasts to an end, let me say for all of us that we wish the bridal couple all of God's blessings and a long and happy life together. Ladies and gentlemen, I give you Leslie and Rick McKee!" Father Tim's voice was jovial, his white clerical collar already unfastened in the late afternoon heat as he raised his wineglass to toast the newlyweds yet again. Leslie and her groom acknowledged the applause from the assembled wedding guests and took their places on the dance floor for the first waltz.

"Thank heaven that's over," Bette said sotto voce while she smiled and waved at a newly arriving batch of distant cousins who'd spotted her across the room.

"It was a beautiful wedding," Alanna insisted, sipping warily at a glass of her own champagne. "Leslie looks absolutely lovely in that gown." She was already on her second glass of the sparkling wine and, as tired as she was, she'd decided it would be her limit.

"Yes, she does. Were hoop skirts in fashion for wedding gowns when we were that age?" Bette asked interestedly as if she couldn't remember being twenty.

"More like when our parents were that age," Alanna corrected with a little gurgle of laughter produced as much by exhaustion as amusement.

"I guess you're right. My wedding gown had an empire waist, a straight skirt, and is about three sizes too small even without the baby." She sighed and waved to the batch of cousins once more. "Well, the lake must have settled down pretty well. They don't look too green around the gills."

"It's still a rough ride over today."

"Ummm." Bette's attention was diverted to David and Billy who were back for a second trip past the wedding cake. "I'd better take Billy home with me. Doctor's orders after my little scene this morning," she added with a flush of embarrassment tinging her fair skin. "And for once, I'm not going to put up a fuss. I'm beat. I just wanted to wait until the speeches were over and the cake was cut."

"You go ahead. We'll see to everything here," Alanna stated firmly, although she wondered how she could manage to stay awake much longer herself.

"It's been one hell of a day," Bette said, rubbing the small of her back.

"You can say that again," Jem remarked, coming up behind the two women. "This place looks great, Alanna. The whole family wants to thank you for giving Leslie and Rick a great reception."

"I didn't have much to do with it," Alanna confessed. "Everybody pitched in while the paramedics were checking the boys out this morning. When I got back over here, Mrs. Ackerman had a huge breakfast started, and about half the town was tacking up crepe-paper streamers and tissue bells." Alanna shook her head, a smile growing inside and spreading across her face as she recalled her father's comments when she'd first walked in on the industrious work detail.

"Can't go back to bed now, Lanny," Malcolm had called from where he was supervising the arrangement of the punch and cake table as well as choosing the most convenient spot to display the gifts. "It's going on seven. Morning's near shot. May as well get something accomplished." He'd laughed then, and so had Alanna, but the next moment a wave of dizzy fatigue had caused her to miss a step and once more she had found Kyle at her elbow.

"Nap time," he'd grinned down at her. "David's out of the bath and needs to be tucked in. I'm going to make sure your mom and dad get some rest before I crash myself. What time's the ceremony again?" he'd asked as they walked out of the winery into the bright, clean new day.

"Two-thirty," Alanna had answered dutifully.

"I'll set my alarm for one," Kyle had decided and left her at the foot of the stairs with a quick kiss on the tip of her nose.

The sleep had done everybody good. The wedding had been beautiful and blessedly short because the day had grown hot and sticky after the breeze that shook the tall cottonwoods and maples in the yard had died away. Leslie had looked as lovely as only a new bride can look, and she'd cried nearly as loudly as Bette when David came solemnly through the reception line and begged her pardon for damaging her wedding cake in a serious and contrite little speech.

"Leslie's gonna start blubbering again if she sees us," her son's voice broke in on Alanna's reverie. He was voicing his opinion on much the same subject that had been occupying her thoughts. "I mean, she bawled all down the front of my jacket at the church and I don't want to go through that again."

"She kisses me every time she can get her hands on me," Billy seconded with a scowl as they plopped down on folding chairs beside Alanna. She was sitting at a paper-covered table at the back of the room watching the festivities while she pulled the edges of a pink crepe-paper streamer out of shape without even being conscious of what she did.

"You did the gentlemanly thing, apologizing to Leslie for the way you acted the other day," Alanna said, deciding she had to make one more attempt to bring home the gravity of the situation.

"Yeah, well, Leslie really did just about yank my arm off. I reminded her of that," David said unrepentantly. "Where's Kyle?" he asked in the same breath. He downed the last of a glass of punch, leaving a pink mustache along his upper lip. Alanna leaned forward with a napkin and David jerked his head back.

"Mom, I'm not a baby." He grabbed the napkin and scrubbed at his mouth. "Better?" he asked with a grin that took all the sting out of his words and showed the gap from his missing tooth.

"Better. I guess I just have to touch you a little more often today," Alanna chuckled as she scanned the crowded room for Kyle's tall, dark-jacketed form. "I want to park you in one spot where I can keep my eye on you and not worry for a long, long time."

David put his arms around Alanna's neck and surprised her a little with a resounding hug and a kiss on the cheek. "I'm sorry we ran away, Mom. It was stupid. But it seemed like a good idea when Billy and me decided to go," he confessed ingenuously. "We were so mad at everybody. And you didn't listen to us either," he added accusingly.

"Yeah, nobody listened," Billy added his own grievance. His clip-on tie was hanging out of the pocket of his shirt and he'd spilled something unidentifiable down his front at one point in the afternoon. In his hand he was carrying a pink sugar rose he'd confiscated from the wedding cake, and there was a smear of frosting on his chin.

"I understand how you feel, David. But it doesn't change the facts," Alanna stated with loving firmness. "You were wrong to have spoken to Leslie as you did. And you were very, very wrong to have taken the skiff and run away. You scared us all half to death."

"That's why I feel bad. I didn't think of you or Gramps or anybody," David frowned thoughtfully as the first glimmerings of adult accountability stirred in his brain. "I'm glad you didn't cry, Mom. But don't ever hug me that tight again. I thought my ribs would break. I bet Hulk Hogan can't give a bear hug like that."

"My mom cried all the time until the paramedics sent her home to take a nap," Billy added unnecessarily. "It was embarrassing."

"You were a bawl baby too, wasn't he, Kyle?" David pronounced, looking up to see Kyle standing quietly behind his mother's chair.

"We all felt like crying," Alanna said firmly as she smoothed the crepe paper back into a semblance of its original shape. She felt Kyle's hands on the back of her chair but he made no move to touch her and she was grateful. She did lean back slightly and felt the sharp edges of his knuckles through the thin lime-green silk of her dress.

"It was neat, wasn't it, Kyle?" David's attention returned to the fascinating subject of his rescue. "Just like *The A Team* or *Rambo* or something. The coast guard guy came down that rope—'cause the wind was blowing so hard they couldn't land the helicopter," he explained for his mother's benefit for at least the twentieth time that day. "He hooked this harness thing on to me. I had to go first 'cause Billy was so scared."

"I wasn't that scared," Billy broke in, compelled to defend himself. "I figured if that skinny old rope broke, I could catch you when you fell."

"That was very thoughtful of you," Alanna said in a strangled voice. Kyle could feel her shoulders shake with suppressed laughter as she leaned against the back of the chair, trapping his hands between the wood and the angle of her shoulder blades. "You were both very brave, but I'm relieved I didn't have to see either one of you dangling at the end of a rope a hundred feet over the water." She leaned forward to emphasize her point and Kyle lifted his hand to touch her shoulder lightly and quickly. She covered his fingers with her own for a moment, then stood. "Billy, your father and mother are looking for you. I see them across the room. I think you should all go home and get some rest."

"But the dance is just starting. It isn't even dark yet," he complained. "The band is gonna play *Wipeout* just like they always do." The sixties classic was a favorite of both youngsters.

"It's a tough life, bud," Alanna joked, and pointed Billy in the direction of his parents.

"Say good-night, David," she urged.

"Night, Billy." David looked ready to pout. "I'm not tired," he insisted.

"I am," Alanna said, leaving no more room for argument. "Go find your grandparents and say good-night."

"Cripes," he grumbled. His hair, so close to the color of Alanna's, stood up in tufts above his ears. She reached out a long slender hand to smooth it down but he ducked away. Alanna stiffened and then shrugged philosophically, accepting his little bid for independence, although it plainly hurt her. The bond between mother and son was never more apparent than it had been today: strong and resilient, like Alanna herself.

"Can't you steal away for a while too?" Kyle asked, pitching his voice so that it didn't carry to the other guests sitting around them in the big main room of the winery.

"I think I can arrange that," Alanna nodded, her eyes following her parents and her son. Phyllis signaled that she would keep David with her and Alanna acknowledged the arrangement with a wave of her hand. "I'll have to come back and oversee the cleanup so we can open tomorrow as usual, but that won't be for a couple of hours yet. Let's go outside. It's getting stuffy in here."

Kyle didn't touch her as they made their way toward the door leading to the balcony. He knew that his presence in Alanna's life was causing heads to turn as it was. He wasn't about to give the gossips and well-meaning friends any more grist for their mills. He'd let Alanna break the news of their relationship in her own way, in her own time.

They were blessedly alone. Alanna looked around the veranda with its murals of vineyard scenes and old sayings lettered in Gothic script that somehow seemed not to have been much affected by the passing of the years or the elements. "Everyone must be inside for the dollar dance," she explained, resting her arms on the veranda railing to look down at the cars parked along the roadway below.

"Dollar dance?" Kyle asked, leaning his elbow on the railing beside her. He'd taken off his tie, and the combination of white shirt, tanned skin, dark jacket and silver-gray hair was an intriguing one for Alanna.

"The guests line up and each one gives the bride or the groom a dollar to dance with them for a moment or two. It helps the newlyweds get off to a good start. Or really have a blowout of a honeymoon." She laughed and turned her head to watch Kyle's profile as he stood beside her.

"Would you like to dance?" he asked unexpectedly. "We've never danced together."

"It would be very nice." Alanna went into his arms and rested her head against his shoulder. "I can't seem to find the energy to truly enjoy this celebration." She wondered fleetingly if she looked as tired as Kyle still did. Very likely she looked a great deal worse, even though she'd taken pains to hide the dark circles under her eyes and disguise the pallor of her skin with a blusher several shades brighter than she normally used. "We'll be the talk of the island if anyone comes out here," Alanna murmured against the skin of Kyle's throat, deciding she wasn't quite so tired when she was standing in the circle of his arms. She pressed her lips to the spot where his pulse beat strong and slow beneath the skin, then daringly repeated the light caress higher, just below his ear. Kyle shuddered and pulled her tighter against him.

"I'll have to make an honest woman of you then." He heard himself say the words and realized they had a far deeper meaning than he consciously intended. They hadn't spoken of what passed between them in the tower room. Mostly because the day had been far too hectic for private speech, but also because Kyle wasn't sure how Alanna felt about making love to him the night before.

"You don't need to feel obligated to me because of what happened last night . . ." Alanna moved out of his arms so that she could study his expression.

"I wanted you very much last night, Alanna." Kyle swallowed to relieve the painful tension in his throat. "I feel the same way today."

"I wanted to make love with you too, Kyle. I needed you and you were there. But needing was only part of the way I feel about you . . ." Alanna held her breath. Perhaps this was where they passed the last hurdle? Perhaps now Kyle could tell her he loved her, because she found she was suddenly too shy to speak the words first.

"Alanna, come away with me, to Dutch River, to meet my family, and let me take care of you for a little while," Kyle said impulsively, resting one hand on the porch railing, one hand above her head where she stood with her back against a thick supporting beam of darkened oak.

"You're already taking care of me." Alanna's arms came around him and she lifted her face for his kiss. "I can't thank you enough for what you did... helping me get through the night...keeping back the darkness for my son." She stopped speaking abruptly as sensations from the night's passion blazed between them again.

"Last night was just the beginning." Kyle's words held a wonderful promise. "But we do need some time..." Why did they need time? he asked himself. Because he wanted to ask her to marry him and he was just too unsure of her response to risk saying the words tonight? They'd come so far in such a short time, too quickly perhaps, and he was afraid to chance his future on one throw of the dice. Was he even ready for that kind of commitment? Sometimes he felt so mixed up inside that he couldn't be sure. He'd tuned out the prompting of his emotions for so long that he wasn't ready to cast all caution to the winds and follow his heart. He'd never asked a woman to marry him; he'd never told Alanna he loved her. He was just plain scared, and he was playing for time.

"I can't leave David, not so soon after last night...." Her eyes were cloudy with indecision. He could see she was torn, and cursed himself for even implying by omission that he didn't want David with them.

"We'll bring David, too. I know you don't want to be separated from him right now." Kyle's stomach was a mass of twisting knots. "We need time together, Alanna," he repeated. He was afraid of asking her to marry him because he couldn't be positive she still didn't compare him to David's father. He had to be sure.

Alanna continued to watch him closely. She saw his hesitation and she sighed but summoned a faint ghost of her lovely smile. There would be no more talk of love and commitment this evening. "I think we can get away for a few days. David will enjoy the trip. Yes, if that's what you want, we'll come to Dutch River with you, Kyle. We'll be ready to leave whenever you are."

Chapter Ten

Sunset came quickly to the west bank of the Hudson, Alanna had discovered over the past three days, but twilight lingered a long time, shading the sky from gold to amethyst with countless subtle variations of hues. The molten fiery ball of the sun itself was long gone behind the bluffs that towered over the little town of Dutch River, yet its rays limned the far shore of the mighty waterway, sparkling off the chrome of cars passing along the highway. In the peaceful rural setting surrounding her and spread out in panorama below, it was difficult for Alanna to believe they were only a little more than a two-hour drive north of New York City.

She closed her eyes and leaned back against the blue-and-white striped cushions of her lounge chair, letting the flirtatious breeze of an August evening play with stray wisps of her hair and touch lightly on the exposed skin of her neck and throat. Alanna rubbed her fingers lightly over a reddened patch of sunburned skin below her khaki shorts. She'd fallen asleep in the sun that afternoon and the aftereffects were making themselves felt. She stretched with lazy grace like a happy cat and smiled to herself. She hadn't done much at all since they arrived but eat and sleep and indulge

in a busman's holiday touring Derek's small, but very productive, plantings of *Baco Noir* and native Niagara grapes.

The Staffords had been farmers and vintners first, and
then businessmen for many generations, she remembered
Malcolm telling her when she had first sought the Foundation's help. You could trust men like that to do what was
best for Island Vineyards. Kyle's grandfather's success on
Wall Street had allowed his two sons to follow their own
paths in life. Kyle's father had chosen to work within the
Foundation and had eventually taken control of it when the
old man retired. Derek's father, the eldest, had chosen to
remain at Dutch River, and Derek later followed in his
footsteps. The Hudson River Valley had once been a very
important wine-growing area, and it would be again if there
were many more inventive, talented winemakers like Derek
Stafford around.

Off to her left, a lively volleyball game was in progress.
Catherine's and Derek's boys, ages ten and twelve, were
teamed with David and Kelly against Irene's twin sons, who
were almost twenty and already in their second year at Cor-
nell. The younger children were holding their own with
Kelly's help. She was, she'd announced to Kyle the night of
their arrival, going to be a starting player on her high
school's varsity team in the fall. And as an added precau-
tion, she'd shrewdly handicapped the elder boys by allowing them to use only one arm apiece.

Alanna focused her attention on Kyle's daughter. She
seemed to be forever on the move, flitting from a part-time
job in the village hardware to parties and dates with a young
man who drove a battered pickup truck and had aspira-
tions to become a nuclear physicist. They'd seen very little
of her since their arrival and Alanna knew it hurt Kyle, but
there was nothing she could do to change the situation.

Kelly was a lovely child: tall and graceful with none of the coltish awkwardness of many girls her age. She was very slender, with high, firm breasts and hips still as narrow as a boy's.

"Drat! Where is that knitting needle? My ankle is itching like the very devil." Irene Stratton's deep resonant voice cut into Alanna's thoughts with slicing quickness.

"Here it is." Alanna reached over the side of her chair to retrieve the lost instrument from the slate patio floor.

"Thanks! Nothing else I could find is small enough to reach down into this blasted cast. I'll never go waterskiing again, I swear to God. My sons are right, I'm too old for that kind of thing. From now on, it's bridge and shuffleboard for this woman." Irene Stafford grimaced, then sighed in relief as the point of the knitting needle found the source of her discomfort and alleviated it. Irene dropped the needle back onto the iron table separating her lounge chair from Alanna's and retrieved her wineglass with a contented sigh. "Marvelous."

"I think so, too. And I understand Derek's *De Chaunac* is quite similar to my own. Kyle and I were discussing it this afternoon. I'm looking forward to a tasting." Alanna lifted her own crystal taster's glass to study the color and sniff the bouquet of the dry red *Baco Noir*. "I'll have to remind Kyle about the *De Chaunac*. I wouldn't want to miss it if it's as good as this one."

Kyle's sister drained her glass. "I was referring to the pleasure of being able to scratch whatever itches." Irene broke into a hearty peal of laughter when she saw the disgruntled look on Alanna's expressive features. A scoring altercation between the volleyball combatants diverted her attention before she could call attention to Alanna's discomposure. "Your David seems to be getting along very well with the Stafford brood," she remarked instead, her glittering black eyes fixed unblinkingly on Alanna. Irene was a tall woman, thin and angular, with a head of dark Stafford hair streaked dramatically with white at both temples. She was nearing fifty and looked ten years younger despite her deprecating remarks about her age. She'd been divorced for many years and had returned to the use of her maiden name. She was also, according to her brother, the driving force behind the Stafford Foundation since their father's death twelve years ago.

"He's a very happy child," Alanna said, setting down her glass and letting her gaze wander back to the game.

"You never married." Irene was nothing if not blunt. Alanna didn't know exactly what to make of the other woman, or any of the Staffords for that matter. Derek and Catherine had welcomed her graciously into the large, extended family group that shared the huge old house and extensive grounds during summer vacations; but they had also been understandably wary of Kyle's sudden appearance. Irene, Alanna suspected, was also slightly wary of her brother's involvement with Alanna, but showed no hesitation in voicing her concern.

"I'm not married," Alanna replied.

Irene was silent a moment longer, then apparently came to some decision in her mind. "I know all about you; Kyle told me. That's why I also believe you're very special to my brother. We Staffords aren't the kind of family to confide in each other without a very good reason for doing so."

Alanna decided to be equally candid. "I love Kyle. I want to make him happy."

"I hope that's possible." Irene seemed to be watching the volleyball game in her turn. "I know about Kelly." She spoke in sharp, bitten-off sentences, as if she feared Alanna might interrupt her words. "I've never told Kyle what I suspect. She is his child, isn't she?" This time her steady dark gaze speared Alanna to her chair.

Alanna wasn't sure how to answer, how much to confide in Irene. Evening sounds rose around them as the volleyball game ended in a chorus of ragged cheers from David's victorious team. Bees buzzed in the perennial border behind the patio; a bird called in the trees, leaves rustled overhead. Alanna watched a jet's trail turn from white to pink as it moved across the evening sky. Knowing she must respond eventually to Irene's query, she studied the older woman's face for a clue to her feelings and found only love and concern written there. Alanna made the decision to trust Kyle's sister in the space of a heartbeat. "Kelly is Kyle's daughter. I didn't think anyone else knew."

"I've always thought so." Irene shook her head and gestured with her hand. Diamonds winked with pale fire in the clear light. "I was going through such a bad time myself when it happened—trying to decide whether to hold my marriage together or go it alone with two small children—that I couldn't do anything to help Kyle. I don't know the details." She made a second, more violent gesture with her crimson-nailed hand. "I don't want to know anything else—it will only make it harder to go on lying." She leaned forward, drawing her uninjured leg up under her chin. The sleeves of her emerald-green, bat-wing top covered the smooth tan expanse of her skin.

"He wants Kelly to know she is his daughter. I think he's making a terrible mistake."

Irene nodded sadly. "So do I. But he's a stubborn man, and he's hurting. He won't listen to me even if I had any intention of speaking to him, which I don't." She turned her head to hold Alanna with her gaze yet again. "But you must. He's fallen in love with you, any fool can see that. Do you have the courage to make him understand that silence is the greatest gift he can give Kelly and her parents?"

"I hope I can . . . I'm not sure." Alanna didn't want to admit to this cool, forceful woman that she was scared to death. "He's tired and sad and unhappy. He might not want to listen to reason." Their relationship wasn't firmly enough established for Alanna to give him all the support she wanted to provide, to assert herself so greatly. "I'm afraid he won't listen to me."

"MOM, DID YOU HEAR THAT? Everyone's going on an overnight and they invited me. Can I go, please?" David's spoon clattered back into his dish of mint chocolate chip ice cream. He picked it up hastily and smiled an apology in Catherine's direction. "Please, Mom!" He lowered his voice to an agonized whisper.

"We've been promising the boys all week, Mrs. Jeffries." Irene's eldest son, Tyler, smiled charmingly at Alanna. "We'd be happy to take David along, too. We've got plenty of gear and it's just down the road, really. The town has a small camping area along the river. We'll take good care of him."

"Hey, what about me, aren't I invited?" Kelly pretended to pout. She was wearing an aqua blue sundress that set off her deep tan and her blue-black hair that swung from a ponytail caught up in a fanciful knot at the top of her head.

"The last time you went camping with us, we had to bring you home before dark," the second twin, Timothy, interjected. "No girls allowed. Right guys?"

"Right." The three youngest males chorused in unison.

"I don't want to go anyway," Kelly said with haughty grandeur, lifting a spoonful of ice cream to her mouth. "I have a date." She did look very much like Kyle, but there were enough differences that the resemblance wasn't striking. She had a defiantly snub nose and a scattering of freckles across her cheekbones as well as a dimple in her chin that were exact replicas of Catherine's.

"A date? With whom, may I ask?" Derek teased. He, too, resembled his cousin to a marked degree. He reminded Alanna painfully of Kyle as he'd been when they had first met. Yet Derek's thick black hair didn't even hold a sprinkling of gray. He was two or three inches shorter than Kyle and heavier, more solid. Alanna studied the blunted angles of his features with curiosity veiled behind lowered lashes.

There were no chameleon shadings in this man, she was coming to realize. His countenance might darken with passion or anger, but Catherine would never have to deal with a myriad of complicated layers of intensity in his personality. Is that why Catherine and Kyle had never been able to form a lasting bond despite sharing a child? Was Kyle too multi-faceted, too introspective and complex for her to deal with successfully?

To say Kyle's personality was more complicated was an over-simplified judgment, but it did sum up in a single word the most obvious differences between the two cousins. Complexities. Derek was less intense, more open, more easily understood and evaluated than Kyle would ever be. Sounds of chairs being pushed back from the table intruded on Alanna's assessment of the two men.

"Mother, can we help you to your room or are you going back out on the patio?" Tyler Stafford's eyes were a deep cobalt blue, several shades darker than Timothy's. It was the only benchmark Alanna had found so far to keep the two blond young men separated in her mind.

"Back to my room." Irene sighed theatrically. "I have work to do. I want to go over Alanna's grant requests and give them my approval so Kyle can take them back to Virginia with him and get them in the pipeline."

"You work too hard, Mom," Tim scolded, offering his parent his arm with a courtly flourish.

"If I didn't keep my nose to the grindstone, who'd pay for your tuition, young man?" She silenced her offspring with a playful slap on the wrist and sailed out of the room in a flurry of good-nights, her savoir faire not one whit diminished by the heavy cast impeding her right leg.

The youngsters followed in a mad rush to find and pack up all the camping gear and foodstuffs necessary for a night under the stars. David didn't seem to be suffering any ill effects from his night on the island. He was as eager as the others for the adventure.

Kelly lingered on to finish her ice cream and make arrangements to take the family car to volleyball practice in the morning. She kissed Catherine a quick good-night, but stopped behind Derek's chair to slip her long slender arms around his neck and hug him tight. "I'll be home by midnight, Daddy, so don't worry. Ron Bellows is taking me to the movies and out for pizza."

"Drive carefully, princess. And no beer for Ron while he's got you in that darn pickup of his. Understood?"

"He knows the rules for dating Derek Stafford's daughter." Kelly laughed merrily and kissed the top of Derek's head again. Beside Alanna, Kyle stiffened in his seat and stared down at the glass of wine he clutched by the stem. His knuckles were bleached white under the tautly pulled skin. Alanna's heart twisted in her breast.

"Good night, Alanna. Good night, Kyle. I'll see you in the morning." She blew a casual kiss in their general direction and danced out of the dining room. Silence stretched out and filled the corners of the softly lighted room. Fresh flowers in vases on the cherry-wood sideboard filled the air with subtle perfume. Alanna didn't know where to look so she watched the ice cream in David's dish melt into a sticky green puddle.

"Shall we go out into the living room? It's cooler in there, I'm sure," Catherine suggested nervously. "What a week for the air conditioner to break down. But at least you're out in the guest house so you can sleep at night." Catherine smiled weakly when Alanna raised her head to make a polite reply.

She honestly hadn't known what she expected from Catherine. She'd been friendly but distant and Alanna hadn't pressed for anything more personal. She suspected Catherine looked on their every meeting as being fraught with overtones and hidden layers of texture and meaning. Alanna didn't blame her; it was true. Yet she couldn't completely set aside her wish to know these people better. Under different circumstances they might have become friends. As it was, Catherine would always be the woman who had been Kyle's lover, the mother of his child. That made her of great importance to Alanna, but it also separated them as effectively as iron bars.

"Wait a moment, please, Catherine. There's something I'd like to discuss with you and Derek." Kyle's voice was rough along the edges. Alanna twisted her napkin around her fingers beneath the concealing folds of the ivory linen tablecloth.

"Oh, Kyle, don't, please." Catherine's words were a plea. Tears shimmered in her midnight-blue eyes. Kelly had her eyes, too, Alanna thought with a tiny unoccupied corner of her mind. "We settled this a long time ago. I knew it was a mistake to allow you back into Kelly's life. But Dutch River is your home and Irene's; your grandfather wanted it that way. And I thought you could be trusted to keep your promise to me."

"Damn it, Catherine. I just want her to know who I am. Is that so much to ask?" Kyle banged his hand, palm flat against the linen. Silverware and china jumped and rattled. Alanna reached out to cover his hand with her own.

"Perhaps I should leave." Her voice sounded weak and uncertain to her own ears. She half rose from her chair.

"No!"

"It's all right, Alanna." Derek's voice was gruff but calm. "Obviously Kyle has told you about Kelly."

"He has." Alanna settled back into her seat but didn't lift her hand from Kyle's, although he had balled his fingers into a fist tight with pent-up anger.

"Stay, Alanna." Kyle shot her a quick, commanding glance that raked over her like live current. "We are all involved in this now." His tone gentled on the last phrase, softening the direct order that had preceded it. He said nothing more, but it was enough to stay her retreat.

"We've discussed this before, so often, Derek and I." Catherine pushed her plate away from her, folding her hands composedly on the tabletop. The pale green walls of the room complemented her dark hair and creamy skin, but her eyes were huge pools of anguish. "We don't want Kelly to know about you, ever. There's no reason. Your name doesn't appear on her birth certificate. Derek is her father, legally, and in every other way but one."

Derek pushed back his chair and moved to the French doors that faced out over the bluff. Darkness had smudged the outlines of the Hudson like a charcoal drawing. Lights blinked from across the water. "She's my daughter, Kyle." He rested one large work-roughened hand on the glass. His nails were stained dark with wine. Another tenuous link binding these people to Alanna. The Stafford family fortune had been built in the earth and on the vines, as her family's had been, but the Depression and Prohibition had driven Kyle's and Derek's grandfather out into the business world to recoup the family fortune.

Catherine left the table also, moving to stand beside her husband, rubbing her cheek against Derek's knuckles as he pulled her into the circle of his arms. It was an unthinking, habitual caress that spoke volumes for their love. "I don't want to sound cruel, to hurt you any more than you've already been hurt, Kyle," she said, choosing her words with care. "But you have no place in *our* daughter's life. That's the way it is. That's the way it must remain."

"No! There must be some place for me." All the misery in his soul underscored the words. For Alanna the whole scene narrowed down to the terrible isolation she felt engulfing Kyle. How could she break through it to give him the comfort she so desperately longed to bestow?

"You have a place in Kelly's affections as my cousin and friend," Derek said. "But that's all. Kyle, be a reasonable man. She's sixteen, going on seventeen, the most volatile, the most vulnerable time in a young girl's life. Don't you see we can't allow her to be subjected to that kind of upheaval?"

"She'll adjust." Kyle didn't sound as if he'd convinced even himself.

"You have no right to Kelly at all, Kyle. You promised me that a long time ago," Catherine reminded him, making a pleading little gesture that went straight to Alanna's aching heart. "Derek is Kelly's father. He came to me when you left me in New York." Catherine kept her voice steady but Alanna felt Kyle flinch from the blow of her words. How hard it must be for him to sit still, a static figure, unable to alter the past or predict the outcome of the future. He was used to molding events and situations to his wishes, not be ordered by them.

"I've paid for that mistake every day since it happened."

Alanna longed to reach out and touch him, smooth the layers of silver hair where they rested in stark relief against the navy-blue collar of his shirt.

"We all have. But Derek is her father." There was no compromise in Catherine's voice when she spoke again. "He was with me when Kelly was born. He took the two o'clock feeding every night. He sat up with her when she had colic and when she broke her shoulder the summer she was six. It was never you, Kyle. You're a stranger to her."

Kyle didn't retaliate as Alanna half thought he might. He stared straight through Catherine as if she didn't exist.

"You've never been a factor in her life. She likes you, admires you, but that's all, Kyle." There was steel beneath Catherine's easygoing surface, Alanna was discovering. She would fight to the death to protect her child. "If you love her, it has to stay that way. For all our sakes, but especially for Kelly."

"Damn it, Catherine, haven't I done penance enough for my sins?"

Catherine stepped away from the comforting circle of Derek's arms. She moved forward to kneel by Kyle's chair where he'd half pushed away from the table. "Oh, my dear, yes, you've paid back whatever pain we caused each other all those years ago a thousandfold. *With your silence.* I never loved you and that makes me as much at fault as you were." Tears filled her eyes and rolled down her cheeks. Alanna glanced across the room. Derek's hands were tight along the back of his chair but he remained silent. For a brief moment, Alanna's eyes caught and held his jade-green gaze before his attention returned to his wife. Alanna blinked back hot, stinging tears of her own.

"I'm making the best decision I know how for my daughter's sake. Help me." Kyle covered Catherine's shaking fingers with his own when her voice faltered and broke.

"I want to be a part of her life, Catherine." Kyle's voice was low and deep. Catherine turned her head, seeking support from her husband.

"I'm sorry, Kyle. The answer is no," Derek reinforced his wife. Kyle stood as Derek helped Catherine to her feet. Only Alanna remained seated. She hadn't contributed a word to this discussion, nor did she intend to. Catherine and Derek were right. Kyle must understand and she must help him accept this great disappointment. But how? Alanna had never felt so very far away from him before. If only they'd had a few more days, a few more hours to cement the love growing between them.

She should have been wise enough to see that this trip could only end in the scene she was witnessing at this very moment. With time she'd be more sure of his love, more sure of her ability to break through the icy carapace that encased him. She would be brave enough to go to Kyle and add her arguments to the rest. But they hadn't shared that precious extra time, and the faraway empty look on his face frightened her mute.

"You aren't going to change your minds." Kyle threw his napkin on the table, and Catherine flinched as if it had been made of iron, not bright pink linen.

"We have no choice." Again it was Derek who spoke for the couple. "It's Kelly's welfare we have to consider above everything else. You have to abide by our decision."

"The hell I do. I'll tell her myself."

"Kyle, no!" Alanna was on her feet but the swinging door to the kitchen had already whistled shut behind him.

"Derek!" Catherine turned and clutched at her husband's shirt. "He wouldn't do that."

"No, he won't. He'll come to his senses. He wouldn't hurt Kelly for anything in the world. He must know it would break her heart." Derek's tone was soothing, but his green eyes were troubled.

Catherine sniffed and smiled up into his eyes. "You're right. Kyle's never been a cruel man. He'll do what's best for her."

"Alanna, go to him, please." It was Catherine's hand on her arm. Catherine's clear contralto voice brought Alanna out of the cold void that had kept her silent and rooted to the spot for so long. "He needs you. Don't you see that?" Alanna stared past her. "Kyle has never let anyone see him so vulnerable. I meant every word I said. I forgave him years ago. My blame is as great as his. But he has to forgive himself. We caused each other a great deal of pain, but I'm so lucky. He deserves to be happy too."

"What if he won't listen to me?" Alanna repeated her greatest fear one more time.

"He will." Derek's low voice was strong with confidence. "He loves you. He's shared you with us—Kyle has never done that before."

"He's proud and stubborn, like all the Stafford men." Catherine smiled despite her tears and snuggled back into the comforting circle of Derek's arms. "He's learning about love and loving late in life, but he's learning. Kyle's grown into the man I never had the wisdom to see he could be. We could never have been happy together, but you can. He's still so very wary of love, of being hurt again. Please, Alanna, for my sake, for our daughter's sake, go to him."

Chapter Eleven

For the next hour and a half Alanna clung to those words like a talisman, repeating them endlessly in her head as though they were a mystic chant of great power. *Help him.* Yet how could she help Kyle when she didn't even know where he'd gone?

Alanna moved like a sleepwalker through the final preparations for the boys' night along the river; she suspected Catherine and Derek did the same. Irene emerged from her room long enough to admonish her sons to watch their little cousins and David very carefully. Her intelligent dark eyes scrutinized the pale strained faces of the other adults gathered on the wide-screened veranda at the back of the half-timbered slate and wood house. She made no remark on Kyle's absence, but her lips tightened into a thin straight line. She gave Alanna's arm a squeeze that conveyed a world of meaning to the younger woman as she turned to limp back up the steps into the house.

Irene's silent assessment of the situation only made Alanna's questioning brain scurry in smaller, more frantic circles. Where was he? Where had he gone in Derek's car? She wandered out to the bluff's edge and stared at the rising moon, seeing little, appreciating the beauty of the golden summer night even less. Unable to stay in any one place for more than a few minutes, Alanna made her way to the small A-frame guest cottage where they were staying.

Kyle was there, sprawled in the one comfortable easy chair before the cold fieldstone fireplace, his silver hair falling onto his forehead untidily, his navy-blue shirt unbuttoned halfway down his chest. He was staring morosely at the nearly empty bottle of Scotch in his hands.

"Where have you been?" Alanna was too relieved to keep the sharpness out of her voice. She walked swiftly over the cobble-patterned vinyl that covered the floor, her heels clicking loudly in the silent room.

"What does it look like I'm doing? I'm getting drunk." Kyle was sharp in his turn, although the words were blurred by drink and fatigue. "Doing a pretty good job of it, too. I'm not much of a drinker, you know, but this stuff isn't bad once you get used to it." He held the bottle up to the light of a single lamp on the table by his left hand. "Not bad at all."

"Drinking yourself into a stupor is no way to solve anything." Alanna could count on the fingers of one hand the times she'd seen Kyle take more than a second glass of wine. She'd never known him to drink hard liquor. She didn't like seeing him this way at all.

"Isn't it? Then what do you suggest I do, Ms. Jeffries?" Kyle smiled but the usual jolt it gave her senses was more pain than pleasure. His lips curled back like a wounded animal's and his eyes remained as dark and hard as agates.

"You need a cold shower and a good night's sleep." Alanna fell back on her conditioning as a mother to keep herself from running out of the cottage and bursting into helpless tears. She walked around the fold-out sofa where David had been sleeping for the last three nights and took the bottle of Scotch from Kyle's slack grasp.

"I'm not finished with that." He made a grab to retrieve the bottle, then slumped back into his chair. "I haven't felt this good in ages; numb. I like it." His tone was still aggressive but tinged with embarrassment.

"No you don't, Kyle." Alanna put the bottle on the breakfast bar that divided the small efficiency kitchen from the main room of the cottage. "I realize you need to sort things out, but this isn't the way to go about it." Alanna knelt in front of him, between his knees, her hands on his forearms where they rested along the arms of the chair. Tension drained out of the corded tendons under her fingertips; there was no more anger in his words when he spoke again.

"You're right. Tonight I'm no match for a stubborn Jeffries woman who's bent on saving me from myself." He moved suddenly to imprison her hands in his. "I won't have any more. Maybe a cold shower will chase these screaming imps out of my head and let me rest."

"It couldn't hurt." Alanna managed a smile but it was wistful and not very convincing. She stood up, stepping back to watch him leave the room, hoping against hope that she could break through all the rest of his defensive barriers so easily.

THE DRUMBEAT OF THE SHOWER on ceramic tile set up a ricochetting cadence of pain deep in his head. Kyle turned back to the tile stall with an oath, snapping the faucet to off with a sharp twist of his wrist. "Damn." He leaned both hands on the cold edge of the sink, tendons bunching in his long muscular forearms as they took most of his weight. "What a fool I am." He had no business drinking. He knew better than anybody what it did to him. Alcohol and cold-headed financial negotiations never mixed. That's why he avoided more than a glass or two of wine or beer on most occasions, but not tonight, and now he was paying for his loss of control.

Kyle took several deep, slow breaths, trying to clear his vision, clear his brain. He studied himself through the sheen of steam on the bathroom mirror. Beads of moisture glistened in the tangled mat of silvery hair on his chest. Lord, he looked like hell. He'd scare Kelly to death if he tried to talk to her tonight.

"What a damn fool." Only an idiot would try to recruit courage from a bottle of liquor. His head felt like a stick of wood: dead wood. It was frightening how lifeless he felt inside. Derek and Catherine had to change their minds; they had to let him tell Kelly he was her father. He'd waited too long, it was time to take matters into his own hands.

Soft sounds of movement from the bedroom filtered through the thick gray haze of misery that floated around him, obscuring the edges of his thoughts. Alanna. The knowledge that she was so close was comforting, heating, the only feelings that had managed to breach the chasm of anger and guilt cutting him off from his emotions. He could make her understand, make her help him convince Derek and Catherine that he was right.

He found Alanna barefooted, curled into the easy chair by his bed. Music floated out of the radio on the shelf above the built-in platform bed. It was tuned to a classical station and the quiet strains of a Beethoven sonata filled the room.

"Are you feeling any better?" She stood in a hurry and looked uncertainly toward the door. "I didn't want to go to my room and have you fall in the shower." The A-frame's two bedrooms were separated by the bathroom and a short hallway.

"I feel like hell," Kyle admitted candidly, "but I'll be okay." He stared down at the towel in his hands as if he couldn't remember why he'd brought it out of the bathroom. The spooky thing was he couldn't remember. "I never could hold my liquor." He laughed and the hollow sound sent a chill up and down Alanna's spine. "Is the room spinning or is it just me?"

"It's just you, I'm afraid."

"Figures. I think I'll sit down. At this rate, in a few more minutes I'll have forgotten my own name."

"It's Kyle, Kyle Stafford," Alanna answered with a little gurgle of laughter. "I'm afraid I don't know your middle name." She took the towel from his hands and pushed him gently down onto the side of the bed.

"Everett." He supplied the information much as David might have answered the same query. "After my mother's father." Kyle rested his elbows on his knees and dropped his head into his hands. "I'm going to have one hell of a hangover in the morning."

"I'm afraid so." Alanna took the towel and began to dry the moisture from his thick gray hair.

"What's your middle name?" Kyle asked, his mind drifting back as he solved the puzzle of the towel and allowed himself to relax a little under the touch of her hands.

"You would ask." Alanna sounded aggrieved. "It's Rose." She sighed heavily. "Roses are my mother's favorite flowers. I never use it, it's so old-fashioned . . . so wholesome . . . but I'm equally uncomfortable comparing myself to one of those long-stemmed American Beauty hothouse roses. It was a bad choice all around, but I wasn't consulted on the matter." She made a comical little moue that Kyle couldn't see, but felt.

"I like it. I think I'll call you Alanna Rose from now on."

"Not if you value your life," Alanna said threateningly, then spoiled the effect by laughing softly. "Here, let me get you a comb," she added with a catch in her voice as her hands grazed accidentally along the curve of his ear where his hair curled soft and wavy. It felt so good to be able to reach out and touch him this way, possessively, erotically, as though they were alone in the universe. Before Kyle could protest, Alanna disappeared into the bathroom, returning with his brush and comb. She tamed the tousled swatch of pewter hair with a few swift strokes.

"You're pretty good at that." His voice, too, was rough with pent-up longing. Kyle tried to focus on her features but the room had a sickening tendency to dip and swirl. It was hard to keep Alanna's lovely concerned face from swimming away.

"I've had a lot of practice. David never touches a comb to his head if he can get away with it." Alanna made her voice deliberately monotonous, hoping to lull him to sleep. She kept trying to steer the conversation away from the painful happenings of the evening. She didn't want Kyle to begin talking about Kelly. She didn't want to rekindle a dilemma she was afraid she couldn't help Kyle resolve.

"But you don't let him get away with it," Kyle said perceptively. "David seemed very anxious to go camping with the others. That's a good sign, don't you think? No bad aftereffects from that night on the island." Kyle was all too aware how much he'd like to have Alanna with him like this, always, talking of nothing in particular, comfortable, homey and domestic. He'd like it very much.

"I think it will be good for him to be out tonight with the others. I did it as much to get over my own reluctance to let him go as for any other reason," Alanna replied truthfully.

"He's a great kid," Kyle said a little fuzzily.

"I know. Now, you get under the covers," Alanna ordered, blinking back a sudden rush of tears at the unguarded vulnerability in Kyle's tone. "I'll stay until you fall asleep."

Alarm sirens went off belatedly in Kyle's brain. He shouldn't allow her to stay. He didn't have the right to ask her, not yet. He'd waited so long to find love. They'd overcome so many obstacles in a very short time, yet there were still roadblocks ahead. How could he tell Alanna he wanted her for his wife when he'd never had the courage to say he loved her? "Where will you stay until I fall asleep?" Kyle smiled wryly but allowed himself to be pushed back against the piled-up pillows.

"In that chair." Alanna inclined her head. She felt herself blushing and was thankful for the dim light that allowed the shadows to creep up almost to the bed.

"I'm not going to go rushing off anymore tonight to make a bigger fool of myself than I already have." Kyle caught her hand. "Will you stay with me all night?" They hadn't made love since the night in the clock tower. There had been too many distractions, too many interruptions and almost no privacy here in the small cottage. He needed desperately to feel Alanna beside him, nothing else was so important as that.

"I want to stay," Alanna said with quiet certainty. Kyle propped himself against the headboard and watched her with a dreamy kind of detachment that did nothing to detract from the intensity of the moment. They were crossing another bridge, Alanna sensed, tearing down another of the obstacles still standing between them.

The tiny pearl buttons of her blouse yielded to her trembling fingers reluctantly. Kyle continued to watch as she undressed and Alanna relished his scrutiny. She wanted to run her fingers through the soft gray waves at the nape of his neck; her fingers itched to touch the tangled silver mat of hair on his chest. She wanted to be near him, close enough to touch, to embrace, to savor the nearness she'd missed so acutely these last nerve-racking days. She slid under the covers beside him.

Kyle reached out for her and Alanna went into his arms gladly. He smelled of soap, and slightly of Scotch, and the clean fresh fragrance of his skin excited her even more. He was cold; she pulled him close into the circle of her arms. She reached up to snap off the overhead light at the bedside switch. Only dull strips of moonlight filtered through the heavy drapes to lighten the sudden darkness.

Kyle turned in her arms to fit himself into the curve of her body, seeking her warmth. She slipped her arm under his head, drawing him nearer, cradling him to her. "I'm sorry for everything that happened this evening, Kyle."

"So am I." He was suddenly wistful. "I couldn't have been happy with Catherine. Knowing that was a basic gut reaction I couldn't change. But running away from her pregnancy was an error in judgment I'll always regret. From that point onward I long to go back and change time." He snapped off the words abruptly, hearing himself, hearing the naked emotion in his voice. Alanna sighed, her breasts pushing gently against his back. Kyle wondered again if he'd disappointed her with his admission of past weakness. He hated the loss of control he felt coming closer. Inside it seemed as if he'd cracked into a million little pieces, like a car windshield after a collision. All it would take was a single push to shatter him into fragments that could never be made whole again.

Alanna didn't need words, she could sense his pain and uncertainty. Her hand traced gently over his shoulder, the hard flat wall of his chest. Her lips touched his hair as she rocked slightly, trying to impart to him a portion of her own strength as he'd done for her that night in the tower.

Kyle experienced a wonderful sustaining heat flood through him, easing the cold that seemed to be seeping into his heart from the very marrow of his bones. His head cleared of the throbbing drumbeat of alcohol, leaving him weightless with an odd floating sensation stealing over him. The warmth of her body loosened his restraint, made it easy in the darkness, to say things he couldn't have voiced in the light. "Alanna?"

She caught the musing note of inquiry in his voice. "What is it, Kyle?" She nearly added *my love* but caught herself in time.

"Do you know anything about sharks?" She could feel him sliding toward sleep and considered not answering for a moment before abandoning the idea.

"Not a lot, only what I've seen on *National Geographic* specials." She tried to keep her voice light and low. She wasn't sure what prompted this fanciful train of thought in his mind, but anything was preferable to reminding Kyle of the painful scene with Derek and Catherine.

"Sharks can never stop swimming, they say. They can't rest for any length of time or they drown." Alanna pressed more tightly against the S-curve of his body, savoring the harsh rasp of hair on his legs against the silkiness of her thighs. The taut smooth line of his buttocks pushed against her belly through the thin cotton of his pajamas, filling her with delicious rippling sensations of delight. "Sometimes I feel I can't stop swimming or I'll drown too."

"You can rest with me for as long as you wish," Alanna whispered, knowing her presence meant more to him than the words she spoke. "I'll be here for you as you were for me and my son."

Kyle shifted suddenly. He turned, taking her in his arms with fierce possessiveness. His skin was warmer now, his breathing quick and shallow with building passion. Emboldened by the darkness, she reached down to push away the last physical barriers between them. Kyle held her close, their bodies touching along every inch, not speaking, his lips gliding across her eyelids, the curve of her cheek, the delicate ridge of her jaw and chin. "You humble me, Alanna. I don't deserve your goodness, your warmth and caring." His voice was low and husky.

"Don't put me on a pedestal, Kyle." This time it was Alanna who shivered, who had difficulty choosing her words, stringing them together into meaningful sentences. "I have far too many faults for that. I'm quick-tempered, stubborn and opinionated . . . but I do love you with all my heart." Their lips touched, mingled, their bodies melted closer still. The kiss went on and on as each sipped the nectar of desire within and without. Kyle broke the embrace endless seconds later, but he continued to stroke and arouse her body with tender persuasive hands.

Alanna arched toward him, her hands making eager forays across his chest to the curve of his slim waist and daringly lower over the hard flat expanse of his stomach. Her graceful, instinctive movements begged more eloquently than words for an intimate merging of their bodies, a touching of their souls.

Kyle held himself above her, his weight resting on his forearms as his mouth lowered to taste her honey yet again. "Did I hear you correctly?" he said wonderingly. "Do you love me, Alanna? Or is this only another lovely fragment of my dreams?" Alanna felt him tremble with the effort of keeping his weight from pinning her to the mattress. "I want so badly to believe something fine and good will come out of this whole damn mess."

"I love you," Alanna repeated simply. "I have for a long time, I think. When I could finally look past the awful coincidence of our pasts, I knew my heart had been right from the very beginning. Even good men make mistakes in their lives, Kyle. And you are a good man. I'm very lucky to have found you again."

She had to be the one with great strength tonight. She must be forceful and determined enough to give her love to this man, and overcome his reluctance to show love in return.

"I love you, Alanna Rose." Kyle's voice was achingly close in the darkness, a low nerve-tingling rumble deep in his chest where it pressed so intimately against the lush full curves of her breasts.

"You don't have to say that." Alanna was suddenly very shy and unsure once more.

"I love you," Kyle repeated. "I'll always love you." That quickly, in the space of a heartbeat, the twinkling of an eye, he spoke the words that had earlier seemed an impossibility. "I want you with me. I want to marry you."

"Kyle . . ." More words were beyond Alanna. She pulled his mouth down to hers, welcoming him with open arms, twining her legs tight around his waist, urging him closer with clutching hands and beckoning hips.

He almost forgot to breathe, so intense were the sensations coursing through his body. Kyle's head still buzzed from the alcohol he'd consumed so unwisely, but it did nothing to lessen his pleasure in joining with Alanna. She welcomed him unselfishly, glorying in the straining rhythm of their merging bodies, meeting each thrust with an answering arching of her hips that pulled him farther within the damp heated recesses of her woman's body. That was what he loved about Alanna the most: her sweetness, her capacity for sharing, for drawing him out of himself and keeping his demons at bay. "I love you, Alanna." His words were cut short, his breathing obstructed, as they drove toward the heart of the volcano together.

Alternating waves of fire and ice lapped at the edges of Kyle's brain as he pushed into her again and again. Tiny sighs of ecstasy escaped from Alanna's lips each time he lifted his mouth from hers. Her nails anchored him to her, scoring tiny half-moon indentations on his back and shoulders. He wanted their coming together to last forever and the momentum was too compelling. The climax, when it came, was simultaneous and so shattering, so complete, that they both lay panting in its wake, unable to move, their bodies still fused together, arms and legs entwined.

Kyle wanted to tell Alanna once more how much he loved her, how much he wanted her to be his wife, but sleep stole over him in heavy enervating waves. He fought it back but her soft lilting voice told him to sleep. Alanna twisted in his embrace until his head rested on her breasts. Her scent, warm and spicy, filled his nostrils like a potent soporific. Kyle ceased to struggle against its siren call. Tomorrow would be soon enough to talk.

KYLE WIPED THE LAST of the cooling menthol shaving cream from his face and walked back into the bedroom. Alanna still slept, the sheet pulled high on her shoulders against the morning dampness.

They'd awakened in the small hours of the morning, long after the moon had set over the Hudson, and he'd taken Alanna into his arms again to prove his love in another nearly wordless confirmation of their newfound commitment to each other. Never in his life could Kyle remember being so totally taken up with making love to a woman. Last night had been unique in his experience, because Alanna was the woman he wanted to spend the rest of his life with. He wasn't indulging in a pleasant nonbinding interlude, not merely having sex with a willing, attractive partner. Kyle searched his mind for a suitable simile to explain his thoughts and could find none. That, after all, was an exercise for poets and philosophers. He was only a man.

Kyle draped his damp towel around his neck and wandered over to the bed. In sleep, Alanna was unguarded, her face flushed and rosy, composed and yet so vulnerable. Her cinnamon lashes made dark crescents on her cheek. She darkened them, he supposed. She was by far too fair-skinned for them to carry that shade naturally. He knew her body well enough not to be taken in by the innocent subterfuge. He would have time in the days and weeks and years ahead to learn all these beguiling little secrets of hers—all the time in the world.

Kyle leaned over, placing a light feathering kiss on her parted lips. "Alanna Rose, wake up. I'm not sure what time the campers will be back, but I don't think we want David to find us like this just yet." She came awake instantly, curling her arms around his neck, pulling his head down to respond more fully to the teasing caress.

"I certainly don't want David to find me like this. In case you haven't noticed, I'm naked," she whispered against his lips. The pearly dawn light made shadows in the hollows of his cheekbones that drew Alanna's fingers upward in sensual exploration. "It's getting to be habit when I'm in your company."

"A very pleasant habit." Kyle chuckled low and intimately. The tightening pressure in his lower body increased. "I intend to become very skilled at undressing you."

"I like that idea too." Alanna waited, holding her breath, hoping he'd continue his lovemaking or his love talk. Either would be acceptable at the moment. Kyle pulled her up among the pillows, leaning his weight heavily against her for a long drugging kiss before breaking off the caress to smooth his hands over the gentle slope of her breasts.

"Will you always blush so easily for me?" Kyle asked in a wondering way as he smoothed the pad of his thumb over her breast and upward to sweep her collarbone. A pulse beat wildly beneath his questing fingers.

"I hope not," Alanna replied candidly, regaining a little of her equilibrium when he shifted his weight a little away from her on the mattress. She pulled her knees up to her chin to hide the extent of her own excitement.

"Alanna, last night we made a commitment to each other. I want you to be with me forever. I want David to think of me as his father, you do believe that."

"I do," Alanna said faintly. What was he getting at? Had she deluded herself into thinking the business of Kelly's parentage was solved because Kyle had allowed to hold him and comfort him through the long night? Obviously she was wrong. There was none of the endearing vulnerability in his face that she'd seen there last night. The pain and confusion were gone, hidden away again behind that impenetrable mask of calm he presented to the world. She clasped her arms around her knees and sought to catch hold his hazel eyes with her own troubled gray ones. "What are you trying to say, Kyle?"

"I can't ask you to be with me until I've resolved my relationship with Kelly." Alanna stiffened a little, hugging her arms more tightly around herself. This was Kyle at his most enigmatic, never a stranger again, thank God, but a man too complex to read easily. What did he intend to do? Alanna was suddenly hesitant to ask.

"Kyle, nothing in that respect has changed since last night." Unease jolted through Alanna, congealing the blood in her veins, making it difficult to breathe. She opened her mouth to suck more oxygen into her suddenly constricted lungs.

"I want her to know the truth. I want Kelly to know she's my daughter." This time his words were defiant. "I'm going to talk to her this morning, before Derek and Catherine can interfere."

"Kyle, no! That's impossible." In her agitation Alanna rose to her knees. The sheet slipped to her waist but she paid no heed, only registering the rush of cool morning air over her skin with a small uninvolved sensory unit of her brain.

"Why is it impossible?" He ran his hands distractedly through his hair. Kyle rose from the bed in one swift, fluid motion. He was barefoot and his shirt wasn't buttoned, but it made him no less formidable an opponent. Alanna's mind scurried around in circles, searching for the one argument that would make him see the impossibility of his present course.

"She hasn't a suspicion in the world that Derek isn't her father. You know best of all how much she respects him, how much she loves him. Don't shatter her loving, stable world with a few rash sentences. You can't drop such a heavy burden on a teenager from out of a clear blue sky and not expect it to affect her adversely, perhaps for the rest of her life."

"She'll get over the shock," Kyle asserted as he buttoned his shirt with jerky, trembling movements.

"Possibly, but you'll have destroyed her faith in her parents. She'll never trust either of them again. Are you prepared to take responsibility for the consequences?" Alanna swallowed hard to stave off tears. She could feel Kyle encasing himself in the hard protective armor she'd thought the fires of their love had burned away forever.

"She's my daughter." Kyle pulled the damp towel from around his neck and threw it into a heap against the far wall. "Mine."

"No, she isn't. She doesn't belong to you any more than David belongs to Elliot." Alanna held on to her composure with frantic mental fingers even as it continued to slip from her grasp. She didn't know where she found the courage to say those words but they had to be said. She didn't want to be the one to destroy Kyle's last hope of being a father to his child, but she couldn't let him continue along this disastrous course. "You haven't the right, morally or legally, to disrupt Derek and Catherine's life, to sully the marvelous relationship they have with Kelly." Out of the great void of cold anger building between them she recalled Irene's words and repeated them. "Your silence is atonement for the past. It's the greatest gift of love you can ever give Kelly."

"No." The word was wrung from his gut. Kyle stood in the doorway, his hand on the casing above his head, his fingers clenched around the wooden molding. "My mind's made up, Alanna. Come with me, help me make it easier for all of us. I've missed out on so much."

The last words were a plea but Alanna hardened her heart. "I can't go with you."

"If you won't go with me to tell Kelly the truth, will you be here when I get back?" Kyle's voice was cold, as cold as her heart. Alanna could feel herself regressing back down the path of uncertainty and self-defeat that had held her back for too many years. Could it have been only a few minutes ago that she'd thought nothing could come between them again? Was her love so fragile and weak, so easily destroyed?

"No." Nothing seemed to be able to reach him. She'd failed. Alanna waited, hoping against hope her bald refusal would shock him back to reality. "Kyle..." Her words were lost in the slamming of the door. She heard the car motor start and the clatter of gravel flung against the window as he drove away. Tears streamed freely down her cheeks, falling on her breasts, wetting her clasped hands as she rocked back on her heels. It was over. Surely if Kyle truly loved her he wouldn't have gone.

She wanted suddenly to go home. She wanted David safe with her, back on the island where the world was ordered and serene. She didn't want to feel like this ever again, loving and hurting and dying inside. Alanna swung her legs over the side of the bed, still crying. She began throwing clothes in a bag helter-skelter. As soon as possible she intended to leave Dutch River. She couldn't stay here and explain her failure to Irene, be witness to the heartache that would follow in the wake of Kyle's disclosure of Kelly's true parentage, and worst of all, be forced to confront the ruins of her trampled dreams a second time.

Chapter Twelve

"How long's it been, Alanna?" Malcolm Jeffries questioned with his usual bluntness. Alanna didn't pretend to misunderstand. She whisked back a loose tendril of coppery hair and bent to cup a cluster of purpling Catawbas between her hands. She inhaled their musky sunwarmed aroma for a long time before answering her father's query.

"Four weeks." She supplied the information while avoiding his compassionate brown eyes. Almost a month of very long and very busy days had passed since she'd run away from Kyle in such mental torment. She'd done a lot of thinking in those thirty days and hoped she'd come to some valid conclusions about herself and her feelings for Kyle Stafford. She loved him, she wanted him back and she'd never allow her insecurities to come between them again. Never.

"But when was the last time you heard from him?" Malcolm reminded his daughter of a grizzled old terrier worrying a bone, refusing to relinquish the subject, no matter how reluctant she was to continue it. "When did that last note . . . the one that came with the wine."

"About ten days ago. I've been the damndest fool, Dad," Alanna confessed as she pinched off a small cluster of half-ripe grapes and popped one into her mouth.

"I'm not arguing with you." Malcolm leaned on his cane, opening his mouth for a sample of the fruit. "But making a fool of yourself where your heart is concerned is something that happens to the best of us mortals." It was a familiar beginning to their conversations these days.

Alanna gave a short little bark of brittle laughter. "Some of us more than others. What do you think of these grapes?" She changed the subject temporarily to give herself time to formulate her random pattern of thought. "It's going to be a good year. I'd say another ten days or so before we can begin to harvest. Agreed?"

Malcolm rolled the pulp around on his tongue before spitting it onto the ground at his feet. "Let me smell those," he ordered, sniffing the ripening fruit she handed him. "Eight days, tops." He nodded his head. "Agreed?"

"Agreed." Alanna tossed away the remains of the severed cluster, wiping her hands on her slacks. It was a steamy early September morning, and already the back of Alanna's shirt was stuck to her skin. She pulled at the cloth, being careful not to allow any grape juice to stain the material. Her clothes were totally unsuited to the job at hand, but the first day of school was only a week away and she had promised—ages ago it seemed—to take David and Billy to Cedar Point, the large amusement park on the mainland.

She didn't want to go today, or any other day. She didn't want to do anything but find Kyle and straighten out all the misunderstandings still between them. Yet she didn't know how to go about contacting him. No one seemed to know where he'd gone. He'd left Dutch River shortly after she did, Alanna had learned from Irene when she'd finally summoned courage enough to call the older woman. He'd never spoken to Kelly again.

He wasn't in Virginia, she was told when she put a call through to his office, and they didn't know when to expect

him back. Alanna was frustrated and disgusted with herself, angry with Kyle's reclusive behavior, and deep inside,
she was frightened out of her wits.

"Where is he, Dad?" she questioned Malcolm, beginning again the, by now, familiar litany. "Is he ill? Is he lying
injured in some hospital somewhere? How can a man who's
second in command of an operation like the Stafford
Foundation simply drop off the face of the earth?" Alanna
scowled down at the toes of her canvas desk shoes, fighting
back tears. "I shouldn't have left him. In my heart, I knew
he'd never carry out his threat to tell Kelly he was her father. I should have realized it was a cry for help." Kyle had
sustained her through that terrible night when David had
been lost in the storm, but when he'd needed her love and
strength in return, she'd failed him.

Malcolm gave her the same answer that he'd comforted
her with ever since she told him the entire story of her involvement with Kyle a few days after returning home to the
island. "He'll show up when he's worked it out in his own
head, honey, if he really loves you. And I don't see how he
couldn't, if he's got all his marbles," he always added with
a father's fierce pride. "He'll be back when he works
through it. You've both got some walls to break down. Trust
me in this, Alanna. I've lived a lot of years; I know."

"I do trust you, but that does nothing to change the fact
that you fathered a dolt," Alanna muttered, unconvinced
but willing, eager, to be assured yet again.

For the first few days after she'd returned to Put-in-Bay,
she'd held on to her anger with righteous indignation,
keeping some of the heartache at arm's length. Alanna knew
instinctively she'd been correct in her arguments against
Kyle's desire to tell Kelly the truth about her parentage, but
that conviction did nothing to ease the ache of lonely torment that assailed her each and every night.

A week after her return a box had arrived by express mail. It was addressed in Kyle's bold precise handwriting. Packed inside, in a great deal of Styrofoam pellets that sifted out into the air and stuck to everything they touched, was a miniature hand-carved circus to add to the train village.

Every blue and yellow wagon cage held expertly rendered circus animals. Red pennants flew from the big top, clowns and acrobats in colorful, exquisitely detailed costumes cavorted down the midway. The concession stand even held a tiny balloon vendor. Nostalgia flooded through Alanna when she picked him out of the packing. Her memories of those sun-filled days in Maryland were never far from her thoughts. Attached to one of the figure's bead-like offerings with a gossamer thread was a card.

It read simply: *You are right as always, Alanna Rose. Silence is the greatest gift I can give Kelly and her parents. Forgive me.* It was signed only with his initial. He hadn't said he loved her or that he was ever coming back to her. Alanna felt a cold chill go through her that even the beauty of his gift couldn't stave off. A few days later several bottles of Dutch River *De Chaunac*, the wine she'd been so eager to taste and evaluate, made the same journey. This card contained only a single line in Kyle's handwriting and no signature at all: *I remember.*

After that, silence. Alanna was torn between believing Kyle had meant all those lovely things he'd said to her their last night together and fearing she'd killed such a fragile, beginning love with her rash words and precipitous flight. Unable to locate Kyle, anxious to right her mistakes, Alanna found herself growing more depressed and irritable with each passing August day. Only the joy and excitement of the birth of Bette's daughter—two weeks ahead of time, but bright and perfect as a summer morning in every way— lightened her mood.

The little blond replica of Tracie was a godsend—although Alanna had to reassure the older child repeatedly that the newcomer would never replace her in Aunt Lanny's eyes. The boys admired the newest Harlan dutifully, then pelted off for more adventuresome sport. Never one to be silent when she could speak her mind, Bette took one look at the naked longing on Alanna's expressive face as she looked down at Bette's daughter, and brought it all out into the open.

"You'll have another of your own some day." There were no secrets between them. Bette knew how much Alanna loved Kyle Stafford.

"I would like to have another child," Alanna said, holding the little one close to her shoulder to balance the tiny body more safely. A tight ache spread from her breast to her womb. "But the way things stand between us . . . we're both so uncertain. . . ." Alanna was silent for the space of a heartbeat. "There are so many problems to solve, that a baby would certainly complicate matters even more." Yet she couldn't completely push aside the sharp pain of regret. She'd come so far. A few months ago she could never have contemplated becoming pregnant again; now, the thought of giving Kyle a child filled her with longing.

"Being pregnant certainly would have gotten you off the fence you've been straddling for the last month," Bette said bluntly, reaching out to take the baby and put her back in the bassinet. "You love that man, he loves you. It's as plain as the nose on your face. Talk to him—"

"I can't," Alanna broke in. "I don't know where he is, or if he even wants to see me again. All I have are two cryptic notes . . ."

"That's a cop-out if I ever heard one." Bette swiveled her head to watch Alanna's reaction as her hands continued to fold a stack of tiny shirts and lightweight cotton blankets.

"How hard have you tried to find Kyle?" She put her hands on her ample hips and regarded Alanna with sharp, inquisitive brown eyes.

"I've called...I've left messages." Alanna's voice trailed off. "You don't think I'm trying hard enough to find him, do you?" She watched Bette closely as the other woman turned back to her chores.

"No, I don't. At least, not in proportion to the way I know you feel about the man." Bette fell silent in her turn.

"You're saying I should go after him."

"Maybe you should. He's as scarred inside as you are, Alanna. Women are a lot more resilient than men. We can change our prejudices, our attitudes, if our hearts tell us we're doing the right thing. It's harder for them. It takes longer to heal."

"I'll...I'll have to think about it." Alanna stared off into space, missing the satisfied smile that curved Bette's lips as she bent over the bassinet to coo endearments to her daughter.

ALANNA WAS STILL CONSIDERING Bette's suggestion a few hours later when she tied her father's small cabin cruiser alongside the marina dock at the amusement park. She hoped the crowds and carnival atmosphere would help keep her mind off Kyle and the growing urgency that she do as Bette suggested and go after him, to convince him of her love and bring him back to the island, to make him happy again.

But did she have the time to implement such a bold plan? Harvest was less than ten days away. From the day crush started until the vines were cut back and mulched for the winter, she'd need all her concentration and energy to get through the hectic days. Her father's health had improved steadily over the summer, but there was no way Malcolm could handle the exacting job of vintage alone. And her duty was to Island Vineyards and her son's future but, as always, her heart was with Kyle.

Happily the park wasn't crowded this weekday morning and Alanna's woolgathering went unnoticed as David and Billy romped down the midway ahead of her. She did her best to keep them in sight, sitting on benches in the shade of big old cottonwood trees when they insisted on riding anything and everything that went around in tight whirling circles, joining more eagerly in their conquest of the theme park's half dozen roller coasters.

After lunch she turned the boys loose, giving firm instructions that they meet her at the restored wooden carousel in an hour and a half. For a while she meandered leisurely through the aquarium, following groups of oldsters with grandchildren in tow and family units with whimpering toddlers pushing their own empty strollers onto the heels of innocent bystanders. She vaguely noticed teens in small groups and intertwined couples as she walked along the chain link fence that separated the park from the century-old Breakers Hotel and long stretch of golden sand beach.

She was strolling through the kiddie rides, no longer surprised to find herself mentally juggling schedules and assigning extra work to her field man and winery staff to allow her several days to go in search of the man she loved, when she heard her name paged from a nearby loudspeaker.

Alanna slowed, then halted, causing a split and eddy in the flow of pedestrian traffic behind her. Her first thought was for the boys. She began to walk swiftly along the concrete walkway, dodging groups of happy laughing children. The park was staffed by hundreds of bright helpful teens who were in charge of the rides and concessions. Surely there couldn't be anything seriously wrong with either of the boys.

She slowed her panicky headlong flight. Most likely David had only lost his billfold, with his entire life savings of two dollars and eighty-five cents, and expected her to make good the loss; or Billy had pigged out on cotton candy and iced fruit drinks and been sick all over his shoes. Inwardly, Alanna had begun to rehearse a scolding for her errant charges that would hold them in line for the rest of the afternoon, pushing aside thoughts of Kyle and her newly formed plans to go to him, when her heart seemed to stall completely in her breast.

So acute was the discomfort of the sensation that Alanna stopped dead in her tracks, unsure whether to blame the mirage before her eyes on the sudden erratic behavior of her heart, or the upheaval in her vital functions on the reality of the figure standing just inside the main gates.

"Kyle!" She took a step forward, paused, waiting for the jagged beating of her pulse to slow and steady. It was Kyle. He turned toward her with that clean, fluid grace that always marked his movements as he examined the swelling crowd on the main concourse. His body seemed to be composed entirely of harsh lines and smooth clean angles and static electricity, something vital and elemental that reached out to draw Alanna to him. She tried her voice again. "Kyle." Incredibly, this time he heard her.

Alanna. She was here. The vibrations of his name, spoken in her clear loving voice, echoed all around him. Kyle raised his hand to his eyes to block out the blinding rays of the sun. He scanned the mass of faces, twisting his head to find her standing beneath a small ornamental tree. She was reaching out to him. She didn't run, but her feet covered the distance that lay between them in the flick of an eye.

"Kyle, where have you been? I've been frantic. I was coming to look for you. Tomorrow...today...I couldn't wait any longer." She was laughing breathlessly as she came into his arms. The press of her breasts against his chest, the strength of her arms locked around his waist convinced Kyle that the pull of his feelings for this woman, feelings that had drawn him relentlessly back to her, were even stronger than he'd admitted to himself.

"Kyle." Alanna was speaking to him and he pulled his thoughts away from the sensory pleasures of holding her again to listen to what she had to say. "I've missed you. Please forgive me for deserting you when you needed me."

"You don't have anything to ask forgiveness for," Kyle whispered vehemently, burying his face in her hair to inhale its sweet fragrance. "You told me the truth that night, Alanna. Those words were straight from your heart, even though I didn't want to hear them. You did it because you love me, and I was too obstinate and stupid to understand."

His embrace threatened to crush her ribs but Alanna didn't step away. She studied him carefully, leaning back in his arms. His face was pale—some of the teak-dark tan she was so used to had faded away. He looked tired, as though he'd had too little sleep, but otherwise he seemed healthy and none the worse. "I meant it for the best." She looked around a little dazedly. It seemed impossible that they should be speaking of something so very important in the midst of a festive group of spectators who were watching two clowns in red-striped shirts and baggy black pants juggle oranges and bowler hats.

"Kyle, how did you know I was here? Why didn't you return my calls? Where have you been?" Alanna was half laughing, half crying and trying to say everything that had made her heart so full of mingled joy and apprehension for so long. Tears sparkled on her lashes like tiny diamond chips, brightening her eyes to a silver hue.

"I'll explain later," Kyle murmured against her hair. He held her at arm's length to drink in the clean fresh beauty of her face.

"I love you Kyle Stafford. I want that made perfectly clear up front." Alanna smiled up into his eyes and tugged at his hand, pulling him along in the direction of the carousel. "I have the feeling our time together is going to be severely limited in the near future. I don't want any more misunderstandings in that respect."

Kyle stared at her silently for a long moment. Then his face changed, lightened, and he burst out laughing. He picked Alanna up and whirled her around and around until she was as dizzy as if she'd ridden every merry-go-round in the park. "Put me down," she begged. "I have to collect David and Billy. How did you know to find us here?"

"I called your parents from Port Clinton. They told me you were here. I told a girl at the entry gate that I was supposed to meet you here and somehow we missed connections, so she had you paged." Kyle looked inordinately pleased with himself and some of the sadness faded away, leaving his eyes ringed with gold flecks so numerous that the green irises beneath them almost disappeared.

"Why didn't you answer my calls?" Alanna demanded. It was impossible to keep all of the hurt from her voice, although she didn't stop walking as she spoke. Crowds of people bustled in and out of the turn-of-the-century shops lining the Midway, passing Alanna and Kyle in a blur of color and laughing voices.

"I needed some time alone. I've been everywhere, nowhere, it doesn't matter anymore." Kyle shrugged broad shoulders beneath the heathery blue material of his sport shirt. "No matter how many times I added it up, the answer always kept coming out the same. I have no place in Kelly's life. The most loving thing I can do for her is to remain silent. Someday, if Catherine and Derek change their minds...well, I'll be waiting. If they don't, I'll have to learn to live with it.''

"You're a wonderful man, Kyle Stafford. Have I told you lately how much I love you?'' Alanna held tight to his lean waist as if he might get away from her again. She halted their forward pace, lifting her hand to turn his face to hers. "I love you more than life itself.''

"And I love you even more, Alanna Jeffries. I want you for my wife. I want to be a father to your son, if you'll let me.''

"Why don't you ask him yourself? He's riding the carousel with Billy. He's missed you so much, Kyle, and tried so hard not to show it.'' She led Kyle toward the merry-go-round, knowing David's enthusiastic response to seeing him again would banish Kyle's doubts.

"Mom, Mom! We're over here.'' David broke out of the waiting line, then came to a dead stop. Calliope music nearly drowned out his words, but the look of surprise and happiness on his face when he saw Kyle walking by his mother's side spoke volumes. "Kyle, I knew you'd come back! I'm glad you're here. How did you find us? Want to come on this ride?'' His questions came in such rapid succession that Kyle wasn't sure which one to answer first.

"Thanks, David, but I think I'll sit this one out with your mom. We've got a lot of things to discuss. You guys go ahead.'' Kyle laughed and waved the excited youngster back into line.

"I told Mom you'd be back.'' David raised his fist triumphantly into the air. "I told her.''

Kyle watched the youngster bounce away to reclaim his place in the slow-moving line. "I missed him nearly as badly as I missed you," Kyle stated simply.

"He was so disappointed when you didn't come back... home... with us."

"What did you tell him?" Kyle dropped down onto a wrought iron bench, pulling Alanna down beside him. He stared at his hands, lacing them between his knees, his forearms resting on his thighs.

"I told him you had family obligations that had to be attended to. Luckily, shortly after that the baby came and distracted him. By the way, Jem and Bette have another lovely daughter."

"I'm happy for them," Kyle answered sincerely. Was a family of his own a miracle suddenly within his grasp?

Alanna drew his hand into her own, tracing the pattern of blue veins along the back of his wrist. "I'm sorry for what happened between us. I didn't know how to handle my feelings. They were so intense for so many reasons—everything just got muddled in my thoughts."

"Don't be sorry." Kyle's words were harsh with self-contempt. "I'm the one who was wrong, dead wrong. It took a while to get that through my damnable thick skull, and by then it was too late. You had already left Dutch River, packed up bag and baggage and gone. At first I was so mad I could have cheerfully wrung your neck. Then, slowly, I began to work it all out in my head. You were right, and I love you for the strength of your convictions. I need your clarity of purpose, Alanna, your endless capacity for caring. I said those words that night but I didn't know what they meant, not really. I couldn't give all of myself to you and you sensed that."

"I wanted you to understand so badly. It *is* best for Kelly, but so very hard for you."

Kyle leaned back, closing his eyes; weariness was etched in deep lines at the corners of his mouth. "When I got past all the resentment, understood what you already knew and accepted it—you were gone. I felt as if I was trapped in the center of an iceberg. It's taken me all this time to chip myself out. It isn't too late for us, is it, Alanna Rose?"

"It might be if you keep calling me by that name." Alanna couldn't reply more seriously because the emotion inside her was so strong it might be impossible to check if she released it at all. She squeezed his hand so tightly Kyle winced.

"I promise, Alanna—" He paused deliberately and smiled his understanding of her need to lighten the intensity of their conversation. "I've asked you once before, but this time I mean it with all my heart. Will you marry me, Ms. Jeffries?"

"I'd be honored, Mr. Stafford. The courthouse closes at three. We can make it if we hurry."

"A simple *yes, Kyle*, will do." He laughed suddenly, hugging her close. "I haven't even had a chance to kiss you, much less buy a ring."

"I can fix that. You can kiss me right now, here, in front of everybody and his brother, and right over there, for the insignificant sum of twenty-five cents, you can toss a ring over a Coke bottle and win a genuine imitation diamond ring." Alanna pursed her lips and lifted her face for his kiss. She could feel him smile against her mouth.

"Sounds like a great plan to me. I feel lucky enough to win you a genuine imitation diamond ring for every finger and toe." He kissed her again, long and lingering, oblivious of the interested stares of people passing by. "Alanna, I've waited all my life for you."

"And I for you," she replied when she could speak again. "We'll never be alone again; from now on we'll have each other."

"A family," Kyle murmured, pulling Alanna up from the bench. "There's David and Billy coming off the ride." He looked suddenly ill at ease. "Will he accept our marriage?"

"I don't know." Alanna giggled, a tiny trill of her enchanting laughter. "What I do know is that he's more likely to demand you move in with us immediately, rather than resent you coming into my life. He adores you, Kyle." She couldn't bear to tease him anymore when he looked so endearingly uncertain.

"I'll do my best for him." Kyle made the statement a promise, his eyes darkening with the intensity of his emotions. He ran a hand through the thick layers of silver hair. "I'll be the best father I can possibly be."

"No woman could ask for more."

"Mom! Now that Kyle's here, can we ride the Demon Drop?" David and Billy came to a skidding halt in front of Alanna.

"Right away, please?" wheedled Billy in his turn.

"Kyle's an adult, too. You don't have an excuse not to give your permission."

"What's the Demon Drop?" Kyle asked interestedly. He grinned down at David and ruffled his red hair, looking a little like an eight-year-old boy himself as the lines of sorrow and fatigue began to smooth away from the corners of his mouth.

"It's over there." Alanna shuddered and cocked her thumb over her shoulder. Kyle spun around and scowled over the hedge at the diabolical tower where carloads of screaming riders were dropped over the edge every few seconds.

"My Lord!"

"Exactly," Alanna said forcefully. "I refuse to go."

"Intelligent woman," Kyle mumbled under his breath. "Okay guys, if it's the Demon Drop you want, it's the Demon Drop you get. Let's go!" He held out a cajoling hand to Alanna. "Come with us, Alanna..."

"All right, all right." She forestalled him with a facetious scowl. "But I'm only coming along to watch the rest of you."

"Billy's got a new baby sister, Kyle," David broke in, skipping along ahead of them. "And we have to earn the money to pay for fixing the skiff. That's a bummer, don't you think?" He intently eyed for a moment his mother's hand folded in Kyle's strong grip, then grinned up at the adults.

"I think it's fair punishment for the worry you caused your mother and grandparents."

"That's what my Mom and Dad said," Billy added with a sigh. "It'll take my allowance for the rest of my life."

"We'll work it out," Alanna said with an admirably straight face.

"There it is." Billy craned his neck to watch a carload of screaming riders drop over the edge of the tower and brake to a screeching, unscathed halt at the bottom of a short curved track. "That's awesome, isn't it, Dave? Let's go!"

"I'm right behind you," Alanna's son yelled. "Hurry up, you two."

Kyle took each boy by the hand, stepping into the turnstile ahead of Alanna. He looked back with an unspoken challenge as she grasped David's free hand and followed them inside the barrier.

"Changed your mind, Alanna?" Kyle lifted one dark brow slightly. There was a great deal more meaning in his eyes than the simple words he spoke could convey alone.

"I've changed my mind about a a lot of things. Let's give it a try." He smiled, and for Alanna the whole world seemed suddenly brighter. She smiled, too, so happy she felt her heart would burst. Everything would be all right now. She would have both the men she loved with her from this day forward.

Her husband and her son.

Epilogue

Wind-driven snow chattered against the windowpanes, waking Alanna from a light sleep. Their bedroom in the loft smelled of new paint and slightly of new carpeting from the living area beyond. The refrigerator hummed to life in the kitchen. A log broke and flared in the woodburning stove, sending a flash of warm golden light across the walls through the open doorway. The loft was cozy and comfortable despite the spent fury of a January snowstorm lingering over the islands before heading north toward Canada and New England.

Beside her Kyle shifted in his sleep but didn't waken. In repose he was defenseless, unguarded, with none of the strict composure that was so much a part of his waking self. His eyelashes made dark crescents of color against his cheek in the flickering light from the stove. His breathing was light and even. He snored a little but Alanna didn't mind. She'd always thought she would miss sleeping alone but she had been mistaken.

Carefully, not wanting to disturb her husband's rest, Alanna brushed a light kiss on his shoulder. He was bare to the waist, the covers pushed low on the hard flat plane of his stomach and the sharp jut of his hipbone. Several shades of last summer's tan still darkened his skin. The care lines had smoothed out of his face leaving him so handsome it made her breath catch in her throat.

One arm was flung over his head, the fingers curled like a small boy's; the other hand rested possessively on her thigh. Alanna traced the dull gold circle of his wedding band, then the adhesive bandage she'd put on his thumb that afternoon when he'd banged it with a hammer while finishing off the countertop in her long-dreamed-of galley kitchen.

Alanna moved quietly from his side. Who else had seen her husband this way, utterly at peace, unprotected by the mental barriers he erected against too much caring? Not many, she knew, perhaps no one but herself. In that context, what they shared in the midnight darkness was a greater intimacy than sex—the ability to rest beside each other and know that they were safe.

Wandering barefoot across the wooden floor, Alanna wrapped her arms around her to seal out the chill and dropped onto the window seat. She stared out over the snow-covered vineyards below. The vines rested, too, their gnarled black branches stretched upward as though imploring heaven to end the winter. But it was only late January and there were long bitterly cold weeks to be gotten through before spring quickened in their branches.

Alanna brushed her hand over the soft rise of her belly. Did life quicken also in her womb? It was early, very early, she couldn't be sure as yet. But a baby... Kyle's baby and hers. Alanna smiled triumphantly to herself.

It had been such a busy year, but a happy one. They had agreed, prior to their wedding, to postpone a family until they were settled into marriage and David was comfortable with the idea of sharing his mother, not only with another man, but with a sibling. Alanna's doctor had given her a prescription for oral contraceptives, to be renewed in a

year's time. At first she'd been a little sad at the thought of
waiting so long, but the weeks had literally flown by. When
she suggested to Kyle that she not renew the prescription last
month, his smiling agreement to the plan was all she'd
hoped for.

Yet she was a little surprised it had happened so quickly.
Her work in the vineyard and Kyle's commuting to Virginia
had left them little time to themselves over the past weeks.
Alanna was so tired most evenings after wrestling with the
year-end accounts for the restaurant's first successful season, and Kyle from long days working on their living quarters in the loft, that they fell into bed too exhausted to do
more than kiss each other good-night.

Well, not every night, she laughed to herself, drawing her
chilled toes up under the skirt of her long cotton nightgown. Perhaps it had happened the night they installed the
Franklin stove and made love long into the evening, watching its red glow through the glass doors, savoring their un-
accustomed privacy because David was spending the night
with his grandparents. It would be nice to think that loving
communion had given them a baby.

It had been a wonderful night, but Alanna had been stiff
for days afterward from sleeping on the bare wood floor of
the loft. Now the large open space was far more livable, but
still needed a great deal of work. They'd moved into the
unfinished new home because Kyle wanted to begin remodeling her house within the next few weeks. The too-large
Victorian anachronism was on its way to becoming a bed
and breakfast inn. Island workmen were to be employed in
that renovation, as well as in the continuing restoration of
the winery, providing sorely needed winter revenue for as
many as possible.

Jem and Bette were considering giving up their small
rented home to act as host and hostess for the inn. It was

another of Kyle's ideas that would bring added income and prestige to Island Vineyards. Alanna hadn't the slightest doubt that they would make it succeed.

"What are you doing out of bed, lady vintner?" Alanna jumped and then twisted on the oak seat. Kyle was awake, looking at the bedside clock. "It's nearly two in the morning." His voice sounded as though he was smiling and there was a lazy relaxed grace in the dark outline of his body stretched along the mattress. Alanna couldn't remember the last time she'd noticed that taut, tightly strung look to him and she rejoiced in the knowledge.

"I couldn't sleep." They fell silent, each attuned to the other, listening in the soft darkness to the elemental rhythm that never went unnoticed between them, an awareness that escalated in tempo and intensity with each passing day. Now it beat between them in the cold night air with breathless sweetness as the current jumped from one to the other. "I'm trying to decide where to put the kitchen things," she added in a whisper, although David's room and a third unfinished bedroom were situated at the far end of the big open living area. Kyle pushed his feet off the bed and walked toward her, wearing only pajama bottoms but unconcerned by the chill.

"That's not much of a reason to be up wandering around at this time of the night. Is something wrong?"

"Then would you believe me if I tell you I'm wondering where we'll put your Telex?" Alanna asked with a smile, patting the space beside her on the padded windowseat. "I imagine we're the only nineteenth-century winery in the Historical Register to possess one."

"I can't believe it survived the trip over from the house after being dragged behind a snowmobile," Kyle admitted, folding his arms just below her breasts to draw her back against him.

"I believe I'll take offense—for my friends' and neighbors' sakes—to that remark, Mr. Stafford." Her fingers trailed over the tendons of his hands and wrists, belying her aggrieved tone with their sensuous invitation.

"Don't go getting on your Jeffries' high horse with me, Alanna Rose," came the quick low rejoinder. "I still don't quite believe the entire island turned out to help us move in here, but I'm grateful all the same, and on New Year's Eve to boot."

"You'll believe it when you get the bill for all the food they ate. And the champagne! It was wonderful, wasn't it? I'll never be able to leave this island. I love it too much; I love the people even more." She giggled ingenuously, twisting in his arms to lay her breasts lightly against his chest. "It's a good thing you're rich enough to commute back and forth to Virginia when it's necessary." The thin cotton of her nightgown was scarcely an impediment to the stimulus of his hair-roughened skin against hers.

"Are you telling me you only married me for my money?" Kyle queried, his voice raspy with passion as his lips grazed along her hairline.

"Among other things," Alanna murmured daringly, brushing her hand down the length of his breastbone, letting her fingers dance lightly over his ribs and the hard curve of his hip bone. "I don't like having you away even once a month." She sighed and turned her head to kiss his shoulder.

"Yes, but coming home is worth it," Kyle reminded her with a wicked chuckle that came from deep within.

"Yes, it is." Alanna's voice was dreamy with sweet memories of shared passion. "Look, I can see the moon through a break in the clouds. It's stopped snowing but you'd never know it from the way the wind is blowing the drifts around." Alanna hoped the color staining her face and neck couldn't be noticed in the silver moonlight. Kyle's latest homecoming had indeed been a night...several nights...to remember. Alanna wiggled closer to her husband, sensual thoughts pushing to the forefront of her musings, warming her body within and without.

"You're changing the subject again, Alanna. Won't you tell me what's on your mind?" Kyle's words were low and cajoling. He was learning to read her moods too well. Alanna resisted momentarily, then spoke of the subject closest to her heart.

"Kyle, will you be upset if I'm pregnant already? I . . . I really didn't think anything would happen so quickly after I went off the pill."

"A baby." Kyle watched her expression by the light of a moon momentarily riding free in the cold black void of the sky. "A baby of our own." Yes, he was ready for a family. He wasn't afraid this new happiness he'd found might be snatched away from him as he'd been, unreasonably so, the first few months of their marriage.

"To love and cherish." Alanna closed her eyes a moment, willing the faint darkness that clouded Kyle's features to be gone when she opened them. She needn't have worried because his next words banished the last of her reservations.

"I've been thinking about having a baby a lot lately," Kyle confessed, still in that low quiet tone that hid his growing elation.

"You aren't feeling rushed?" Somehow she needed to hear him say the words aloud.

"Rushed? Do you know how many years I've thought I'd never have a family of my own? That I'd never be able to put my hand, here," he placed a big gentle hand on the rise of her stomach, "and feel my child move inside the woman

I love? So long..." He dropped a kiss on the top of Alanna's tousled head. "So very long. Are you sure?"

"No, not completely." Her smile, tentative at first, grew to match is own. "But yes, in my heart, I'm sure. You are happy, aren't you?" She couldn't quite dismiss the slight uneasiness that had driven her from their bed.

"Yes, I'm happy. A few months ago..." Kyle shrugged in honest bewilderment at the change his feelings had undergone in such a short space of time. "I think it was just too much change to cope with all at once. I couldn't be sure that all of this—that your love and David's love—wasn't just a dream. A lonely man's self-fulfilling dream."

"But now you are sure." Alanna stretched up, leaning her weight against his body to kiss him long and lingeringly. "You know I love you more than life itself."

"And I love you, Alanna Rose." Kyle answered as she knew he would. Her nightgown became a splash of ivory on the wide polished oak floorboards as she stood and Kyle pushed it down over her shoulders and flaring hips. He ran his hands caressingly over her soft white skin, lingering to splay his fingers wonderingly over the sloping rise of her belly. "I love all of you...our son..." He lifted Alanna high in his arms.

"Our daughter perhaps." Alanna rested her head on his shoulder, smiling against the curve of his throat; she tightened her hold on his neck when she heard his achingly sweet response.

"I was referring to the son we already possess: Master David Harris Jeffries Stafford."

David. The adoption would be final by the end of the winter. They had decided between them, her men. For a short time, Alanna had feared that Kyle might resent David's unwavering attachment to him, fear her encouraging their relationship as an attempt to place David in his affections in Kelly's stead. Had her hesitancy been the cause of Kyle's unease, the strain he'd confessed to a few moments before?

If so, she regretted it, but it was all in the past, as were all the old hurtful memories, all the bad times for both of them. She'd made peace in her heart with the ghost of Elliot Mayhew's betrayal. Regardless of what Kyle had suffered she didn't regret her own life choices. Elliot and Kyle were not the same kind of man; she'd learned that, if nothing else, these last months. Kyle had made a mistake when he was young and immature; he'd suffered for it all these years. Elliot was selfish and unfeeling, with little regard for the anguish he caused others. Still, if in the future David chose to want to learn about his biological father, she was strong enough to allow the contact; she wouldn't stand in his way. But some intuition told her that with Kyle in his life, David's curiosity about Elliot would never be very great.

The cool touch of the sheets against her bare skin brought Alanna back to the present in a sensual rush. Kyle watched the preoccupation fade from her gray eyes, leaving them dark and luminescent with passion. "Penny for your thoughts." He bent forward, his hands running over her silky curves, slipping low over her belly.

Alanna caught her breath on a little moan of delight, and Kyle felt his body respond to the sensuality in her expression and the movements of her body. "I can't decide if I want a boy or a girl." Alanna reached up to link her arms around his neck, pulling him down to sprawl across her in heated contentment.

"I don't care, as long as it's healthy and happy and so are you." Kyle's still-rare smile lifted the corners of his mouth, twisting the strong angles of his face into a reluctant grin. "But while we're wishing, how about twins? If Irene could manage, so can we." He kissed her lips, sealing off a response for long delicious seconds while their tongues dueled in sweet combat.

"Twins! Kyle, bite your tongue." Alanna's whisper was shrill with laughter and some surprise, as if she hadn't thought of the possibility until that very moment.

"I'd rather bite yours, if I have a choice." Kyle suited action to words, nipping playfully at the tip of her tongue when he claimed her mouth again. Alanna pushed at his chest, rolling him onto his back, resting her weight possessively against him.

"One baby at a time, if you please." He could barely think coherently as she slipped atop him, establishing a primal rhythm for their eventual coming together, moving to make exquisite pleasurable torment, ecstasy.

"I'll give you all the babies you want, Alanna, love." The words came out low and serious. He lifted her hips to settle her more intimately on him. Alanna's eyes closed in pleasure and passion. She began to move more boldly, her words coming in broken phrases.

"All the love I've ever wanted...or needed...I've found in you."

Kyle eased himself deep into her velvet softness with a groan of fulfillment that echoed again in Alanna's more feminine tones. "I don't think I'll ever hear you say that enough," he whispered. "Tell me again you love me."

Alanna drew him close, enfolding him in her loving, heated embrace. Her declaration of love was for his ears alone, her breath tickling his skin and pushing him farther along the road to completion. Kyle felt them drawing closer still as the crest of loving drew them steadily forward with each thrusting caress. The stinging sweet tension stretched them tighter and at the same time bound them more closely until the gossamer strands broke beneath the swell of mutual desire. They came to rest on the other side of passion, still wrapped in each other's arms.

Kyle pushed a damp strand of hair from Alanna's forehead, kissing her gently. She was already asleep, a small satisfied smile curling her lips. Kyle closed his eyes, his last waking thoughts of the island he'd chosen for his home.

Or had the island chosen him? It didn't matter. Here, where the seasons swirled and changed around them; where life would always be gauged to the lake and the vines, he could be happy. He'd lost the joy of being part of Kelly's life, but he could live with that because it was best for all concerned. And he'd gained so much more in the end.

Now he had David, his son, and children he would share with Alanna. He loved her more with each passing day, and together they would build a life of their own and bring it to fruition, like Alanna's wines, all in the fullness of time.

Harlequin American Romance

COMING NEXT MONTH

#193 PLAYING FOR TIME by Barbara Bretton

Strange comings and goings, odd disappearances—Joanna's New York
apartment building sizzled with intrigue. At the heart of it was
Ryder O'Neal. She tried to maintain a safe distance from the elusive,
mysterious man, but Joanna wasn't safe—from Ryder or from the
adventure of a lifetime.

#194 ICE CRYSTALS by Pamela Browning

Monica Tye's entire life was focused on overseeing the training of her
daughter, Stacie, as a championship skater, leaving her no time to sample
the pleasures of Aspen. Duffy Copenhaver couldn't see the sense of it.
Duffy had his own prescription for happiness—it included lots of love—
but would the Tyes slow down enough to sample it?

#195 NO STRANGER by Stella Cameron

Nick Dorset dreamed of being in Abby's neighboring apartment. He
longed to sit beside her, talk to her, hold her. But when she took off her
bulky coat, Nick knew he would have to care for her, too. Abby Winston
was pregnant.

#196 AN UNEXPECTED MAN by Jacqueline Diamond

When busy obstetrician Dr. Anne Eldridge hired handsome Jason Brant
to cook her meals and clean her Irvine, California, home, she didn't
dream that he would meddle in her social life. But Jason took it upon
himself to protect Anne from her dismal choice in men. Was there a
method in his madness?

HARLEQUIN HISTORICAL

Explore love with Harlequin in the Middle Ages, the Renaissance, in the Regency, the Victorian and other eras.

Relive within these books the endless ages of romance, set against authentic historical backgrounds. Two new historical love stories published each month.

HIST-E-1

ATTRACTIVE, SPACE SAVING BOOK RACK

Display your most prized novels on this handsome and sturdy book rack. The hand-rubbed walnut finish will blend into your library decor with quiet elegance, providing a practical organizer for your favorite hard-or soft-covered books.

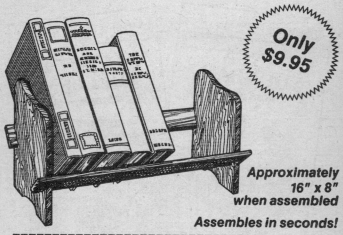

Only $9.95

Approximately 16" x 8" when assembled

Assembles in seconds!

To order, rush your name, address and zip code, along with a check or money order for $10.70* ($9.95 plus 75¢ postage and handling) payable to *Harlequin Reader Service*:

Harlequin Reader Service
Book Rack Offer
901 Fuhrmann Blvd.
P.O. Box 1325
Buffalo, NY 14269-1325

Offer not available in Canada.

BKR-1R

*New York residents add appropriate sales tax.

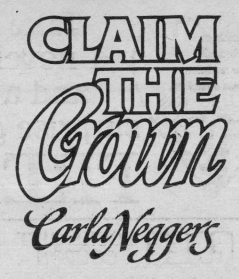

CLAIM THE Crown

Carla Neggers

**The complications only begin
when they mysteriously inherit
a family fortune.**

Ashley and David. The sister and brother are
satisfied that their anonymous gift is legitimate
until someone else becomes interested in it, and
they soon discover a past they didn't know existed.

Take 4 novels and a surprise gift FREE